ELI THE RAT

Jim Meirose

MONTAG

Montag Press
ISBN: 978-1-940233-34-5
Jacket and book design © 2016 Niall Gray
Cover © 2016 Wojciech Magierski

Montag Press Team:
Editor – Charlie Franco
Managing Director – Charlie Franco

A Montag Press Book
www.montagpress.com
Montag Press
1066 47th Ave. Unit #9
Oakland CA 94601 USA

Tawdry and mesmerizing, *Eli the Rat* is as much a commentary on greed and urgent compromise as it is a caper doomed before it begins. The characters and their circumstances may seem all too familiar and yet still pack the power to surprise even after the dust settles. Reading this book a lot like starting a new job, and finding out the truth about the American workplace after obligations and responsibilities make quitting in protest impossible.

—Jane Rosenberg LaForge, author of *An Unsuitable Princess: A True Fantasy/A Fantastical Memoir* (Jaded Ibis Press 2014)

Eli the Rat is a noirish, kaleidoscopic novel, checkered with the allure of money, power, addiction, envy, and longing. Meirose's multi-perspectival storytelling evokes the turbulent lives of workers behind the scenes, churning with misfortune and misguided loyalties.

—James Esch, Editor, *Turk's Head Review*

Using clean, minimalist prose, Meirose constructs the complex dreams—and schemes—of workers stuck on the 9-to-5 wheel. This is poignant yet subtle literary fiction, offering both humor and tragedy as its characters strive for better lives outside the workplace walls. When Meirose holds up a mirror before the workaday world, we see grit in the reflection—as well as truth.

—David Massengill, Author, *Red Swarm*

With wild imagery and his masterful use of internal monologue, Meirose thrusts us in the mind-bending drug-induced madness of his characters. His words, like that which is present in so many of Eli's visions, are fire.

—Corey Mingura, Editor, *Arcadia*

Meirose is a master of interiority, with shifting points of view and meandering states of mind, the unlanguage of thought is the glue that holds his art together—and art it is. Meirose explores the thin spaces between thoughts and words, desires and deeds, motivation is his playground, duplicity his swing set, altered states the quicksand bars of his jungle gym.

—Ruuf Wangerson, Author, *The Pleasure Model*

Repairman

Following in the footsteps of noir, Eli the Rat is a true tale of intrigue; about greed and vice, but also of desperation, desire, and affection. What pushes people to the lengths they go to, to survive? Meirose ponders the question, and still leaves us wanting more.

—Nana K. Twumasi, Co-editor, *Monday Night,*

A Journal of New Literature

To Preston

Contents

1 – VNA Corporation   1
2 – Gene   13
3 – Molly   23
4 – Gene   31
5 – Molly   41
6 – Eli the Rat   53
7 – Bobby and the Packers   61
8 – Panko the Foreman   71
9 – Eli and Molly   79
10 – Franklin and Gene   89
11 – Bringing up the Dragons at Lunchtime   99
12 – The Narco Cage   111
13 – Molly and Eli   123
14 – The Deal Goes Down   151
15 – Eli and Molly   169
16 – Molly and Gene at Dunkin's   185
17 – It is Finished   195
18 – Eli's Last Day   201
19 – New Lives Ending Starting Out Ending Again   219
20 – Eli's Report   223
21 – At the Front Door   225
22 – VNA Corporation   227
Acknowledgements   233

1 – VNA Corporation

At a gleaming conference table high in the headquarters of the VNA Pharmaceutical Corporation, two men sat across from one another, a spread of paperwork on the table between them; computer printouts, copies of e-mails, letters, paper scraps. The men's hands rested on the table and their fingertips drummed the tabletop as they thought of what they had to do.

Massengill sat nearest the window fingering the lapel of his deep brown suit, and glancing out at the cityscape below. He watched the cars going by, far below, like blood cells moving through a set of veins. He took his hand off the table and picked at a small pimple on his cheek as Jacobs, his boss, reviewed the scope of Mr. Massengill's responsibilities as distribution center manager for the eastern region.

"I need you to ensure that our products are kept safe and secure—both as they arrive and reside in the warehouse and that they safely and effectively flow out to our customers—our company's life blood."

Massengill nodded. He remembered when he was first given the job with millions of items involved—how could he possibly keep track of such a huge number of items and control the hundreds of people that were going to be working in the warehouses under him, the items flowing through the warehouses, on conveyors, as though the buildings were alive—the pulsing bloodstream of the company's business, and it was his to safeguard all of this. It was as big a job as taking care of the entire city he could see below his window—with thousands of things going on, both right things and wrong ones, with all the people, and all the stuff—

Jacobs drummed the table louder as he went on, his tight vest straining across his large belly, rising and falling with his every word.

"I need you to ensure me that we are hiring all the right people to handle our products and that they are the type of people who care about the efficiency and security of the processes they are part of—honest, upright, and straight on their jobs each and every day—as I have said, 'the company, and our customers and shareholders are depending upon you!' "

Jacobs' words floated off into the teeming cityscape below.

But, how do I control all this—it's too big a job for just one man like me—it's hard enough to know what each and every person in all the offices and all the warehouses are doing, how am I supposed to do this as well? The people here, up in their glass towers, are good at telling me what I need to control but they are not very good at helping me know how to do it—how does one man do this? How can one man cope?

Jacobs' words floated back to him, "—each one performing his or her appointed role—with honesty and integrity, and with energy that befits the importance of the products we distribute for the health and welfare of the public that relies on the quality and excellence of what we produce!"

Massengill fidgeted in his chair.

God, there must be thousands and millions of individual items to be watched over kept track of and delivered to the right customers—millions of items,—an avalanche of products covering me, smothering me, so that I can't possibly take care of all this—no man could, the standards are too high, too high for me, it's too much for one man, what is the point of all this talk? What is he driving at? Where is he going with all these words? What is the point of pouring all this responsibility in the lap of one man? Millions of items flowing over me, smothering me, suffocating me—

Jacobs continued, "—yes, the general public relies on us—for our products to find their way into their lives and into their bodies to keep them healthy—our products must not damage our customers, our products must not harm them—"

So what is his point already? Why drum this into me? Why are we here?—I am already a nervous wreck in a job that is too big for me, why is he beating, pounding, slamming the shit out of me? What is the problem here? Tell me already, what, why, are we really here—

Massengill bit his lip hard—almost bloody.

Suddenly, Jacobs, obviously finished with his preamble, pounded the table, leaned forward, pointing at the paperwork lying between them.

"Do you see what those reports show?" he said, tapping the papers.

Massengill looked over the spread of papers openmouthed and dumbfounded, searching for the right words.

What—what—what kind of reports are those? I haven't seen those reports, what kind of reports are they—they are showing all kinds of things I have not seen, how can I be responsible for reports that I have not seen—

"I—I don't believe that I've seen those reports," stammered Massengill.

"Well, look at them there! Look at what they show us! Look at these pilferage rates, loss rates! Look, man, its part of your job! Focus! Look!"

Massengill ran a finger over the papers.

What? All these numbers are a blur—what is the pilferage rate? What, where—here; first I'll turn the papers toward me, so that I can see the columns, yes, now point at something, yes, now point again—the pilferage rate? What pilferage rate? Where what number which number? There are columns and columns of numbers what damned numbers damn—

"Don't you see that, Massengill, there—and there—and there and there—?"

"I'm trying to follow the columns—not so fast. I'm trying I'm trying—"

Jacobs' eyes blazed.

"There and there! Five hundred and twenty units of thirty three thousand, four hundred and sixteen—in the first half of this year alone—"

"What product code is that?" said Massengill, pointing at the number 33416.

"That number is the hard stuff—it's the Oxycodone! Don't you know your numbers man? Don't you know your important numbers—?"

"We use the company inventory codes on the floor. That looks like a vendor number; it's not one of ours. That's how many cases of Oxycodone that is missing?" said Massengill, grinding his finger into the number. "From which distribution center—?"

Jacobs leaned back smug.

"From Somerset. One of yours—"

"I know Somerset is one of mine. But, Oxycodone?—why aren't they showing up in *my* inventory reports as missing—"

Jacobs threw up a hand and leaned back further.

"They, whoever they are, must have figured out a way to defeat your inventory system—I found out about this from our vendor delivery reports—the numbers that we get before they go into our system, and see those numbers, the delivery numbers, and your numbers, the inventory numbers, they don't match—your starting inventory numbers are off to begin with. They are stealing their way towards correcting our inventory numbers, so that when we do inventory, everything appears to match. Now it's yours to fix, Massengill. I want you to get to the bottom of this and find out who is robbing us blind! After all you are the boss there! Or am I wrong? Your very office is in the Somerset facility—isn't it?"

"I—I am and it is," said Massengill. "I don't know how this is happening, but I know I will get to the bottom of it—I will—the problem has to be somewhere when we first get those inventory numbers put into our system."

Massengill was completely stunned.

How could they, it had to be more than one person, defeat our inventory system? It must be somebody with brains doing it, especially if it's in Somerset—that's where my office is, I see those people going in and out of the warehouse all the time. Are they carrying the stuff out right under my nose? And now, because of this, I have to sit here and be lectured by this fat fool? I will get to the bottom of it all right—I'm not going to worry about whether stealing is a sickness or whether it's a disease, they could be getting into a lot of trouble taking that stuff out of my warehouse like they're doing—but who is doing it? And why? They must be doing it for money why else would somebody take so much? It's a lot more than you would need for a personal addiction, so no it's not a disease, it has to be something else—greed.

Massengill remembered that he too used to steal sometime from work—even it was just for a candy bar now and again, it was still stealing. He had had a job at the IBM annex and one of his responsibilities was that he used to fill the Kotex machines in the ladies rooms and when he did, he used to take some of the change that was in there and use it in the candy machines to get himself a candy bar, as a treat, for a job well done, so he knew the thrill of stealing, but at the time it didn't seem like stealing, at least he didn't think of it that way, he was just a kid, it was just a natural thing to do.

I don't think I had much of a conscience back then, that must be how these pilferers in my warehouse are, and they've been doing it for at least a year and a half now—how long have they been doing this? How long has this been going on? From before I got here? Where is that in the report—?

"Mister Jacobs," said Massengill, "how long has this much Oxycodone been missing from the Somerset warehouse—how long has this been going on?"

Again Jacobs pounded the table.

"At least a year, more likely a year and half once the new inventory numbers come in, and we compare them to the vendor numbers. That's what these production reports show."

Massengill turned toward the window and looked out at the clouds above.

I took the Kotex money for at least a year and I remember that job was really crazy—I used to get there really early, I'd drive my 1959 Ford out into the country where the annex was located and I would drive around and look at the farm girls on the farm down the road from the Annex getting up to their morning chores and the farm boys would see me slowly driving by and get mad and jump in their jalopy cars and chase after me and I'd hit a hundred or more miles an hour on those back roads getting so far ahead of the farm boys that my motor would start to overheat so even with them chasing me I'd stop dead in the road and get out with a jug of water that I kept just for this reason and lift the hood and put ice cold morning water in the radiator and those angry hicks would be getting closer and closer and at the last minute, I'd slam down the hood and throw the jug in the back and get in and take off again just as they reached me—it was crazy the things kids do, the things people do, it's almost comical—I'm sure they would have tried to kill me, they were that mad thinking that I was gawking at their girls, their girlfriends or sisters of whatever they were to them, or why else would they have chased me so—It wasn't that I was a bad guy—I wasn't any kind of a damned bad guy—I just used to like to cruise their farms in the mornings before work, to get me started on my day.

Jacobs sat back watching Massengill impressed by what appeared to be the amount of silent concentration Massengill was putting into this grave loss-prevention problem. And Jacobs was happy to see this because he himself had promoted Massengill five years earlier from the foreman job in the Wilkes-Barre distribution center and Jacobs had no use for thieves—he half-closed his eyes watching Massengill think and relaxed, clasping his hands over his wide belly.

That damned Rennie stole my boat—Rennie-the-walker, he was, Rennie-the-walker everybody called him, and I had my boat in the cove of the brook where I used to go out trout fishing and I caught Rennie in my boat, I knew somebody had been taking my boat and I caught Rennie red handed, so I went up and grabbed him by the arms and threw him into the muddy water where he was up to his neck in the muddy water and it was cold, and his boots were stuck in the mud and he was shivering trying to get out—but he deserved it—the damned thief. Then there was the time when I was just a kid down the bridge by the dam with my brother's sailor cap on that he had brought back from his tour in the Navy and these big kids from down the street came by and snatched it off my head and threw it down into the water right above the dam—just to be mean to me because I was a little kid, and the hat floated to the lip of the dam and went over and after it went over I saw it floating down below the dam so I ran down the slope to the ground under the dam and I tried to find a long stick I could use to reach out and get the hat but I couldn't find one so I asked Lob who was fishing down there if he would cast out and try to snag the hat and he looked at me with his eerie eyes and cast out once, twice, then said, "looks like you're out of luck kid," and the hat floated down under the low trestle and out of sight and so my hat was gone all because of those rotten bastards and I told my Navy brother what happened and he said "Damn! Damn! You should have fought harder to keep the hat, you should have popped them one in the mouth or kicked them in the balls or the shins—it's your fault my damned hat is gone, it was the last one I brought from the Navy and you lost it—now get down there beyond that low trestle and find it," and I told him that I didn't know how to get beyond the low trestle, and he said, "go up past the tracks to the Rexall parking lot and you'll see that the water on the other side of the dam will be there and the hat will be there hung up in some weeds or snagged in the bank, I'm sure of it, so go get my hat, kid, I want my hat back—" and so I went up past the tracks to the Rexall parking lot and sure enough there was the dam water from the far side of the trestle bridge and true enough the cap was snagged up in some mud skunk cabbages and lily pads. But that was on the other side of the brook, which was about forty feet wide at this point, so I decided that the hat was important enough to my brother for me to take off my shoes and socks and pants and to wade across the brook to get it. And so I did this without realizing the depth of the water and in the middle of it I was up to my neck and my shirt was soaked—I really should have taken off my shirt, but when I was on the other side and I had gotten the hat there were those boys again laughing and point-ing at me as they took my shoes socks and pants and went up behind the bank and disappeared. So now what was I going to do? Something else had been stolen from me, those mother fucking thieves, and Mom wouldn't like hearing how my clothes were stolen and besides, how was I going to get home? I'd have to walk up Washington Avenue with just my briefs on and a soaked t-shirt—and so that's what I did, but I wore that Navy cap proudly. I had gotten the hat back but the trauma of having to walk all the way home in just briefs made me forever hate to high heaven anybody that would steal from anybody else—thieves are scum who made me walk home in my underwear and after that my Mother would ask me when she was doing my laundry, "What happened to those jeans? What happened to those shoes and socks?" And all the while they were probably laying in some garbage can someplace, thrown there by those kids for what reason? I hate thieves but I've since learned that you've got to be smart to catch'em— as for me, whether I am the culprit, whether I stole the cases of pills, aside from the candy bars, I've never stolen nor would I ever—it's the lowest activity known to man and so yes, I pledge that we will find who's stealing these drugs and they need to be put in jail just like I thought those boys who first took my brother's hat and then stole my pants, shoes and socks needed to be put somewhere—somewhere where they would suffer torment and then suffer and suffer some more—

"So do you have any advice for me on how to catch our pill thieves?" I asked.

"To flush them out, you need to plant a Rat in the warehouse— that's the only way you'll get them," Jacobs said with confidence.

"A Rat? What's a Rat?"

Jacobs leaned over the table, the buttons of his vest almost bursting.

"A Rat is a planted informer," said Jacobs, pressing his forefinger into the table "you need to go to a security firm and hire out the services of a professional Rat—"

"And what would a Rat do?"

"Flush them out! For Christ's sake, he'd work in the warehouse. He'd be just another worker, watching everybody, getting to know everybody—a good Rat should attract the bad guys—making the bad guys in the warehouse think they could use him to their advantage—a Rat's got to have a bit of a sleazy side and stay relaxed around everybody—should seem selfish and stupid—talk about needing extra money a lot—and be given a responsible job in the warehouse that would draw your criminals to him—like I said, there are companies who will supply professional Rats—I want you to get on the phone and talk to some of these companies and see what they charge—you need to get a man who will fall in with your offenders and who name names and all of that and then he will be a witness when we prosecute—"

"Prosecute—?"

"Yes—of course, prosecute! We want to see these people in jail. We're talking about Oxycodone, an illegal drug with a street value of nine hundred thirty six thousand dollars, according to security, for what is missing. Nine hundred Gs is no small potatoes—so go back to your office, get on the phone, and get this started—oh and one more thing—one more just one more—"

"What?"

"Panko the foreman shouldn't know about it, nor should Jackson the assistant foreman—they could very well be in with the pilfering scheme, as could anyone else. The only one that can be trusted, in my mind Massengill, is you and only you! You need to understand that the Somerset distribution center, your Somerset distribution center, is a bed of thieves, okay?"

"Okay, I got it," said Massengill.

Jacobs rose and thrust out a hand.

Massengill rose and shook the hand.

He said "Can I take the reports to review them?"

"—yes, of course. You should definitely study them—" he said, sliding them over.

With that Jacobs strode to the door of the conference room, flung it open and walked away. Massengill stood there thinking of all he had to do—to study the reports that he had in hand—to talk to security companies—and so he left the room making a mental note of everyone that reported to him and made his way through the maze of corridors, elevators and stairways toward his car.

Why on earth are these places built this way?— they're like a rats nest, built just for rats, but Jacobs said he trusts me to find these thieves— who can I tell about it—I'm going to have to tell someone about it—but no, I can't talk about it—I am a professional—I am supposed to hate thieves in this job, just as I have always hated thieves—I have to listen to Jacobs—he is my boss—and then there's always the customers and the shareholders—I was not supposed to raid the Kotex machines for candy bar money—I am not supposed to steal ornaments of tombstones from cemeteries and carry them though school all day and bring them home and put them up around the back yard like I did—but because, in some ways, I am a thief, I should understand thieves—to be clear, I do not steal any more—unless you call accepting my overblown salary, with the unearned time and half overtime, stealing where I stack my extra hours onto weeks that are already full up, or that have holiday time in them—something that everyone that can does—I will get to the bottom of this—just like that time I caught the meanest bully in the school, there were a couple, masturbating up in the beams of the trestle bridge—and I said what is it you're doing, because I had never seen anyone masturbate before—and he yelled down to me, I'm working up a boner—but don't tell anybody about this—make sure you don't ever tell anybody about this—because if you do, I'll make sure that you'll have Hell to pay—and I didn't, so I know I

can be trusted—I won't be telling anybody that somebody is masturbating
VNA off—jacking all those pills off.

Kotex and Candy bars. Who imagines it could start with Kotex
and candy bars—but I'm clean now—and I'm the big shot. This big su-
per quiet Mercedes car that I drive makes me the Somerset big shot—it's a
company car, of course. A street value of nine hundred and thirty six thou-
sand dollars stolen—from MY warehouse. That's a pretty sweet haul. It's
getting dark—twilight—best time to steal—you can't see people right in
the twilight, let alone what they're doing. But I will catch our thief. The
Rat man; I wonder what he will be like? Large, strong, tough talking?
Older or younger—a big mouth I bet. Bait is all he is. Bait is what he
is. Bait to attract the bad guys, get in good with them, and then squash
them; a Rat. Then boot him the hell out.

"You need to get a good Rat," Jacobs told me. "And then,
boot both him and the crooks the hell out! You can't trust a crook,
but; a goddamned rat is just as bad. A crook at heart is a rat! So
watch it, he could be just as dirty!"

2 – Gene

The picking line in the warehouse is a long winding conveyor belt of silvery steel rollers that hiss and whine between two sloping racks loaded with the pharmaceuticals they handle in the Somerset distribution center. The workers walk on a long rubber mat beside the conveyor and load green trays from the racks with the drugs for the order they are working. A large stack of orders is in a brown box at the head of the line and when a worker is finished with one they would go get the next order, grab an empty green tray and start pulling the items off the racks the new order called for—and when that order is filled the worker let the green tray flow away down the steel rollers toward the order checking station, where their orders are double-checked for accuracy by another worker, of a higher standing. There's always someone of a higher standing—that's how corporations work. Some orders require multiple trays. Neon lights hang above the pickers, the racks are dark green, the rubber mat black, the conveyor wheels silver, and the bulk of the drug items are in yellow boxes, with black or white topped plastic bottles popping up occasionally. Gene is one of the two order pickers working the line today. He moves deftly in his blue uniform filling the green trays and bantering with Rose, the other line picker. She wears her grey smock and had grey hair, thin hands and a long peach-fuzzed face. A glitzy pair of silvery glasses sat on the tip of her nose.

"Hey Rose," blared Gene, as he filled a tray. "Got a big date tonight?"

"I don't think so Gene," she said as she let a loaded tray roll down toward the checkers. "Anyway—what's it to you if I have a big date tonight?"

As they talked, they did not look at each other, but only at their orders. They walked quickly up and down the line picking their orders and their words came out easily, squeezed out of the intense boredom of the job. Through their whole shift, they bantered nonstop as they filled the orders, signed them with their respective stamps, and sent them off down the line to the checkers.

"Cause I care about you Rose," said Gene, as he filled a tray with a dozen large white bottles. "That's why I ask these things. I want to make sure you get yourself a good man."

He smiled up at her, and she smiled back.

"Well thank you, Gene, for caring so much—but it isn't really necessary. What if I had a big date—I mean, so what?"

"Like I said, I'd want to know all about him—I'd want to make sure he was right for you. You deserve the best."

Gene was a fortyish slightly built man with graying hair, reading glasses hung from a chain around his neck, a five-o'clock shadow and a bulbous large-pored red nose, swollen from years of boozing. Rose was likewise fortyish with dark hair, heavy lipstick, and a small pot belly that made her appear perpetually pregnant. Their hands quickly loaded the trays as they moved along the line, talking over the mild clatter of the work.

"And what would make a guy right or not right for me, Gene?"

"Oh," said Gene, cracking a grin, "I don't know. Why do you think I would know what would make a man right for you or not?"

"You're the one who said it. You must have known it when you said it."

"Well I guess I already forgot."

"You really do have a short memory."

"I know."

"Gene—you really are something else, aren't you?"

"I know."

"Hey, listen—I heard on the radio that there was a big accident on route 35 going down the shore this afternoon," said Rose. "Is that going to affect you?"

"Nah—I'm sure it'll be cleared up by the time I go through there. Besides I'm putting in overtime tonight."

"You took the overtime?"

"Sure, why not?"

"Eight hours of this crap is enough for me. You ever thought of moving up here closer to the job? It's a long drive to the shore, isn't it?"

"Nah—I like living down the shore. I relax during the drive. After the overtime, the rush hour's over. There's no traffic. Straight shot all the way down."

"Doesn't that eat up a lot of gas?"

"No it's not too bad. Hey, you know—when I get extra overtime money, it pays off."

"Yeah, and I guess that sharp BMW you got makes the drive sort of fun. I'm not ashamed to admit it, but I've wondered how you bought that car, with cash, all brand new, like you told us you did."

"I tell you, I'm rolling in cash," he snickered. "After work, I tend at my buddy's bar in Point Pleasant on the weekends in the winter. I also do few other things, too. And even though it's all small here and there stuff, it adds up quickly when you don't spend it."

"Oh, that's right—you work the wheels on the boardwalk in the summer—you've already told me all this—that, plus the extra overtime here—boy you really must be rolling in it, Gene."

"Hey—some people got it, some people don't."

"Got what?"

"A knack for making money. Hey Rose—you really ought to get into this overtime. It ends up making a big difference on payday. Really, you ought to."

She put up her hands in protest.

"No way! I get enough of this crap in forty hours here. On my feet for eight hours a day, my feet want to explode by the end of the day! Gene, we're not all spring chickens like you—some people, like me, just aren't meant to drive a fancy BMW like you—I still can't believe you can afford that car on what we make here. Even with all the other stuff that you do."

Gene reached high to get a bottle of drugs on an upper rack.

"That's OK if you don't believe it. It is true. I won't be working this weekend though. Going up to my place in the Poconos for the weekend."

"Must be nice. That the same place you inherited from your Dad?"

"Yeah."

"You still have to pay property taxes on the place, right?"

"Oh, yeah."

"Are they high?"

"Not too bad. I'm going right up from here Friday. I'll meet the wife there."

"Where does your wife work Gene again—I can't remember, I know you told me once."

"She doesn't."

"Oh that's right. Was she going to start working?"

"She's not. She does crafts from home. She sells her stuff at street festivals and craft fairs."

"Does she make good money?"

"Nah, not at all. It's mostly a fun thing for her."

"Doesn't it cost money?"

"How?"

"For materials and stuff?"

"Oh that—oh yeah—but I make enough for the both of us."

"Boy, you really are rolling in it, aren't you?"

"I am. And I earn every penny, square, and honest."

His eye glinted into hers as if he were going to say more when a curly haired man in a blue VNA t-shirt and manager's pants came down the line from the checking station. He carried an order slip in his hand. Gene's face brightened as he turned away from Rose.

"Bruno!" said Gene smiling, "Did I screw up again?"

"Why does it always have to be yours, when I come down here Gene?" Bruno said smiling in return.

"Because Rose never screws up."

"Well, this time it's for Rose."

"What?" said Rose, pausing and leaning on her line. Bruno showed her the order.

"There," he said pointing to the order sheet, "it says twenty-four tubes. Look. You only gave me twelve."

"What is that? The Kenalog cream? The big tubes?"

"Yah, the Kenalog."

She turned to the rack and got down a second yellow wrapped twelve pack of tubes.

"There you go Bruno—hey Bruno?" she said.

"What?" he said, taking the pack and stuffing it into his tray.

"You still lifting?"

"Yeah Bruno," said Gene from down the line, "You still doing that weight training?"

Bruno tossed the tray on the line, and struck a pose, flexing his large biceps.

"What's it look like, eh?" he said, grimacing, "what's it look like? And you ask am I still lifting?"

"I'd say yes," said Gene. "What do you think, Rose?"

"I'd definitely say yes too."

"Damned straight," said Bruno, relaxing with a smile and a nod of his greasy head. "So how you been doing, Gene—heavy day today eh? You guys are really pushing down a heavy shitload of big orders."

"Haven't you heard, the drug business is booming, Bruno. What? You guys down the end can't handle the load?"

"Hell, yes we can handle it! Keep it coming. See you at break."

Bruno turned and went back around toward the checking station.

Rose waved to him as he left, and then she turned to Gene.

"Bruno's looking really good," said Rose. "If you ask me, weight lifting pays off."

"Better him than me," snorted Gene. "It's all too much effort for me."

"Pays off great, though—did you see his arms? Christ, they are huge."

Gene flexed his arms.

"What, Rose—are you turned on by Bruno's manly arms? Hey, here, look. I got arms, too."

"Oh, yeah, sure you do." said Rose with a smile, as she turned away and began picking again. They both began working again and worked in silence for a while until Rose walked past Gene to get an item, and spoke softer.

"I tell you though, I should have married you. That's all I got to say."

She winked at him with a smile.

"Why, what do you mean?"

"Your wife gets to stay home and do what she wants instead of working a God-forsaken job like I have to."

Gene turned to her holding a tray of big brown bottles.

"Oh, this job's not all that bad," said Gene. "We could be tossing hundred pound hay bales."

She shook her head, pushing her sparkly glasses up her nose, and said, "I guess I shouldn't complain too much though. And besides, I already had that life. When my Willy was alive I didn't have to work either. Then I just worked because I wanted to, you know. Not because I had to, not like now."

"Yeah. I get it Rose."

They talked on without looking up from their working hands.

Rose mumbled as the drugs flowed through her hands, "It's different when you're working because you have to, from when you don't have to. It's tougher somehow when you have to. The same job can be okay or miserable, depending on that. You know what I mean? Funny, isn't it? Because in the end it's the same job."

"Yeah," said Gene, as he arranged a large number of tiny boxes in rows on his green tray. "Say, how's your son? Is he still studying that atomic stuff out West? What's that place called? You told me but I can't remember—"

"At Sandia you mean? He's the boss over a bunch of scientists there now."

Gene paused his work and glanced over.

"Scientists, huh?" he said. "I wonder how he likes his job."

"He hasn't complained about it. He must like it. He studied for it like mad for years."

Gene pressed his forefinger onto the top of a pack of drugs.

"I know. But, I mean, does he really like it? I don't complain about this job either, but I don't like it at all."

Her eyebrows rose.

"Oh no?" she exclaimed. "I thought you said you loved it!"

He pointed at her.

"Well—if I said that I loved it, the only reason has to be that I get to work with someone as amazing as you, my dear."

"Awwww."

They grinned and bent back to their work.

A slender brown haired young woman appeared at the opposite end of the line from the checking stations, over by the large refrigerators used for the insulin. She wore the same type of grey smock that Rose had on.

"Gene," said Molly, as she slid the cooler door open. "How's it going? I haven't been by here today."

"Molly," said Gene. "Good morning. Things as usual, are great!"

"Good morning Molly," called out Rose.

Molly held a piece of paper clipped into a clipboard in one hand and a pen in the other.

"I need to find out what you guys are low on," she said, as she walked the line gazing at the stock racks. She stooped and stretched up on her toes to see what was getting low and she wrote the numbers on the clipboard.

"Nothing in particular is low on my side," said Rose as she filled a green tray. "The vet stuff at the end might be, but that always moves slow."

"I'm good with my stuff," said Gene, pulling up the next order sheet from a brown bin.

"Hey Gene," said Molly, coming close to Gene.

"What?"

Molly nodded, winked, peeked over toward Rose to make sure she was busy, and whispered to Gene, "Got it?"

Gene nodded, smiled, and Molly winked with a smile, then turned away just as Rose finished loading down some medications into her tray, quickly turned, and called out to Molly.

"So, Molly. When do you suppose you'll marry that prince of yours?"

"Oh Rose, I don't know," said Molly, cheeks reddening. "What prince are you referring to?"

"Rose—don't embarrass Molly," said Gene, with a wink.

"Well, I'm just asking. Molly, I'm talking about that guy you been seeing for a while now."

"Oh him," said Molly, pushing a hair from her eye. "That's been over for a week now."

"Broke up? Why would a man break up with such a fine girl like you?" said Rose.

"I dunno," said Molly, "He didn't say why. And he didn't do the breaking up. It was actually sort of mutual. He got boring to me. I told him. He said he was bored, too."

"Oh—look you've caused her to blush," said Gene to Rose. "Let's change the subject!"

"Molly, I hope you know I'm just joking with you," said Rose.

"I know, just bad timing nothing more."

Molly worked her way down the picking rack making notes on her clipboard and got to the end of the line and turned around and made her way back.

"Okay," said Molly. "I know what you guys need."

Rose touched her arm and their eyes met.

"Really, Molly" she said softly. "I hope you know, I was only joking."

Gene smiled and looked down as he tried to pretend that he was not paying attention.

"I know it Rose. Don't worry," said Molly, as she hurried down to the insulin cases and left the picking line. Her scent lingered in Gene's nose.

Young girl. Young girl scent. Nice good young girl scent—

"It's tough for a kid like Molly today, you know Gene?" said Rose.

"Yeah, but she's got a great attitude. Imagine being that age again and having that shit job buggy-lugging big filthy cases all day, making sure these racks are all full."

"I know. Her attitude is great. Hey—you don't think I hurt her feelings, do you?"

"Nah. She's tough as nails with that guy shit."

"Well, I feel a little bad. I didn't know they were broke up."

"Don't feel bad Rose. If you feel bad, I'll feel bad."

"Okay."

They worked on in silence. The morning wore on until it was ten minutes to ten, the morning break bell about to ring. Gene folded his arms and leaned back against the line to wait for the bell. Rose did the same.

"Not a bad job we got here Kiddo, don't you think," said Gene. "Panko never bothers us, workload is about right—"

She pulled off her fancy glasses and smiled.

"Yes, that's true."

Franklin, the assistant foreman who fed Gene and Rose the orders, came around onto the line wearing his white shirt, red tie, and solemnly set black face, clutching a fat sheaf of blue tinted orders in his hands. He dumped the sheaf in the box hung off the start of the line, then looked up waving to Gene and Rose. They shot him smiles, as he spoke.

"Heavy day," he said thinly. "Think you can keep up? Or do you want me to ask Panko to put one more on this line? Don't be afraid to say if you need that."

"We're good," said Gene. "We'll yell if we need help."

"Yeah, we're keeping the checkers busy." added Rose. "Bruno even came up and asked what's with all the orders today."

"There is a lot," said Franklin. "But—"

Just then the break bell cut through Franklin's words. Rose and Gene left their line and headed for the break room, while Franklin lingered, thumbing through the orders counting them; he shuffled them and rearranged them until they were in a satisfactory order, and then he left sniffing at something that seemed to linger in the air.

3 – Molly

Molly slashed off the tops of the cardboard boxes of medication that she pulled out of the bottom level of the tall green and orange rack, and piled them onto her cart. Molly was a pick-rack-stocker, a PRS they called her, and she was good at what she did. She worked in back of the long sloping racks that fed the pickers and filled the racks with open boxes of medication; from behind they slid down the racks to the end where the pickers could get them. Her job was to see to it that the pickers always had the drugs they needed to fill the orders. She worked alone in the stock racks, moving up and down the aisles all over the warehouse gathering the boxes of drugs she needed, surrounded by the maze of tall green and orange racks that reached to the ceiling holding hundreds of pallet loads of every kind of drug. Her feet pressed hard to the concrete floor as she sat on the cart and worked steadily using her long thin fingers to slide her cutter along the length and width of the box tops, slicing them off smoothly. As her hands moved gracefully over the boxes, her long red nails shone.

—must get enough of what all of us need, all that I need too. I need to get past today—oh God may the break bell ring—oh God may the day come to end and the week end too with the end of Friday and then two days off—not slicing and slashing and grasping at box-tops—

Molly worked one side of the picking line; Frankie, the other PRS, worked the other side. Occasionally, they would meet up in the back racks. Molly would push around a corner and there would be Frankie, stacking boxes on his cart, slashing the tops off them the same way Molly did. Frankie was the youngest in the warehouse, a little more than eighteen, potbellied with short black hair and a protruding upper lip.

—there are only thoughts of getting enough of what is needed but oh look, there's Frankie—Frankie boy hey! Hey Frankie—

"Hey, Frankie!" said Molly. "How's today going for you eh huh?"

Frankie paused, looked up, his plum lips ejecting words.

"Not much. Lots to do today. Hey, you got a watch? Is it break time? What time is it?"

She regarded him with a smile.

—see he's the same as me, straining for the break bell to ring, straining for the day to go by, these endless days we all strain through why must I see it all, all this pain—

"The bell will let us know what time it is," she said, pushing back her hair. "I don't have a watch. Don't you have a watch?"

"If I had a watch would I be asking you the time?"

"I know you're not wearing one. I mean, do you own one?"

—why do I care do I really care I don't really care why'd I ask this why—

"Yes I do own one, it's at home."

—who wants to know why oh, talk need to talk go go go—

"Then why don't you wear it," she said solemnly, "If the time is that important to you?"

He cracked a smile.

"Oh don't give me a hard time, or are you in some kind of mood this morning?"

She smiled.

—huh, what? Everybody's always in some kind of mood, all the time—what kind of a question is that, why do you ask that Frankie? First you need to know the time, now you ask me something about my mood, what's in that fat face? Answer me that Frankie—

"Everybody's always in some kind of mood, Frankie. I just want to know why you don't wear your watch?"

"I never wear my watch to work."

"No? Why not?"

"It could get messed up. I could bang it against something while I'm pulling these boxes, and break it."

—huh what? You could just be careful—all it would take is to be careful, you could just as well bang your wrist, slice it and draw blood, and then you'd wish you had a damned watch on you to protect your wrist, or you could just buy a cheap watch and it wouldn't matter if it got banged up—

Molly turned from him, saying nothing, and pulled her cart up to the pallet she'd come looking for containing the drugs she needed. She lifted her box cutter. She touched the blade tip.

—dull, yes dull, damned dull—

"Hey Frankie. You got any blades for these cutters?"

"In my locker I got some. Why, you got a dull blade?"

She bit her lip and looked hard at him.

—now why would I have asked it if I didn't have a dull blade and so what that they're in you locker—they're no use to me when they're in your locker when I need one now—

"Frankie, tell you what. Why don't we trade cutters? It's almost break time, and then you can go to your locker on break to replace the blade. I haven't got any blades and mine is so dull I can't even use it. See here? Look here. Feel."

She went to him slowly, holding out the box cutter, and he lightly felt the blade.

"Yeah I see. I'll tell you what, I got a couple boxes of blades I'll bring you a whole box after break."

—no I want your cutter now, I need it now, give it here now—

"Let me use your cutter, Frankie. You don't even need it until after break. You got all the tops of your cases open. You won't even need your cutter until after break."

"How do you know I won't need a cutter before break?"

"Frankie," she said, "It's ten minutes until break. Ten minutes won't kill you."

His plump face looked up; his eyes sat slitted in their fatty sockets.

"Well, Molly," he said slowly, "—then it won't kill you neither."

Her eyebrows rose as she backed towards her cart and sat down with eyes to match his.

"Oh, please, come on Frankie? For your little pal Molly?" she cooed in a low flirty voice.

"Molly, I told you" he said. "I'll bring you a whole box after break—"

An orange forklift suddenly buzzed from around the end of the aisle. It was designed for narrow aisles, with the operator standing up. A tall man in a dirty torn undershirt, a buzz cut of hair and a grizzly mustache stood on the forklift, as he swung it around and stopped on the other side of Frankie. The man hopped off the machine and stepped towards the duo.

"So what do you need, Frankie?" said Carl, the forklift operator.

"Eleven twenty fives," said Frankie, pointing up. "I need that load brought down."

"Okay—hey Molly—what are you up to here with Frankie?" said Carl.

She smirked and looked away.

—lord God Carl, you do smell bad, day after day after day you smell really bad—

"Working," she said, hacking at a box top. She sniffed back hard. "Why?"

"Oh, I thought you were over here flirting with Frankie."

"Please."

"Hey Frankie. Is she flirting with you? Word is out that's what goes on in these racks all day. How 'bout it, Frankie—"

—lord God please take your smelly chauvinistic pig comments and go—

Carl turned away wearing a huge smile before Frankie could answer, as he got back on his forklift, he moved it into position with the machine moaning and groaning, sighing and rattling, rolling and rocking, as he lifted the forks, slid them under the pallet, and got down the load that Frankie wanted. After setting the load into an empty slot he jumped down, pulled the inventory slip with a flourish, and drove off the way he had come without a word or a look at either Molly or Frankie. In seconds the smell dissipated and he may as well have never been there.

"Did you smell it, Frankie?" asked Molly, hacking at another box, the dullness of her blade temporarily forgotten.

"Smell? You mean Carl? Oh yeah. Every day it's the same. Maybe there's no plumbing in his house."

"No, I don't think it's his plumbing," said Molly, amused. "He's just a damned pig."

"Yeah, I guess. He's got a really shitty attitude to go along with his stink too."

She nodded and watched Frankie's hands move deftly slicing through box tops with speed and grace.

—attitude yes, but really I'm the one here that's got attitude, try me Frankie, I got an attitude, God damn it do I have an attitude—

Her interest in his hands dissolved as do all passing thoughts about nothing and they both slashed at their respective box tops as they waited for the break bell to ring. While they worked and waited, a portly man with slicked back greasy hair in a white shirt and striped tie came into the aisle and went up to Frankie.

"Frankie, I need you after break on the packing line," said Tom Panko, the foreman.

Molly worked slightly faster as she looked toward Panko.

—it's a good thing we were just now working, Panko is a pain in the ass, he thinks people should be working all the time, if we had just been

talking he'd have been upset but you know I bet he saw us talking before and he probably doesn't think there's enough work for both us stockers back here today—

"Okay, Tom," said Frankie to Panko.

Panko rubbed his pot belly with one hand and waved the other toward Molly.

"And Molly, if you would, take care of both sides of the racks for the rest of the day while Frankie is packing, that would be great. Okay?"

She rose with her cutter in her hand and pushed her cart slightly.

—what do you mean, if you would—what if I said I won't— then what—

"Okay Panko," she said, sitting back down on the cart stacking the boxes of drugs.

"Great!" said Panko, slapping his fat thigh, and he turned and left the aisle, proudly swinging his arms by his side.

She watched him go as her hands automatically resumed slicing the boxes.

—another pig. The world is full of Goddamned pigs—

A fly distracted her. It buzzed at her face, and then was gone. Her eyes landed on Frankie.

"Guess you'll be taking it easy the rest of the day, eh Frankie?" she said.

"Hardly," he said, slashing the last of his box tops. He rose and stepped over and handed his cutter to Molly.

"What's this for," she said, taking it.

"Yours is dull, and I won't be seeing you after break to give you a blade—so let's trade like you said before."

She grinned at him, nodding.

"Okay Frankie, thanks," she said, handing him her dull cutter with a grin.

—he remembered what I asked. He remembered. That's so nice, he's so nice—

Frankie returned the grin, nodded, and pushed his cart out of the aisle, leaving her alone. She sat back down and used the sharp blade. What a difference. The cutting was sharp, clean smooth and absorbing.

—*some would say this blade cuts like a hot knife through butter. It's the little things in life that count you know—I bet Frankie doesn't really have a watch, he's always talking like he has no money, I remember the day he was telling me he has no money and I said there's ways to get money, extra money and he asked me what did I mean and I never answered him I feel sorry for him, it's not good to have no money, this job pays nothing which is why I'm lucky to be hooked up with Gene like I am, you know like I—enough said——*

The break bell rang at last, making Molly jump. She stood and pushed the cart out of the aisle toward the racks she would be filling. On the way to the break room she passed the large caged-in area filled with pallet racks of cases of narcotics. She glanced over at the caged racks as she pushed her cart past the slid-open unlocked door.

—*and I'm trusted which is a good thing, Panko trusts me and leaves that one cage open all day or I wouldn't be able to do my job of stocking the pick racks and I wouldn't be able to get money one of those other ways that I was talking about, to get money like I told Frankie, since nobody can hear me think why not think it—that cage is full of fucking money, it feels good knowing that, good hot warm like a good light gentle touch someplace, what place? that place—*

She dropped her loaded cart off by the back of the pick racks, and went through the gate into the hall that led to the ladies' locker room. Rose, the picker who worked with Gene and several other women were in the locker room. Lockers were opening and closing, slamming and crashing, as Molly pulled her keychain and worked to unlock her locker to get her snack.

"Why do you keep that locker locked all the time Molly?" Rose asked. "You're the only one who does that. Why go to all that trouble? Nobody's going to steal anything from you."

"It's just a quirk," said Molly, turning the Master lock key and slipping the lock out of the hasp. "You know, one of those things—I always keep my house locked and I always keep my car locked, so I guess it's just my nature to like to keep things of mine locked up you know?"

"Don't you trust us?" smiled Rose, opening her bag and taking out her apple.

"No, it's not that. I know all of you are honest."

She opened her door revealing her large lunch pail and got it down.

"It's just a quirk," she said again. "Call me silly."

She slammed the locker door back shut.

4 – Gene

Gene climbed into his powerful BMW sedan, threw the lunch pail into the passenger seat, and left the Dunkin' Donuts parking lot, burning rubber. He smiled as he headed for the ramp to the Interstate, having made his one mandatory stop after leaving the distribution center. He had what he needed again. He had it.

Power—power—it's all about power—I'm damned lucky to have this but don't I deserve it—luck has nothing to do with it, it's power—power—some of us are just more powerful than others and when you are powerful you deserve more—you deserve more and you get more—Rose asks me how I can afford this car—they all ask me, the small ones back in the warehouse and even down by the boardwalk and in the bars—people envy me, they envy my car and the way I flash my money around, but it's not about the money, it's all about power—some people have it some people don't—I had nothing growing up so I figure that I deserve something now, I deserve to have more than the rest of the little ones, working their small jobs for an hourly wage and counting on that pittance of money to drag them through their miserable days—and after taxes they only get to keep half their money and what will that buy them?—that will buy them nothing, that is what, nothing—

He sped up the ramp to the Interstate and in seconds was cruising an easy eighty five. The hum of the road sang by far below.

—Massengill thinks he has all the power, but he's under the thumb of the man just as much as the packers and the men who work on the

loading dock—and that Tom Panko—what a joke—bossing around a bunch of nobodies doesn't make you a somebody, it makes you a nobody as well—the way he walks around all pumped up with his nose stuck in the air, wearing those silly button down shirts and fancy ties that he bought fifty five pounds ago, checking that everything's flowing—that the orders come in the front get digested in the middle turn into products and get shit out the back—it's just a big shithole, a really big shithole and the loading docks are the anus—the sphincter, you know; and you know those germs they say you have in your gut that help you digest your food? That's what Panko is, he's a germ, a big stupid wad of bacteria just like that other one, Franklin, who gives us the orders at the head of the picking line, at least he serves a purpose—Panko and Massengill they serve no purpose but to be bacteria in the gut of the system—dirty filthy bacteria, germs—look at how philosophical I have become—

Gene smiled as he squeezed the wheel, approaching the Route One crossing.

—but the damned system is bleeding there's a ulcer in the gut of the system, they don't even know about that, they can't see hear or feel the pain—like I said I'm damn lucky to have this —this stuff—

He patted the heavy lunch pail on the seat beside him. The rattling handle mixed with the whine of the engine and tires as Gene sped along, crossing Route One, heading for the Parkway. He squeezed the wheel hard holding his head high.

—I'm so lucky that I can cruise along at eighty five and no cop will touch me, I know that it's not in my future to get stopped or get ticketed, that's for the small ones, the weak ones, the slow ones—I can feel the curve of this lunch pail right beside me, and it's thanks to that little Molly, that little squirming Molly germ, that this lunch pail is full—Molly's a germ, she's a bacteria, just like Panko and Massengill, nutrients in the blood stream, keeping things rolling, that's her role, to bring the nutrition to the organs moving the shit through the gut—that's the way it is the way it is—the nutrition leaks into my lunch pail and I take it out and here it is on my car seat, now what if I got stopped and the officer said

'mind if I look inside that lunchbox,' I'd be a dead duck, better to slow down now, besides there's a turn up ahead, what would the copper see if he opened the lunchbox? Just ten yellow boxes that say on the boxes what they are, but I'm not going to get stopped because I've got a lucky charm around my neck, I should pull it up and kiss it, the scapular, just in case. I always wear the scapular of Our Lady of Mount Carmel and she always rides with me and that's why I'll never get stopped and I will never have to open the lunch pail for anybody but the ones I deal with down on the boardwalk and in the bar and even there, in a shithole of a place like that, Our Lady of Mount Carmel protects me—what does it matter this is nothing but a drop in the big bucket of blood of the even bigger corporation, I'm bleeding it for its health, years ago they would bleed people for their health and I think I remember them saying that the people they bled were the better for it, so what's fifty bucks here, fifty bucks there, fifty bucks for her to pop me a full lunch pail once a week—it's nothing to pay her, if she only knew what she's buried at the bottom of—

Gene took the off ramp for the Parkway south. He powered down onto the main road and slowed to cruise through the toll booths with his EZ pass.

—yes they used to bleed people for their health, why they did that makes no sense, but I know why I'm doing it, I'm bleeding the system to line my pockets with what my pockets should be lined with, where did that expression come from—line your pockets? There's that old plant on the right I pass every day, it's big and abandoned now, but somebody certainly thought they were a big shot in there once too, but where are they now? The place is crumbling—maybe they just moved, like us, they been talking about moving the VNA warehouse to Cranbury, I don't care if it's not set up the same after the move, more's the better if it's set up different, we'll figure it out, there's always some way to bleed the system and nobody knows the blood is gone until it coagulates in my pockets, in my wallet—I like the way money collects on my pockets, I could add it up but not now, I'm too tired now—a full day on the picking line doing an honest days' work makes you tired, I don't do anything wrong, no I don't, she does what's wrong to make me

right—I could go for her, she's a sweet little thing but for that sassy mouth, I could lay with her just as I can with my stick of a wife, full of vodka, with her sassy mouth—when I spin the wheel on the boardwalk I'm going to be taking in a few quarters, but when they come to my wheel with twenty dollars in hand and ask me for the blood, I give it to them and I do that, one pill at a time, ten, twenty, thirty times a night—if she only knew, she would shit herself—a thousand dollars a day isn't bad money as I stand at the wheel giving out teddy bears to the lucky ones but I give out little drops of blood to the ones that need it—I wonder what that big abandoned factory used to make, I wonder if its system had any bleeding ulcers like ours does, every system probably has its share of bleeding ulcers—slow down there's another toll booth ahead, cruise right through it and go back up to ninety, this BMW is smooth as silk, the ultimate driving machine is right—I have to watch out now, my turnoff comes up fast around this here big curve— where are the bacteria of the big factory now? Probably bacteria someplace else, every system has a mouth, a gut, a stomach, a cunt, a dick, an ass, it all clicks into place—who is the mouth and who is the gut and who is the stomach and who is the cunt and who is the dick and who is the ass—kiss the scapular again Our Lady of Mount Carmel—my daughter, before she died, dated a scumbag who used to wear of a scapular of Our Lady of Mount Carmel just like me and it wasn't right, I wanted to rip it off him damn him—but he's gone now, just like she is, don't think about it, don't think about, don't think, just drive—

The Parkway wound around and the Route thirty seven exit was a few miles away—but at ninety, like he was, ninety felt almost like standing still it all got so unreal, all stretched out; he would reach it quick.

—damn I'm at ninety and people are passing me, there's a state trooper right on the other side, he doesn't seem to care, still I'm slowing down, there's a big white H in a blue square up ahead, that's my turnoff thirty seven south—

Gene turned off onto Route thirty seven stopping at the first red light. He was surrounded by cars of every size, color, and shape, make, and model, but none of the other cars were like his black BMW.

—the red light says to stop, like heart valves stopping the blood in the heart, opening closing opening closing, and here I sit with a pail of blood in my car—the lunch pail is cold but what's in it is hot —now it's green, good go, there are a lot of stores along the route here, a MacDonald's, a Burger King, but there will be food on the table when I get home, she might like vodka for her dinner, but she fries up a good chicken for mine and it's almost time to pull into the driveway, get out, go into the house, and peck her on the cheek, the vodka as her only food started when our daughter died—

The black BMW crossed the Bay Bridge and he was almost home. He kept to the right.

—almost home now, almost at the house we're going to be moving out of soon, I've got my eye on a nice big house with six bedrooms and four baths—she says to me why do we need that when I showed it to her but I said it's because we deserve it—I got my eye on it, and when I'm making a thousand a night tax free why can't I get it, she says it'll be too much to take care of and I say we'll get a maid service, and she says where are you getting all the money for this, and I say I'm working all the overtime, yeah right, bull shit, I'm bleeding the system, don't you know, can't you tell, I'm bleeding the system dry—

Gene turned off onto his street and pulled up in front of a small green and white house. He pressed the automatic garage door opener and pulled the car into the tight-fitting garage and turned it off, got out, leaving his lunch pail on the passenger seat, closed the garage door and went across the pebbled yard and up onto the porch of his house. A woman in a black buttoned shirt and long skirt met him at the door.

"Oh Gene," she said. "It's good to see you."

He pecked her on the cheek.

"Hello, Sarah. What's for dinner?"

"I thought we could go down to Blondie's tonight. I didn't make anything."

"That's fine—what's that?"

He pointed to the two bottles of vodka on the counter. One was half full.

"What do you mean what's that? It's my vodka—you know what that is."

Gene said, "Oh" and bit his lip, leaning against the table regarding her.

—*right and she's probably already soused like every day when I get home—it's not my fault Wendy died, why is she taking it out on me by being a damned drunk? she knows I hate her drinking and tonight there's not just one but two big fifths of vodka, one already half full, as if she's flaunting it to me, why can't she be like she used to be sober as a judge? She never drank before that night we stopped at Solly's after Wendy's funeral, we never should have stopped there that night, that's when she had her first vodka and I remember she said that she felt pretty good—I didn't even feel like our only daughter had killed herself she said just like that right out of the blue, and I said to her that Wendy hadn't killed herself and Sarah said yes she did, she did with the liquor and I told her that Wendy didn't have any liquor because I don't drink and back before Wendy died there was never a bottle in the house and Wendy was underage so she couldn't have bought any liquor herself, but Sarah said what about that damned Danny he was driving when he was driving drunk and I said that's true and she said Wendy got in the car with that drunk and she should have known what was going to happen, and I said yes I'm sure she had an idea of what could happen, his blood alcohol was three times the limit, so she said, she killed herself when she got in that car with that damned drunk Danny behind the wheel— Gene don't tell me no that's not what happened, that's what it was—*

"You know you shouldn't just leave that out on the counter like that," said Gene.

"Why not," said Sarah. "—who's going to see it?"

"I see it. You know I don't like you drinking."

"Would you rather I snuck it behind your back?"

"I'd rather you didn't do it at all."

She walked across the room and got her bag.

"Come on Gene. Let's leave it and go to Blondie's."

"Which car should we take—I put mine away already."

"We'll take mine."

"Give me the keys. I don't want you driving drunk."

"I'm not drunk."

"Yes you are—why is half the vodka gone?"

She held out her arms. Her hands were steady.

"Gene—look—what's drunk about me?"

"Sarah, drinking won't bring Wendy back."

"What are you talking about? Why are you talking bad about Wendy?"

"I'm not talking bad about Wendy."

"Yes you are—you're saying I drink because of Wendy."

"So you agree that drinking is bad?"

"I—ah—I don't know Gene. Let's just go to Blondie's—you can drive, if you must."

She rushed to the door, and went out, leaving him behind to watch.

All right, all right, what's your hurry, Jesus Christ is the house on fire and you haven't told me, or what—

"Sarah!" he called after her, grabbing up the keys of her old brown Chevy from the crystal bowl on the counter and rushing after her, pausing to lock the door, only to turn to see that she was already in the car. He went down the walk, around to the car, got in and thrust the key into the ignition.

"What's your rush?" he said, starting the car.

"I'm hungry," said Sarah, smoothing down her skirt.

Yeah, he thought, gunning the car—*and why does she always wear black? Ever since Wendy was killed she's been wearing black like a weirdo—*

"Okay," he said, as he pulled away.

—I mean you've got to get over it when someone dies, people get over it, she was my daughter too, and you don't see me drinking myself to death and always wearing black do you? God damn it—but I don't dare say something heaven help me should I say something, Sarah's always right I ought to know—she's always right, like all the women all the Goddamned time, the women are always right—or else there's hell to pay if you say otherwise—

"What do you think you'll have to eat?" Gene asked.

"Steak," Sarah said. "Blondie's has the best steaks."

Gene smiled looking straight ahead as he drove.

—and you'll probably order it bloody raw like you always do, with a plate of blood in front of you with a piece of meat floating in the blood, you're disgusting Sarah, do you know that?—you know that, don't you know—disgusting—

"What will you have?" Sarah said, as the car bounced over a rail crossing.

"Hamburger and fries."

"Is that all? Gene, you are as thin as a rail."

He glanced toward her.

—yes that will be all and it'll be cooked good and black just the way I like it, I like my meat well done not like that swill you eat, that bloody rag of meat—reminds me of something that comes out of you once a month—that bloody rag—

"Yes that's all I'll get, I'm really not that hungry tonight."

"Oh. Well, anyway, how was your day today? Did you kill yourself in that damned warehouse?"

"Yep, you know it."

"You know you could get a better job, one that pays more. I don't know why you thought it was a good idea to buy that BMW when you've got the kind of job you got. I don't get how we can afford that."

He turned to look at her momentarily, as they thudded over some potholes.

—who is she to question me? Who is she to ask what I do—

"Listen—I handle the money, don't I? Are you lacking for anything?"

"Well, no, but I wonder."

"Wonder what?"

"How you can afford the car and all that."

"All what? There's just the car."

"Well you been talking about a new house—a big house—I wonder where all the money is going to come from, I don't want to end up in the poorhouse."

His jaw dropped.

—you don't want to end up in the poorhouse? You'd be in the fucking poorhouse if it wasn't for me—what the fuck else can you do but suck down that shit—

"You're not going to end up in any poorhouse, Sarah—remember, I also work the wheels down on the boardwalk and I bartend every weekend, give or take."

"But, Gene, I don't want to have a life like that, a life where I never see you. It's that way now. You're always working—it's already bad enough that you work all the overtime at the warehouse."

He raised his hand.

"What's bad about the overtime? It's easy money!"

She raised her voice, hollow and grainy.

"You get home too damned late! I hate being alone all day. It's so damned quiet. The damned walls close in. You know what that's like Gene? When the walls all come closing in?"

He glanced at her as he pulled over in front of Blondie's, finding an empty curb spot to enter, he threw the car into park.

—alone all day with your vodka, right? Well home is where I want you, no wife of mine is going to work, the next thing out of your mouth better not be how you're going to go out and get a job to keep yourself busy, isn't it Sarah? That's the next thing that's going to come out of your mouth—

"Sarah, I have to work to bring the money in. That's how life is."

—although that would be nice if you said that you'd get a job if I wanted you to, to help out, even though I would never allow it, not so that you could share with some sympathetic co-worker how sad you are in your marriage, it would show some ambition some emotion, not this black, drunken disgusting whiny way you are—

"Let's please not argue," she said, "we're here, let's enjoy ourselves."

She got out of her side of the car without saying anything more and headed for Blondie's front door, leaving Gene in the dust. He watched her tiny shoulder blades sway under her black blouse.

—damn you Sarah, you're crazy, you're damned crazy, you're like something I would win at a wheel on the boardwalk, that's what I can tell people when they ask me where I met my wife, I'll say that I got her when I won her on a wheel on the boardwalk, because she's so loopy spinning crazy, and I mean crazy—

"Wait up Sarah," said Gene, slamming the car door. "Why are you always in such a damned rush?"

"To get there," she said, her large eyes blinking innocently, her hand on the door.

She pushed it open.

"To get where," said Gene.

"Wherever we're going—why? What do you think?"

—crazy, thought Gene—*she's crazy—just crazy—*

The night had just begun.

5 – Molly

The bell always rings to signal the end of the work day. Always, without fail, the same bell, shrill, and insistent. It's the same bell that rings at the beginning of the work shift, but at the end it invokes entirely different emotions in the warehouse full of workers. It sounds the same; but it is not the same. Like twilight and dusk; the same, both half-light and dim, but not the same. At the sound of the final bell Molly rose from her cart and put down her cutter and started walking up the aisles between the green and orange racks toward the locker rooms. A lighter feeling filled her; time to go home, time to rest. She walked slowly; no need to rush. The others all half-ran to the lockers when the bell rang to get there first, but not Molly. She had reason to go slowly. What was in her locker could not be seen by all the others, locked-in behind the steel Master lock they all teased her about. She didn't really need to lock it—everybody was honest—but she needed to make sure. What was in there was secret and to her as important as gold. She went in the locker room, and took her time, washing her hands and face and brushing out her hair; taking care to do it right, taking care to do it slowly. Molly took off her grey smock, revealing a green long sleeved sweater underneath. She took out her big key and twisted it in the lock and there was the lunch pail, on the top shelf. With her standing there, there was no danger it would be grabbed down and looked into by any of the other women; though Rose, who always talked to Molly when she was around, teased her about it as Molly arranged her sweater and got out her jacket and gloves.

"Why do you have that big lunch pail up there? I always see that up there but I see you taking your lunch from a bag. Why the big black lunch pail? Going to brain somebody with it out in the parking lot?"

Molly smiled and tossed back her head.

"I bring my lunch bag in it," she said. "It belonged to my Father. From when he worked, he used it every day—sometimes I think it'll bring me luck. Plus, like you said, it's a good weapon—somebody messes with me out there on the way to my car I can brain 'em. Like you said."

Rose chuckled a moment.

"Funny, that," said Rose, slipping on her overcoat. "Anyway Molly, see you bright and early tomorrow, okay?"

"Of course Rose. I'll be here, for sure. You have a nice night."

"I will."

Rose turned away smiling, and slipped from the locker room, and so did the few other women remaining, finally leaving Molly alone. She swung the lunch pail down from the shelf onto the bench with a heavy clank, and looked inside. They were all in there; she ran a finger over them; over all ten little pretty cute bright yellow boxes. The locker slammed shut and latched, and she clicked closed the big Master lock, put on her black jacket and red gloves, picked up the lunch pail and left the locker room. She smoothly glided out the door from the warehouse into the front office, padded down the aisle between the empty desks and their dark computer screens, and went out the door to the outside. The brisk air lay in layers, and a cold wind blew; not really biting cold, but cold enough that she appreciated having brought gloves to work today. She walked down the sidewalk between the rolling lawns, got to the parking lot and into her red Pontiac.

The cold and wind made her feel she had been holding her breath walking out of the building, and that she was now safely outside she was free to begin breathing again. With each step toward the car the tightness in her lungs faded until she gave it not a single thought, as she reached her car and opened the door and swung the lunch pail over to the passenger side. Once behind the wheel, she took the car up the driveway toward the stop she would have to make in the Dunkin' Donuts parking lot, up around the corner on Easton. Nothing to do with donuts, no—though a donut would be nice she always watched the calories; and after Gene pulled up and switched her full lunch pail for an empty one, he pulled away, and she opened the lunch pail and there it was, again, as every time; a brand new looking stiff crisp fifty dollar bill. She pocketed the bill and headed out of the parking lot toward the short drive home; and the trees and the ramp to the interstate and the feeling of being in control and moving in the car so easily oh so easily, took away whatever pang of guilt that may have shot through her the instant before she twisted the starter. The fifty dollars was good. Fifty dollars, twice a week, easy money, the extra four hundred a month were really helping, because money was very, very tight. She moved fast enough on the highway but once turned off heading for Millstone, she was lucky enough to get behind a large filthy orange cement truck moving at exactly, five, miles—an hour.

Pokey, pokey, pokey, pokey. Might as well just stop dead, sit and relax, as go this slow.

She drummed the wheel to keep from becoming too tense and too angry, until at last she came to her turnoff, powered with the pedal to the floor up the incline, past the big cemetery to her street, making the left turn wide, but it was okay nobody was coming; thank God where they lived, nobody was ever coming— and was home. The house was far back, alone; no neighbors, just the deep woods and the neighboring cemetery, a big old fashioned one with many crypts draped in black moss and years of mold, among a great field of leaning stones. When Molly was younger she felt that living so near to the cemetery was creepy; but not anymore. She had outgrown such fears; and as she went in the house, she got ready to greet her Mother, who would be lying on the sofa in the living room under a great handmade comforter, knitted with the images of a white-tailed buck and a pretty doe standing alert and watchful upon it; she would not see her Father right away, because he would be in the front parlor—his sacred room into which no one else was allowed to venture—and it was just as well Molly came to Mother first, because she was the more gregarious of the two. Molly came in the room, swept off her coat, and flung it over a chair along with the same words she said once home, every day for years now.

"Hi Mom," she said, wringing her hands.

"Hello Molly—did you work hard today?"

"Oh, yes."

Mother shook out her great shock of blonde hair. Her form shifted under the comforter.

"Must be nice, to be able to work, to be able to work hard, like you do. I used to work hard too, remember?"

"I know Mom—I need to go in and put on dinner—what would you like?"

"Some of that leftover stew from yesterday—you made a great stew."

"Okay Mom. Think Dad will like that too?"

"Oh, who knows what he'd like?"

Molly's mother laughed and Molly laughed back. Father never cared what he ate. He was too ascetic. "I am above food," he had once said years ago. "Food just makes you age and after your allotted food has been consumed, then it is time for you to die."

Molly remembered this every day. It was annoying to remember it every day so she always spoke over it and smothered it down, fast, saying the first thing that came to her; and, thank God, it always made some kind of sense, like now, as she said, "Would you like me to put on the TV for you, Mom? It's time for the evening news—"

—yes then we will eat and once we've eaten enough, it will be time for us to die—

"No," said the prone woman lying on the couch, raising a hand, stopping Molly's thought. "It's always all bad news—and the weather—why on earth would I want to know the weather? I can't go out in it anyway."

Molly just smiled, for some reason suddenly happier, lighter, as if Mother had just tried to tell her a joke. "Okay," she said, leaving Mother, and going into the kitchen. Mother had been crippled years ago, in a fall from a scaffold on a house painting job she had gotten. She was a house painter—way ahead of her time as a woman. She used to do tall steeples on churches and tall houses where the rich people lived. Like that one that day and all kinds of painting jobs. Then that one day the scaffolding guys put her scaffold up wrong. She should have checked, but she didn't, and she was up three stories when the scaffolding folded dumping her to the ground, and she severed her spine in the fall, permanently paralyzing her legs below the waist. There she lay on the ground, unable to rise, thrashing her arms and head all around, yelling, cursing and pointing at the pastor of the rectory she was painting, who had come out to help her, and she cursed him, saying, "I will sue the church and you! I will own your house!" But nothing came of it. The lawyers took her money, months went by, and at last they just told her she did not have a case, and that the fall was her fault. She had only been twenty five when the fall happened, and Molly had been three. Dad had done his best to raise Molly, and take care of Mother and work a job, all at the same time. When she was younger, Molly's Grandmother used to watch her during the day while her father was at work and she used to play and watch TV in the room where Mother lay under the same comforter she has used up to this very day, with the buck and doe standing alert—and Molly had often struggled to watch her kids shows on TV while Grandmother and Mother yelled bloody murder at one another, because Grandmother never approved of Mother being a house painter and going up on high places to work, and she used to always say, "Something awful will happen to you. This is not women's work. This never was women's work," and then after the accident while Mother lay there helpless Grandmother would repeat the same thing, that she had had no business doing men's work and that was why she was paralyzed now, and not some guy, as it should have been, and then Grandmother would always say that she hoped she was happy disappointing George, her husband, like she was, being paralyzed and unable to have sex with him, and Grandmother would give Mother hell like this, the whole time, all the time, each and every day, from when Molly was three to sixteen. Then, when Molly turned sixteen, Grandmother died and Mother refused to allow any of the family to go to the funeral—she had hated Grandmother even though she had been the one caring for Molly, doing all the housework, and preparing all the meals—the daily comments about forcing George to go without sex in his marriage cut through Mother like a butcher's cleaver, and she never forgave Grandmother for that, nor appreciated any of the things she did for her daily. But Molly did go to the funeral without telling her Mother because she loved the old woman for having raised her, and for having played so many board games with her, made so many puzzles together with her, and having watched so much TV with her, and having helped her with so much of her homework, and all those kinds of things that made sure Molly grew up right and stayed on the straight and narrow, so she decided to see Grandmother in the casket one last time. She was amazed that the casket lining, padding and pillow were all hot pink. It was just perfect! Pink was Grandmother's favorite color, and she looked so happy lying there engulfed in it, in a matching pink dress, with a pink rosary around her neck and a pink band in her hair. After that, Molly had left the funeral home and gone home to Mother and even though she was only sixteen going on seventeen, she immediately took over where her Grandmother had left off, and began taking care of Mother and making the meals and cleaning the house until she got her job at the VNA corporation in the warehouse. With the extra money she then made, her father hired a nurse to spend the days with Mother, until first George came home and took over from the nurse, and when Molly came home she'd take over from George. Molly made dinner and cleaned the house on the weekends and this was how they had lived for the last twelve years, up until now with Molly at the age of thirty, Mother fifty two, and Father, God knew how old he was; he had the ancient stooped down look of old people from long ago and his beak of a nose stuck out and hung down, his eyes shifted and blinked nonstop as though judging everything around him, as though his brain was crammed with thoughts and judgments and criticism and complaints, and he carried a pocket holy bible everywhere he went, as if he'd always been on the pastor's side against his wife about the accident. He talked about retiring from his job as an airplane engineer, but Molly had no idea how many years away from retirement he was. She just knew he had to be at least ten years older than her Mother.

In the kitchen, Molly put on the stewpot and got the table ready for her and her father and got a tray table ready for Mother out in the living room as she asked, "Mother, have you taken all your pills? Do you need help into your wheelchair? Do you have to go to the bathroom? Is there anything I can do for you?"

Every time Molly asked her Mother this, her Mother's eyes transformed in such a way that brought love for Mother into Molly's heart for a sharp instant.

"No," said the old blonde woman, her eyes slowly fading back away.

Love lowered; hold on.

"No to which one?"

"No to all of them."

Love sank away behind sharp words of concern.

"You didn't take your pills?" said Molly, sternly.

"No."

"Why not?"

"Too much trouble—besides, you give them to me when you come home."

"No, no. You're supposed to take two in the morning and two at dinner. You shouldn't be taking all four of them at dinner now. And you need to take two of the little white ones at noon— doesn't your nurse give them to you?"

"I tell her I don't want them, and that I would throw them all away if I had legs—and if you didn't have them all locked up so I can't throw them away—maybe that's why the nurse doesn't give me them."

"No the nurse has a key—Mother, you can be a real pain in the ass."

Mother smiled a wry smile, again her look shifted.

"What," she said, "—about taking my pills on time?"

"Yes."

The old blonde woman rolled her eyes away from Molly's and out to the far wall.

"Time, time, time—that's all you talk about. You know what time is, Molly?"

"What?"

Mother's eyes rolled back and locked onto Molly's, as she answered, saying, "Time is something that rushes by, disappears, and leaves us for dead."

Molly reached out, touching Mother's cold veiny hand.

"Mom, listen—it's not that bad—that's no way to think."

The cold hand withdrew from Molly, as Mother added, "Yes it is, yes it is, Molly—as you get older, time goes faster and faster and it just speeds up until its racing and then when it's going as fast as it can, Pop! You're dead!"

"Well—it probably seems that way. Hey, listen. Where is the mail? Was there mail?"

"Yes. There. It's on the coffee table."

Molly went over and looked through the mail and saw it was mainly medical bills. In the years that passed after the accident, Mother had no less than ten back surgeries. And each time, they were told it would be the last one, and she would walk, but it never was; and she never walked. Mother's last surgery was six months ago, and the bills just keep coming. The VNA insurance was piss poor, and Father's insurance was nonexistent, because he was an independent contractor at the airplane factory now, because the firm had wiped out all the union jobs when the last of those guys had retired. And now, again, the doctors were talking about another surgery for Mother—one that might give her some limited partial use of her legs, whatever that means.

"Limited partial use?" said Mother. "What good is that? What does that even mean? Limited partial use? I mean, either they work, or they don't! What's limited partial?"

"I don't know," said Molly.

Mother's head rolled back, her voice thinned to a whine.

"I'm a wreck—just a bundle of aches and pains."

Mother often talked like this, and then weakened, and started saying, "I should just die, you know that? Yes, that's what should happen. I should die."

"Don't say that Mother," Molly would snap. "Don't ever say things like that, at least not to me."

"Okay, Mom," Mother replied, grinning sarcastically. "I need my little Mom Molly to keep me in line."

"It's not a joke, Mom," said Molly, turning away.

Even so, Mother grinned. Molly felt it coming hot, on her back. *No. None of this is a joke—*

Mother's grin faded by half.

None of it, yes! Just like that, like that!

And at last, was gone completely.

Yes none of it!

Molly moved toward the kitchen, leafing through the bills. Luckily, Molly got most of Mother's pills for free, at least—she would spirit them out of the VNA warehouse, along with the other stuff. Every little bit helped. Every little bit.

The bills shuffled through her hands.

Thank God for Gene and his fifty bucks.

Thank God.

Once into the kitchen, Molly stirred the stew which was bubbling up and heating rapidly. For some reason, the bubbling brown stew made her think of the fires of hell—and the sight of the old crumbling cemetery through the kitchen window did nothing to kill this image in her mind. It always made her think of Father, who had never been the same since Mother fell from the scaffold and who claimed, almost bragged, that he'd never had had sex with a woman since. He had been brought up by a religious woman, a fallen nun who dropped out of the convent to get married, and she and her husband adopted George, and raised him as though he had a halo on his head. My little saint, his Mother would say; my little Georgie is an absolute saint. She raised her little saint to see everything as a sign from God, to the point that when Mother fell and got paralyzed, he took it to be a message from God that he should be celibate for the rest of his life and lead a monastic existence in the midst of the family. And so, as though he were a priest, he wore black shirts and pants exclusively and would have donned the ecclesiastical collar if it had not been that God had told him in a dream no, no, that's going too far—but instead he promised God that if his wife died first, he would take holy orders. That was his big dream. While Molly was in the kitchen stirring the stew, and while Mother was on the couch refusing to watch TV, he was down the hall, in the front Parlor, his Sacred Room, with the shades drawn and a dim light lit, the room crammed tight with heavy dark furniture and a mothball smell and crosses—hundred of crosses peppering the walls, and pictures of Jesus, his Mother and the Saints all along the wall as well. And there was the smell of candles and one wall full of a bookcase of prayer books, books on the lives of the saints, bibles and every other kind of holy book you could accumulate in a long holy saintly life, as well as statues and pictures of the rest of the saints, and crosses holding little compartments that contained everything a priest would need, when summoned to a deathbed in the night. All these things had belonged to his Father and Mother. In the midst of all this, he wrestled with the flesh, wrestled to maintain his celibacy, because he was, as seen by some, still a reasonably young, strong man and the flesh tortured him with the fires of its demands—he sat rocking back and forth, mostly, back and forth, struggling.

A knock came on the door.

"Dad?" said Molly through the door, "It's dinner time."

"I'll be right down." he said loudly; the first words he'd spoken all day.

Her voice went away, and her footsteps sounded on the squeaking floorboards moving back down toward the kitchen. He turned up the electric lights and blew out the candles in the room one by one; as he did so, an old friend of a thought grew in him— that he was God-like—and that he just might be God put on earth—but this truth must never come out until the end times, which he knew would come in his lifetime. But, he must first take holy orders. He must first be a priest. That was his fantasy, and as the smoke from the blown out candles swirled upward, upward, with his thoughts, his eyes swung upward as well, following the ribbons of smoke, until he could see through the ceiling, through the second floor bedrooms and the ceiling of those rooms and on through the floor of the attic, and the roof, and he was able to expand towards everything and take in God himself, who he was privileged to know personally—as the candle smoke faded, he gripped the doorknob, opened the door and made his way toward the kitchen carrying his pocket bible, towards where Molly waited with the steaming stewpot on the table that reminded him too, as it had Molly, of hell.

My daughter Molly knows. Yes, she knows—

"Molly," said George. "Bless you, for this food."

"Sit down Dad," said Molly. "Let me bring Mom's food out to her, and I'll be right back."

She left the room, perfume hanging behind her. The smell brought up bad thoughts in George's head; he shook it and clenched his fingernails into his fists under the table. He could hear the women talking in the other room; women's talk; nothing important. Molly returned to the room and sat down across from him at the table. Her hair; the curve of her face; it might have been Mother, back when she was young and lithe and ran free across the grass around the stones of the cemetery, urging him on, and then she'd turn, and come back laughing, laughing towards him. Greedily he gripped the ladle and spooned out his stew over two slices of thick white bread, that lay atop one another on his plate, and the warm thick liquid ran over them, smothering them; and he did not look Molly in the face, but ate in silence, one hand on the bible in his lap, his eyes set beyond the walls, like a lone prisoner in a cell.

6 – Eli the Rat

Eli rose and got tea; thinking of this, the first day of his assignment, made his hands shake as he lifted the cup to his lips. What would it be like? Who would he meet? He knew they were stealing Oxycodone, and he knew roughly how much. Massengill had briefed him already. He was going to put on the uniform of a working man. He would be a fork lift driver; this would give him ready access to all the areas of the warehouse. He sat at the table in the kitchen of his apartment and pushed his glasses up his nose. The newspaper open before him was full of stories he was too nervous to care about. He rubbed his long sideburns as he read, and there was something in there about a helicopter crash, and an eclipse which would take place tomorrow; partial, not total. Not worth looking out for. He sipped the last of the tea and got up and put his cup in the sink and ran hot water in it. He would need to get his morning smoke; he had to fortify himself. He went into his room and in the sock drawer was a small cube wrapped tight in tin foil. He brought it to the kitchen table and laid it on the open newspaper and got his pipe out of the drawer where the cutlery was. He used a regular briar pipe, brown, with a black stem; nothing fancy. After getting a single cigarette out of a pack he kept up on a shelf with his bills and address book, he sat down. He was not a smoker per se; but he kept a pack of cigarettes on hand just for this purpose. Last, he took a small envelope of fine white powder from behind the salt in the spice cabinet that he had written *MAGIC* on it in pencil. After rolling some of the tobacco from the cigarette into the bowl of the pipe, he unwrapped the small black cube from the tin foil and sliced off a small piece of Lebanese from the cube using the warm spoon he had stirred his tea with. This went into the bowl of the pipe with the tobacco; he sprinkled some powder on top like icing sugar. The pipe went in his mouth; the matches came into his hand; he lit the bowl, and he smoked it. He had learned this method of smoking hot blends when he was in the Army in Germany; where they had been no weed for him. Since then the strong stuff was all there was for him in this regards. He smoked down the entire bowl fully and powerfully, as the room expanded around him; and he fought his way through the roaring flames licking at him from under the floor boards to put away the remaining materials into the sock drawer, being careful to avoid the hissing writhing snakes squirming inside. He put away the pipe, cigarettes and matches, snatched up his car keys, and went out the door, which was now made of a great slab of hairy flesh, and came from a place he never wanted to go, and locked the hairy door of flesh behind him.

Lucky for him, the VNA pharmaceutical distribution center was about twenty minutes from his apartment. Flames boiled about his car, as he drove down the highway toward the place, but he was not afraid, he never was. A woman sat beside him, she too had come from the pipe's bowl. She wore no clothes and covered her breasts with her hands and her privates with her crossed legs. "Why do you want to go to work there," she asked, as the flames boiled unnoticed around her as well. "Why don't you want to spend the entire day with me? You have more than half a cube to smoke, back home. We could have so much fun, you and I." He shook his head hard to say no, shaking her from his mind and she disappeared in a wisp of curling smoky vapor.

High on his private mixture, he drove to the VNA compound and when he got there he parked his car and saw that flames were also rising from the roof of the warehouse, smoke pouring from the loading dock doors and large shattered windows of the office block. Undeterred he got out and locked his car and shuffled his brand new steel toed boots toward the front door, up the now red hot walkway between the walls of fire; and he thought for an instant he may have made a mistake and had added a little too much PCP to his hashish for breakfast, this being his first day in this assignment, but no—he would be all right, he always was. Looking sober as a judge, he opened the doors, went in and slid straight up to the receptionist's desk, and stopped, and faced her, his hands clasped before him.

"I'm the new hire starting today in the warehouse, do you know anything about where I'm supposed to report to?" he said—she smiled at him with too much lipstick, her teeth already stained red with it and her whole face roughly smeared with thick pink pancake stuff, and she said out this red hole of a face, "I will call the foreman, Mister Panko. What is your name please?"

"Eli. My name is Eli."

"Just a moment Eli."

She held the fancy black phone to her ear, as she punched in the numbers into the buttons.

"Mister Panko? There's the new hire for the warehouse up here. His name is Eli. Yes. Yes. Yes. All right."

She put the phone down.

"Mister Panko will be here for you in a minute, Eli," she said.

"Thanks."

Eli sat down unharmed in the midst of the smoke and flames around him and sat there unconsumed, until a portly man with his hair smoldering came out of the door to greet him. His shirt buttons were straining over his belly, and his tie was unfashionably short and wide.

"Eli?" said Tom Panko, extending a hand. Eli stood and took the hand. Panko stepped back with his hands on his broad hips looking Eli up and down and said, "I see you've arrived all ready to start work – new boots and all."

"I sure am," said Eli.

"Okay then," said Panko, flames hissing. "Come on back, I'll introduce you to Carl, our other fork lift driver. He'll be training you on the company fork lift."

"I've driven a fork lift before."

Panko lifted a hand.

"Yes, I'm sure, but Carl will train you. There are procedures you need to know—but it's good to know that you've driven a fork lift before—how else would you have gotten this job, seeing that no one asked me if we even needed another driver, nor did I get to review your qualifications. Regardless, follow me."

Eli followed Panko into the warehouse; and that was how it all started. He survived the first few days hidden in the midst of flaming racks on both sides of the aisles as he met Carl and read procedures and got lectured, but by day three he was fully trained in VNA operational protocol, and was able to cruise around the warehouse, getting to know its people. He was learning the ropes fast. Obviously the first person he got to know well was Carl, since he had trained him on all the processes and procedures, and he was now the senior fork lift driver.

"Eli!" said Carl, "clean the bulk stock area!"

"Eli!" said Carl, "load that first trailer in bay one!"

"Eli!" said Carl, "gather the empty pallets!"

"Eli!" said Carl—

"Eli!"

Tall lanky buzz-cut mustachioed Carl would charge across the loading dock, filling in bills of lading, pulling inventory slips, barking at everyone, not just Eli. In his filthy undershirt Carl would race his forklift into the racks to get loads for Molly, or

Frankie, or for Panko. At break time he would stand in the loading dock door smoking a cigarette, the morning sun pouring in on him, Eli standing beside him.

"A bunch of shit, Eli, don't you think?" said Carl, "Working for a living is a bunch of shit."

Out toward the flowing sunlight past the loading dock doors the blacktop loading pad stretched out to a wide green lawn, and on to a tree line in the distance, and further.

"I don't know if it's a bunch of shit, Carl. It brings in money—"

"That's about it! You know if I was twenty years younger and knew what I know now, things would be different!"

"Oh yeah, how so?"

Carl blew out smoke.

"Yeah! See that smoke? That's how."

After working with him for the first two weeks, Eli had ruled Carl out as a suspect in the pill thefts. The grizzled man was gruff, smelly, rude, a bit stupid, and generally disgusting—but he was no thief. Eli would need to dig deeper into the others to find the culprits.

"Someone's slowly bleeding off the drugs," Massengill had said. "They're taking ten to twenty bottles a week—it's clearly a small time operation, someone stuffing them down their pants—but it adds up—and whoever's doing it is making good money off those pills. I'm sure of it. And that, my friend, is shit that needs to stop!"

One day when Carl had not given him a full shift's worth of things to do, he sat on his forklift in the rear of the bulk stock area, the warehouse spread before him, taking in the dead quiet.

What about these warehouse thieves—where do I start—should we stop everyone going out every day and check if they are carrying anything that they shouldn't?—No, they would just stop them from taking the stuff—I need to catch someone, anyone in the act—I need to catch someone doing something wrong—I can't do anything to stop them from do-

ing something wrong. It's crazy—the need to catch, humiliate, prosecute, punish them for all that they have gotten away with so far, and not just to stop it. If you just make them stop stealing then they will have gotten clean away with everything they have already done—it is an interesting puzzle—bringing people to justice—these thieves, whoever they are, have gotten thousands of dollars worth of drugs out of here over the last couple of years—they have to be made responsible for that—even if it takes a rat like me to make friends with them, to start in with them—and then the boom drops—one day, they will walk right into the arms of the law. God, this place is massive. I need somewhere to start, I need to gather facts—about who has the money, who has a bit too much money—who has the access—who has the opportunity—I need to get on the stick, this is the way it works, you come in, work for a while, and without digging or doing anything suspicious, without asking any questions that would make them wonder, why'd he ask that? Why's he caring about this, or that? I can't talk to Panko about it because Panko might be in the middle of it—he controls the whole place and he drives a good solid Cadillac, top of the line—that makes him a suspect—and whoever drives that big black BMW out there—I don't know whose car that is yet but when I find out, that guy will be a suspect—and who's got access to the narcotics cage—I know Carl does but honestly Carl seems too stupid, but what if he's not? I don't have enough to go on yet, I haven't been in here long enough yet— what about those people who work on the packing lines? They have the opportunity. Or what about the people who work in returns—they also have opportunity. Or, what about the people picking the orders up on the picking line? I don't even know their names yet—what about that girl and that guy who go around with their carts all day getting stuff to load in those picker's racks? What about those people in the checking station? What about down on the docks? What about the garbage men who come by every day, they could be being fed stuff to take out in the trash. They're young, hairy, stinky and smelly, and laugh out loud all the time. Yeah, they got the look, but—there are so many possibilities. They don't even have guards at this place to check people coming and going. Maybe it was someone who set up the piss poor security here? What about those great big sweaty guys who run around picking cases all day? They handle every drug in here. The narcotics cage is wide open all day, or at least most of the day, from when Panko opens it in the morning, to when he shuts it at night. But no, I could be full of shit; I could be all wrong—see I don't even know how this place works. I've got to knuckle down and figure it out—here comes Panko—what does he want—better straighten up, look busy—I'm the rat. Who's coming—

Panko shuffled up into the quiet and spoke words, sending the quiet scurrying away in all directions away from Eli.

"Eli. Bring some number one two and three boxes up to the packers. They're running low."

"All the packers? Both sides of the line?"

"Right. Can you handle it? Carl always did it, but he's out today. You done it yet?"

"No I haven't, but there's always a first time."

Panko turned nodding grimly, and disappeared behind a wall of mineral oil, cough syrups and digestion aids. As he disappeared, Eli pushed the lever and spun the wheel and started off to get the boxes.

Can I handle it? Sure I can handle it. Now I get to schmooze with the packers—but come on, I mean—can I handle it? Of course I can. What kind of fucking question was that?

He sped up the forklift.

I can handle anything. I'm a rat.

Eli headed off toward the packers.

7 – Bobby and the Packers

Fat bearded Bobby stood at his packing station, tapping a rusted staple hammer on the hard steel table top, bored stiff with the job he'd been doing for fourteen years, and would probably be doing for at least fourteen more. He stood bellied up to the table facing the conveyor line that brought the packers the trays of drugs to be packed and sent away. The steel tabletop was rubbed shiny—the green paint was all gone from the years of boxes sliding across and across and across—as they would, forever. Across the line, at the next table, Jim Jolly, small and black, stood facing Bobby through the tall shelving between them that the line ran under. Jolly shook his staple hammer at Bobby, and spoke strongly, reacting to Bobby's latest teasing attack.

"You ought not talk to any man like that, fat boy—you ought to have respect—I'm a damned man! Not a boy! Never call me a boy."

Bobby leaned back, holding out his hands in appeasement, and spoke with a thin grin.

"I only asked you how it is to live in a lean-to against the wall of Rahway state prison, in that shithole of a town—hey Cynthia! Cynthia, turn around! We got a question!"

He turned to a small white-haired woman in gold rimmed glasses, who stood facing the two men from across the next line, where she worked alone, packing.

"What, Bobby?" said Cynthia, unable to hear what they'd been saying. She leaned forward to hear better. She wore the same grey formless smock as all the other women at VNA.

Bobby waved the staple hammer and yelled to her, saying, "Jolly over here's getting mad at me, just because I asked him what it's like to live up against the wall of Rahway State Prison—"

"You said more than that," barked Jolly, through the shelving. "You said a whole damned lot more than that, you bastard!"

"What?" yelled Cynthia, her deeply lined pale face tilted, still straining to hear them clearly over the rolling hiss of the surrounding steel conveyors.

"Oh, never mind—it's just Jolly acting up," said Bobby, pointing at Jolly, and he smiled at his great joke an instant, before lifting his hot mug to his lips. He drank, swallowed, and then spoke low to Jolly.

"Calm down, Jim," said Bobby, putting down his mug. "I'm just teasing you."

"You do too much damned teasing," said Jolly, wide-eyed. "Just do your damned work—you make me fucking nervous with your damned teasing. You don't tease a grown man the way you do. I am a God-damned grown man not a child!"

"What?" said Bobby, leaning in at Jolly.

"I said, just do your God damned fucking work, and I'll do my God damned fucking work, and we'll be fine and get to the end of the day when I don't have to see your filthy pig puss any more today! There!"

"Pig puss, heh," said Bobby. "That's a good one. Pig puss."

"Keep laughing, fat man! Someday you'll be laughing for the last fucking time!"

Grinning broadly, Bobby pulled a green tray containing an order of yellow boxed drugs off onto his shiny steel table, and turned around to the stack of folded cardboard shipping boxes behind him. He gripped up a box and turned back to Jolly, and spoke as he began forming the next of the hundreds of boxes he stuffed the drugs into every day.

"We're almost out of boxes," said Bobby. "Didn't you say you told Panko we need them?"

"I did tell Panko," said Jolly, pulling off a two tray order onto his table.

"So why don't we have boxes? I mean you're sure you told him?"

"I said I told him. How the hell should I know why there's no boxes here yet?"

"You don't have to yell at me, Jim."

"I'm still aggravated from before! It's hard to calm down when you got to spend all day across from a fat boy son of an asswipe, like you!"

"Jim," said Bobby softly, lifting his mug toward his lips, "like I said, you need to learn to relax. You'll get chest pains if you keep it up, the age you are. You should be careful."

Jolly bit his lip, glaring, and said, "Just can't stop, can you Bobby? I think you better just shut up right now!"

Bobby drank, nodded, then put the mug down and looked down, stabbing a button on the tape machine set to the side. The tape shot out and he swung it over the opening of the box, sealing perfectly the flat brown line before him. He tore the label from the paperwork, glued it to the box, and tacked the paperwork down on the box that then got shoved it off onto the line next to them, which led to the UPS labeling, weighing and shipping station, where the next worker would do what was needed to keep each order moving. Their lines and stations were surrounded by tall green and orange racks laden with hundreds of cases of drugs. The racks stood in ranks stretching out over the whole warehouse, with just enough room for forklifts to come and go in the aisles between. A tall loud orange forklift with a huge stack of boxes suddenly shot out of the aisle nearest to the packers, and pulled up behind Bobby. The forklift driver wore a small black beard and thick dark framed eyeglasses. Holding onto the glasses, he jumped off the machine, and stepped up, bent, and started sliding the empty pallets out of the way.

"You're the new guy," said Bobby. "Didn't you just start just this Monday?"

"Yeah, I'm the new guy, I'm Eli," said Eli.

"Carl always brings us the boxes. Where's Carl? Off hiding someplace?"

Eli chuckled with sparkling eyes at Bobby, saying, "I'm sure he's not hiding. He's just busy doing some other stuff so Tom Panko told me that you needed boxes."

"Okay—hey, I'm Bob, and this guy behind me is Jolly— say Jolly, introduce yourself to Eli, shake his hand or something— have some manners, where's your manners?"

Jolly leaned out at Bobby and said loudly, "Settle down, Bobby. I just told you—fuck with me one time too many, and you'll get a big surprise!"

"What? Hey Jim, don't curse at the new guy—he might be religious—"

Jolly leaned to the side, ignoring Bobby, and said, "Sorry about this loudmouth here, Eli. Welcome to VNA!" which he pronounced *Ve-Nay*.

"Nice to meet you." said Eli, his grin unbroken, "and who's the young lady over there?"

"That's Cynthia," said Bobby, turning and yelling past Jolly, saying, "Hey Cynthia—meet Eli—our new fork lift driver."

Cynthia called out "What? A new fork lift driver? What happened to Carl? Did they finally have the sense to fire him?"

She left her station and came over next to Jolly and all three now faced Eli's shiny grin.

"It's like I told these guys, Carl's doing something else. There are two fork drivers now."

"Young man," said Cynthia, "that's a cute little beard you got! If only I was twenty one again."

"What do we need two fork lift drivers for?" said Bobby, hefting his hot but cooling mug, and raising his eyebrows.

"I don't know," said Eli, "the big shots decide those things. All I know is, I got a job."

"Yeah—big shits, you mean," sneered Bobby.

"Yeah, whatever," snickered Eli, eyes narrowed.

Eli got busy tossing the few remaining bundles of boxes off the pallets, so he could take them away and bring in the full one. The crashing of the bundles and pallets sliding and slapping down to the floor mixed with the general din of the lines. They all drifted back to their jobs and Eli slid the forks into the stack of empty pallets, and quickly backed the truck off out of sight around the towering piles of cases.

"Seems like a nice guy," said Jolly, tacking an order onto a box with his staple hammer and pushing it off down the line.

"Yeah," replied Bobby, pushing a tray of big black bottles into a box. "But I don't see why we need two fork lift drivers, plus if they did, why they didn't offer the job to one of us instead of hiring someone off the street. I would have taken that job in a minute, it's better than being tied to this table. Plus, it pays more."

Trays, boxes, tape and labels deftly flowed through their hands as they continued chatting.

"Oh, you know why Bobby," said Jolly, waving the staple hammer, "It wouldn't be safe around here if you were driving one of those damned things!"

"What do you mean?"

"You'd be crashing into things, running with the forks up, all set to spear somebody, not looking where you're going, dropping loads down off the racks, crippling people, maybe even killing somebody. That's how it'd be with you Bobby—you're too damned crazy to run a fork lift."

"Why? Do you think you could do it better?"

"I'd do it damned good!"

Bobby picked up his mug again.

"Oh, well, we're never getting off this packing line, anyway. Hey, what did the new guy say his name was anyway? Levi? Yeah, Levi, that was it. Levi."

"No," said Jolly, "It's Eli."

Bobby took another sip from the nearly cold mug, then snickered, "Eli? What kind of God-damned name is Eli? It's like He-Lie. As in, Eli's no good, he lies down on the job all the time."

"It's his name Bobby—don't go ragging on the guys name."

Just as Bobby put down his mug and started to speak back to Jolly, Eli drove the forklift back around the wall of cases, a full load of number one boxes, that he was going to drop right behind Bobby. As he pulled up, and let down the load, Bobby couldn't help but speak up.

"Hey Levi—well done—not bad for a new guy."

Eli said "The name's Eli—and thank you."

Jolly waved his staple hammer and called out to Bobby, "God damn you Bobby! Making fun of a man's name—what's wrong with you to make fun of a man's name right to his face like that?"

Bobby threw out his hands.

"I wasn't making fun—I thought his name was Levi—isn't that right Eli—don't Levi and Eli sound about the same?"

"Yeah, I suppose they do," said Eli, as he slid his forks out from under the load and disappeared back around the wall of cases to get the next load. Bobby, Jolly, and Cynthia left their stations and hungrily surrounded the new stack of boxes, sliding what they needed off and tossing the bundles across the floor.

Jolly waved his hands sharply towards Bobby.

"What are you doing, fat boy?" said Jolly. "You're taking so many bundles of boxes, there won't be any left for me and Cynthia!"

"You'll have plenty, Jolly—the way you pack you don't need that many anyway."

"What do you mean the way I pack—what do you God-damned mean?"

As they faced off, Eli distracted them, racing back around with the next load of boxes, and dropped it with a loud slap down on the concrete. Bobby ignored Jolly, turned to Eli, and shook a bundle of boxes in the air.

"You do good work, Levi!"

"It's Eli", grinned Eli. "E-L-I—Eli."

"Oh, gee, I'm sorry. I keep forgetting," he smiled, and he turned around and brought the bundle back to his area with a wide grin on his face. Jolly scowled. He turned to Eli.

"Eli, he's calling you Levi on purpose! Like I said, he thinks he's a real card! Meet Bobby, the jackass of jokers," he said, waving his staple hammer towards Bobby.

Eli smiled leaning on the fork listening as Bobby dropped the bundle and pointed to Jolly and said "You've got a lot of nerve calling me a jackass in front of the new guy, Jolly—you best look at yourself first, unless you want me to start talking about you next."

"Bobby, you're just one fat young fuck. I ought to—"

Eli called out, "Boys, don't fight on my account. I'm not mad—"

Bobby threw up a hand, saying, "I know you're not mad, Levi, it's just this damned Jolly has me all nervous—all shook up, you know. Like the damned song. Besides Jolly, did you just hear that, the new guy called you a boy? You going to give him the same shit you give me when I call you a boy?"

"Bob," said Jolly, carefully controlling his anger, "His name is Eli, not Levi. And there are no boys in this warehouse."

With a smile Eli straightened the forklift and zoomed back around out of sight around the wall of cases, as Jolly went on pointing at Bobby, saying, "Why do you have to teasing that man like that Bob—he's new here. Let him be. There's something wrong in your head. You just got to tease everybody."

"I really do get the names mixed up Jolly—I can't help it if I get the names mixed up!"

Just then Panko came around from the end of a rack with his hands up in the air.

"Guys," he said, "the lines are getting pretty backed up— what seems to be the problem?"

"Problem's not me, Panko—problem's not me," said Jolly.

"Yeah?" said Bobby, slicing the straps off the new box bundles with a knife. "Who is the problem then, Jolly? Who? Hey Panko, come here. I got a question for you."

"What?"

Panko came up and stood with his hands on his broad hips, listening.

"What are you doing hiring a new fork lift driver off the street instead of promoting one of us?" said Bobby, pointing off toward the racks, "and also, why do we need two fork truck drivers?"

Panko threw back his head, buck teeth shining as he answered.

"We needed two drivers to handle both the bulk stock area, and to load trucks when it gets busy. In the afternoon there's too much work for just one."

"Okay. But why'd you hire someone off the street? Lots of us would have bid on that job."

"Massengill's decision. Go talk to him. We needed somebody with fork lift experience right away. We got no time to train new guys."

"But, what about Carl? Carl used to be a picker, and you put him on a fork—you trained him didn't you?"

Panko flung out his arms playing with the shadows from the overhead fluorescents.

"Bobby, I told you. It's a Massengill decision. I asked him the same question; he gave me the same answer. Just keep your lines moving and cut out the chit chat."

Cynthia had been listening to all this as she steadily worked her line. Finally, she called out to Bobby.

"Hey, Bobby, stop pumping Panko. He told you he doesn't know."

Bobby shot a look at Cynthia, who seldom spoke.

"What, are you sucking up to Panko now, Cynthia?"

"God no—I'm just using common sense—you and Panko got the same answer. Why go on and on about it? Why not just let the poor man be?"

"Hey, listen guys," barked Panko, slapping his hands together and backing away. "I don't really care, just get to work and clear these lines. It's late in the day—these orders need to go out now. Back to work everybody, right now! We don't pay you to jibber jabber."

Bobby turned back, scowling, to his packing station. Jolly smiled at seeing Bobby put in his place. Cynthia went back to her industrious work. Just then Eli drove up with the final pallet of boxes, dropped them up against the other loads, and without a word started pulling back away, but Panko called out to stop him.

"Eli!" called out Tom, "Come around to my office! I got another job for you!"

"Okay Boss," called out Eli, who quickly back out away gone, as Panko turned around and headed toward his office.

When they were gone, Bobby leaned in to Jolly.

"Something's up Jolly. It don't feel right to me, about this. It's all fishy somehow."

"Listen Bob, why don't you just do your job, it's none of our business why Massengill and Panko do what they do."

"It's my business if it affects me," said Bobby. "I could have had the lift job and they could have brought the new hire in to pack."

"No way that's true, Bob, Panko would not have put you on a fork lift—come on, forget it, let's just get busy. We'll all be in hot water if we don't clear these lines."

Bob pulled the next order off onto his table, saying "I still think its fishy Jolly."

"Maybe it is, maybe it isn't." said Jolly. "But it's not our business. So let's just work."

At last agreed on something, they continued with heads down, chipping away at the full line. Bobby continued to wonder in silence.

Fishy. So fishy. Something stinks about this. It's off somehow. Way way off—

8 – Panko the Foreman

Panko fingered his wide tie, and his fat body quivered as he rushed through the racks toward his glass office in the dead center of the warehouse. It was time to prepare for next month's inventory; and he needed Eli to start working on it.

—*got to keep going keep on going Massengill notices he always notices he moved me up once he can move me up twice—three, four, five, six—move me up twice!*

As he rushed onward between the towering racks, he wondered about Eli as much as the others did; why had Massengill suddenly thought they needed two fork truck drivers and why had Massengill pushed to hire Eli? Panko tilted his head and smiled, catching the answer.

—*hey yeah that's it, Eli's somebody Massengill knows outside of here, probably some big shot's son all out of money, needing a job, and Massingill figured what the hell, the budget's there, so sure. That's how people get jobs these days. You got to know somebody to get a job. So there's the answer—three four five six seven racks gone by—walk faster. Damn these worn out shoes, need a new pair—but so what, I can use Eli. Massengill always knows best, God damn him, touch of gold he got, touch of gold, he knows best—*

As Panko's aching feet got him to his office, Eli pulled around up on the forklift, ran a hand back through his curly black hair, stepped in through the door, and spoke.

"Okay, boss, here I am. What do you need done?"

"Do you see those pink tags on the bottom of each load, up in the racks, all around the warehouse?"

"Yes indeed," said Eli, looking up. "Carl told me those are inventory tags."

"Did he also tell you to rip off the pink top sheet when you bring down a load to be used for orders and leave behind the green tag underneath? And then to give me the pink sheets at the end of the day?"

"He told me to give him the pink sheets. He was probably going to give them to you himself."

"Right," said Panko. "That, he does. The thing I need is, well, inventory time is coming. I need you to go around the warehouse and check all the loads in the racks that are not on the bottom level and make sure they all still have their pink tags. Also check back in the bulk stock area, and in the narcotics cage."

Eli's eyebrows rose.

"What's the narcotics cage? I didn't know there was a narcotics cage."

"It's where the harder drugs are—you know—pain pills, psycho pills; all stuff like that. I lock it up every night."

"Is the cage open throughout the day?"

"I open it in the morning—actually, Carl usually opens it. He also has a key. I lock it up after everybody's gone, before I leave every day."

"You mean the narcotics cage is open all day?"

"Yes. The pickers need to go in and out all day to get stock. The case handlers too. And the forklifts need to go in, and—long story short, it would be too much of a pain in the ass to unlock and lock it every time somebody needed something. Massengill knows we do this. He approves."

"Okay," said Eli, shrugging.

"Why did you ask if the cage is open all day?"

"Oh—no reason—I just wanted to know for when I need to get in there to check the tags."

"Okay, good."

Eli got back on the forklift and pulled back away, headed out toward the bulk stock area to start checking the tags. Panko went into his stark bare office, sat down, and stared at the newspaper spread open on his desk that he had been reading earlier.

—let's see, where did I leave off, what have I read or not read, yes, here—why is this new guy asking questions about the narcotics cage; no, no, that's not where I left off—here, maybe—new people don't usually ask so many questions, but—what the hell the world is full of pill popping weirdos anyway maybe he's a pill popping weirdo yes maybe with that beard, that voice—those eyes—yes here is where I left off, right here—

The newspaper story he'd been reading pulled him back in. It was an interesting story about the CIA and some scandals involving Cuban baseball players in the major leagues. The story absorbed him full for about ten minutes, then he folded over the newspaper and took a sheaf of paperwork and a blank yellow legal pad from the top desk drawer, and spread them out before him. He shuffled through, found what he wanted, laid it next to the legal pad, and pressed it with his fingers. There was nothing else to do right now, no excuse to stall any longer. He laid one hand on the paperwork, and picked up a pencil in the other. It was the right time to work a while on Massengill's inventory plan. All it ever involved was taking last years' inventory plan, changing the date, and some of the names of who was going to do what, because people had come and gone since then. This would take Panko less than an hour; and it wasn't due for two weeks. He stared at it.

—yes, time to make up another fat document to pass up the chain, symbolizing that something's really happening way down at the bottom of VNA; way down here yes, Mister Massengill, there is a real warehouse at the very bottom way way down below you, and this paperwork will come to you and prove that the place actually exists, and in the place everything

goes on every day after day after day all year the same—but this paper-
work will become the new new inventory plan that I have produced, that
will be in the massive list of both our accomplishments this year—and
on your bosses list, Mister Massengill, and then on his bosses list, so on
and so forth, and you will come to pat me on the back, come to my glass
box office in the dead center of the filthy noisy warehouse, where you come
once a year, maybe sometimes twice but mainly never—you will come and
finally say it finally say what I've been waiting for; You know Tom, you
know, I have been watching you. I have been thinking of you. I do see you.
Maybe, Tom, you're ready for the next step up. Yes my God, yes—the next
step up already God—

A knock and a voice came.

Shit! No—

"Tom," said a weak voice.

What? What—

The eyes in his face which he had not known were
clenched shut in despair opened to see a woman in grey leaning
against the doorframe; something else had just rushed away,
what was it, what is it, what—his voice followed all by itself.
The woman listened.

"Rose, what's wrong, you look pale—what is it?"

Something is wrong, very wrong, gone, yes, but no—it's her. It must be
her—yes—it is nothing but her, so listen to her you asked and she will tell—

"I need to go home," said Rose weakly. "I'm sick—I'm having an asthma attack—my puffer's not working."

"Should I send you to medical?" asked Tom. "They'll take
care of you there."

Her hand slowly came up palm out.

"No, no, no. I need to go see my own doctor—he knows my
condition—medical won't do anything but send me to him anyway—I know when it's that bad Tom, I always know."

"Okay Rose," said Panko. "I hope you get better. And be
sure to punch out."

She nodded, turned from the doorframe, walked down the aisle, turned the corner at the far end, and was gone. Alone as before, Tom clenched his lip in his teeth. The emptiness and silence of the room crept up from the concrete floor, entered him, and made him rise.

Okay, well—need to go do my job—shuffling people cards and sheaves of lost money people and cards and what—go to the pocking line look see do—my function—

Passing his desk as he moved toward the door, he tossed his pencil atop the yellow pad, and it rolled and bounced as he walked on, and fell to the floor and slid under the cheap plastic molding ringing the office, never to be seen again. Outside the office, the hiss and bang and whine of the warehouse encased Tom tightly, as he stuffed his hands in the pockets of the slacks that just like the shirt, were a couple years too tight on him. He breathed in the noise and the bang and crash and whine of the fork trucks and miles of conveyors snaking around and over the entire length of the warehouse, and headed toward the picking line, where Rose usually worked. For some reason it felt good to get out of the glass box and out onto the floor—to manage people—to wonder about the workload—to worry about the tall stacks of orders needing to be filled—yes, out on the floor it was better; his glass box office was just all silent nothingness full of make-believe work. Panko got to the line, up on the black rubber mat, and turned, and Rose's picking partner Gene stood alone between the stock racks, his dyed black hair slicked back shining under the neons, and a pencil tucked back behind his ear, just like the one just lost forever in Panko's silent glass box.

"Tom," said Gene. "You sent Rose home? I hope so. She really is sick. I can see it."

"Yeah, I did," said Tom. "Can you hold down the fort here by yourself or do I need to bring down one of the checkers to help you pick?"

"I think I will be okay, Tom," said Gene. "I'll yell if I need help—we got a lot done before Rose felt sick—plus the day's almost over and the lines are already almost full."

"I'll leave you then. Yes, like you say, the day's almost over anyway. I'll leave things the way they are. I think we're about clean at this end."

"Good decision, my man!"

Gene grinned toothily and patted Panko on the back, the way he always did; the exact way Panko had always hated. It was the same way Gene had slapped him on the back before he was promoted, when he was still a picker working where Rose was working now. Gene grinned and slapped in a way meant to make Tom feel inferior—like Gene was the boss. Gene always had a way of talking down to people, of bossing people, making them feel small. Panko backed away.

"Okay Gene—you're it then!" said Panko.

"Sure thing."

Gene bent back to his work and pulled the drugs smoothly out onto the green trays and pushed the trays down the line away from Panko, as if to say okay now, Panko, I'm done with you, you can go now, I don't need you here. Panko turned from Gene and left to go back to his glass box, shoulders hunched slightly more than before he had seen Gene. He stretched his neck and shoulders to ward off the growing sense of fatigue and weakness. He needed to get to the desk and chair in his glass box and sit down quickly. He turned the last corner leading back, and stopped short as a young woman's face turned up and smiled large brown eyes into his.

"Molly," he said. "How's it going today, Molly?"

She sat on her cart holding a box cutter, that until Panko had appeared, had been quickly pulling her hand back and forth over the top of a large dark brown case.

"Oh, it's great. It's always great. You know."

"Yes—"

Eyes, her eyes, I love her eyes I—

"Hey I'm glad you came by," she said. "I see we got two fork lift drivers now. What's the new guy's name?"

"Eli."

Why do you want to know to want—?

"So if I need a load brought down, do I ask Eli now?" said Molly.

—she wants and answer yes she wants from me something yes she wants—

"That's right, Eli's assigned to your area. I see you are keeping the racks nice and full."

She looked up and down the racks, smiling.

"Well, I try."

"Good work. Keep it up."

"Will do."

Her smile, yes, her smile got the knife sliding in her hand again back and forth back and forth—

He turned from her. He walked different.

I gave her something the smile back and forth the smile eyes—she had said, well, I try.

The racks flowed by.

—I am the boss, yes, try to please me please this woman yes try—

He rushed into his glass box to work more on the plan. The door slammed loosely shut behind him and the silence brought her up in him louder.

—please me yes please me—

The yellow pad lay atop the paperwork, but where was the pencil, where was it gone—

Where? Where? There—oh there, yes, there—

At once he came awake somehow, and found his hand under the desk rubbing a great erection that he abruptly became aware of, all crushed in and hidden in the threadbare cloth of his too-tight pants. He paused, he looked around—

Yes yes there is no one, no—

Luckily no one was around, thank God, so he just went on gently fondling himself, back and forth and back and forth, and glanced at the watch on his other wrist—twenty more minutes; no time really to get a bite on the inventory plan; back, and forth, a little more quickly, closing his eyes, yes going much much higher than the whine of the conveyors, of the boxes sliding by, sliding by, and it all came back to him in a single violent rush.

—yes maybe it is time for your second step, Tom—

Her eyes, her hand, him, the quiet, the moments, yes—

Yes. Maybe yes, it is.

This is what it's really all about.

9 – Eli and Molly

Molly pushed her cart to a slot in the rack that should contain cases of antibiotics, and found an empty pallet. This was not unusual; normally she would go seek out Carl to bring a load down from up above with the fork lift; but since he was out, today she'd get Eli, the new fork driver to do it, as Panko had told her. She peered through the racks but saw no fork lift. She left her cart and walked up and down the narrow aisles, turned one last corner, and there was Eli, standing by the tall old banged up orange fork lift, holding a yellow legal pad before his face. He held a pencil in one hand and was writing on the legal pad. By the way he held the pad so close to his face she figured that Eli must have very bad eyes. She stepped up.

"Eli?" she said—

The yellow pad dropped down, and Eli said, "Hi—yes, what do you need?"

"I need a pallet load of eleven twenty fives dropped down—the pallet is empty."

"Okay—lead the way. I'm new, you know. Got to learn the place."

"I know. I'll show you. It's in rack three—follow me."

He put the yellow pad of paper on the fork lift shelf, got on the machine, and followed her back into the racks where her cart was waiting. She pushed it out of the way, pulled out the empty pallet, turned to Eli and pointed up at the load to bring down, raising her box cutter in salute.

"There, up there. That's the one," she said. "By the way, I'm Molly."

"My name is Eli—"

"I know. The foreman told me your name.

"Oh."

He pushed out a hand for her to shake. She shook it. It felt cold and dry.

"Good to meet you, Eli."

"You too."

"Step back now—while I get the load down you need."

She stepped back. He raised the forks and turned the truck, and she watched as he smoothly inserted the forks into the pallet, brought down the load, and put it in place.

"So—is that it, for now, Molly?" he said.

"Yeah, that's it—say, when did you start? Is this your first day or what?"

"No. I've been here about a week. Carl was showing me the ropes. Now I've been turned loose on my own, so here I am. And where do you hang out? What do you do?"

"I keep the picking racks full of stock."

"Aha," he said, leaning over the edge of the truck. "So, what is a picking rack?"

"You don't know what a picking rack is?"

"No. I'm new, remember."

"The picking racks are up front, and Gene and Rose up there pick stock down to fill the orders and send them down the line. I do this job on this side of the warehouse, and Frankie does the other."

"Sounds interesting."

"Not really. Every day is exactly the same. There's nothing interesting after the first day."

He brought a fist to his chin, and nodded, looking her in the eye.

What, what, is he thinking looking that way, she thought.

"That's a cool way of putting it, Molly." he said slowly, adding, "How long have you been with the company?"

Oh, nothing, just a good simple question with a good and simple answer comes—

"About six years."

He leaned further toward her as he spoke.

"So what level are you?"

"Level three. Why do you ask?"

"I like to get to know people I meet for the first time. Helps me remember them—Molly, six years, level three."

"And you're Eli, one week, level ten. Fork drivers are level ten, right?"

"Right. Fork drivers are big shots. How about that, look at me, I am a real big shot already, after just here a week. How about that!"

"Yes, that is something!" she laughed—"You must have done this kind of work before. You made it look very easy."

"Sure, I've done this before, had lots of jobs, but; how about you? How long do you plan on working here Molly? Young person like you should be moving on sometime. I'm sure I'll move on if I spot something better. When do you think you'll be moving on?"

—no—why this question, he's about my age, what to say? I have no answer, but really, why this question—

"I don't know. I haven't thought about moving on," she stammered. "I'm single; I still live at home with my parents. I guess I like things the way they are."

He raised a hand.

"But Molly—the money's not good here. Do you pay rent to your parents?"

Why? Why push me, why push me, these questions, I—must stop this—

"No I don't," she said strongly. "I'm not worried about money. There are always ways to make extra money."

"Really. Like what?"

—*God, now I've done it—why did I say that I shouldn't have said that no—*

"Oh—this and that," she blurted. "There's things to do on the side, I'm sure."

"What kind of things?"

—*his eyes are, are trying, to see in me, why doesn't he go, he should just go he is making me tell him what Gene and I are up to, taking the drugs but I don't want to think about it why is he pushing to make me think about that, I don't like what I do but I—*

"I actually haven't the slightest idea," she said, holding up her hand. "I don't really know why I said that. Funny, huh?"

He straightened up smiling, his hard eyes softened and he looked around, then back to her, saying, "You're an interesting person, Molly. But I've wasted enough of your time. I got stuff to do, too. Great to meet you."

"You too," she said, her face relaxing.

Thank you God, thank you God, he can go now—

Eli threw Molly one last grin as he straightened up, pulled the control handle of the truck and swung the forklift around and headed away toward the back of the warehouse. Molly watched him grow smaller and smaller, until he abruptly turned and disappeared around a huge pile of white cases.

—*why all the questions he's a nice guy and all but its one thing to get to know a co-worker but it is really going too far to pry. But he is gone. It is over.*

Rising from her cart, she cut the rope tied around the pallet load Eli had brought down, pulled a case off the load, sat down with it and deftly began slicing off the tops. After doing this to ten cases, she rose and turned her cart toward the picking area to slide the new stock down the racks. The stock was intended for

Gene's area. She pushed the ten cartons down the racks and then went around into the picking line.

—*need to talk to someone, lying is hard, Eli has tired me, tired me, I need to talk*—

She approached Gene, who had his head down working an order. As Molly stepped toward him, she noticed Rose was gone.

"Hey Gene, where's Rose?" Molly asked Gene. He looked up with a smile.

"Hey, Molly—come by for a visit? Rose went home sick with her asthma."

"Yeah, I'm caught up, I just wanted to loaf here a while. So, you're picking alone today?"

"Yeah," he said, pushing his trays down the line and deftly filling them from the racks. Molly followed behind.

"Say have you met the new guy, Eli, yet?" she asked. Gene turned around.

"Is that his name? I heard there was a new guy but I didn't get his name. Eli, huh?"

"Yeah. I just met him. He's odd. All full of questions. He asked me if I made enough money here, was I planning on moving on from this job, stuff like that."

Gene paused and leaned on the rack, his pencil hung in his hand.

"That is odd—what kind of guy is he? I mean—is he okay?"

"He's a nice enough guy, but I just felt like I was being pumped. You know what he asked me? He asked me about if there were ways to make extra money around here."

"What? Why did he ask you that?"

"Well—I kind of led him into it. I said that there were lots of ways to make extra money, after he said that I don't make much money, or something like that—I don't know, we just talked about making extra money on the side."

"What?" said Gene, his eyebrows rising. "Sounds to me like we better keep an eye on this guy—you know, everybody in the locker room's wondering why they hired this guy off the street out of nowhere, for the new fork lift job instead of offering it to one of us. Plenty of us wanted that job. As a matter of fact, when I asked Panko why they got this new guy, he just said it was a Massengill decision."

He pulled off his glasses and looked her in the eye as she spoke.

"So—do you think maybe—maybe he knows something about us?"

"Oh, Molly," he said lightly, "He doesn't know anything. We've been too careful for anybody to know. What it is, I bet Massengill probably owed one of his cronies a favor and this Eli is somebody's son-in-law, or something, who he's made up a job for."

"I just didn't like all the questions. He's a very nosy guy."

"No, probably just a friendly guy—maybe he's interested in you!"

"Oh, please, God, no," she chuckled, narrow-eyed. "I don't need that in my life right now!"

They laughed and chatted a while together, leaning side by side back on the line.

"Still you've just got to watch what you say," Gene finally said. "Just because someone's being friendly doesn't mean he's okay—oops, here's Mr. Panko—"

They stood straight and faced Tom's belly swaying toward them as he spoke.

"What's going on, guys?" said Panko loudly. "Molly—all the racks full up? Gene—picks all done?"

"Working on it Tom," Molly said.

"Yeah, me too," said Gene.

Panko barely looked at Gene and Molly as he started ruffling through the orders in the box at the head of the line.

"Gene," he said idly, "did you do an order for L&H Industries yet?"

"Yeah," said Gene gruffly, pushing his glasses up on his forehead. "I did that one a while ago. Franklin said it had to go today."

"Good."

Panko pushed his way past Molly and Gene and moved down the line and around the bend toward the packers. When he was out of sight, Gene pulled the pencil down and spoke.

"He's got the personality of a fish, doesn't he?" he said grinning.

"Oh yeah," she said. "Big personality. It seems like there's way too many of those around. Gene, I've got to go back to the racks. See you after work."

"That's right," he winked. "Today's Wednesday isn't it?"

"It is. Do you think we are good to go?"

"Its okay, Molly, I'm sure of it. Less said the better. You know."

"Yup."

Molly went down off the picking line and back to her cart. She pushed it past the narcotics cage and around the bend. There she ran into Frankie, who was sitting on his cart pulling Noctec.

"Frankie?" she said. "How's it going?"

"It's going," he said. "What time is it?"

"Not sure. Almost quitting time, I think."

"That's good—I've got no problem with quitting time."

She leaned on the handle of her cart.

"Say Frankie, have you had any dealings with the new guy yet?"

"New guy, what new guy?" he said, scratching his head, "Do you mean the new forklift driver?"

"Yeah. Eli's his name. I met him before."

"Oh yeah? Me too. He pulled a couple of loads down for me today. Why?"

"Did he ask you a lot of questions? Like how long you been here and all?"

"No, not at all—he barely spoke. He reminds me of Carl, except for the age and that hair and big beard—and no smell—thank God there's no God damned smell like Carl's."

Frankie turned back to his work.

"Okay, Frankie. See you later."

"Sure."

Molly pushed away from Frankie, gazing at nothing, heading toward the ladies' room, idly chewing her lip.

Why all the questions for me, then—it's sort of spooky all the questions new people don't usually have so many questions—

She pushed her cart to the gate to the ladies' locker room, left her cart, and went in. No one would be in there yet. There were still some minutes to the end of the shift. She unlocked her locker and opened it and the big black lunch pail came down from the top shelf and went on the bench, and opened, and there they were. Ten little yellow boxes, each containing a sealed brand new bottle of ninety Oxys each; but what Molly saw and smiled down at, was fifty bucks; fifty bucks from Gene—so easy, too easy. The sight of the bottles told her she should kick herself for having said such a stupid thing to the new guy. Yes, she should watch what she said from now on, she would. Just because someone's nice doesn't mean they can be trusted. Especially not in this case, with the fifty bucks on fifty bucks being so easy to make; and that could just as easily be blown away, if anyone ever found out. She closed the lunchbox and sat on the bench. This close to quitting time, there was no point in going back out on the floor. Panko could not come in the ladies' locker room to find her. She sighed deeply and rested her hand on the curve of the lunchbox and let the time slowly fade away.

Three minutes or less now—then time to wash up, get out of this ratty old grey rag, and leave, back home, to the crazy house—until the bell rings, I will sit here. Until the bell rings, my backache will fade and my worn out feet will recover—I hope Gene is not mad—Gene is very important yes—Gene is good to me—

Her hand slid slowly down the curve of the lunchbox.

—what does Gene really do with the stuff after he gives me my money and drives away in that big BMW—he's probably selling them

for big bucks a pill at a time he must roll in the money good old Gene but he deserves it. He deserves whatever he gets. A hundred a week sets me up good enough. What Gene does is probably not easy. He deserves the money yes—and what he thinks matters yes it does—

Her hand rested on the lunchbox.

Yes.

The bell rang, lifting Molly from the bench to begin washing up and changing and all. It even was hard work to get ready to leave the damned place.

Damned dog-tired, but got to get up and go.

10 – Franklin and Gene

After Molly and Panko had stopped by to chat, Gene worked the line, alone, industriously, faster, hoping to clear all the remaining orders by the end of the day. As he worked he thought of how stupid Molly's comments to Eli had been. She might have spilled the whole pot of beans, or pills in this case. His hands moved as quickly as his thoughts.

There are lots of ways to make extra money, she had said—what could that possibly mean, aside from the fact that she's stealing drugs from a god-damned drug warehouse.

Gene's lip curled slightly, as he considered Molly.

Molly seemed a little bit simple—and more than a little bit stupid—and though she's likeable, maybe things have run their course with Molly. That's a damned shame, she's a nice kid, but, can't take chances with what else she might have said, or let slip, or what she'll say tomorrow, or the tomorrow after that, as she gets to know this Eli better. But, without Molly, how else to get the stuff? I got no business going in the narco cage, but she does. And plus, it's set up now that if anyone's going to get nabbed walking out with drugs, it's going to be her—I come out clean if security jumps her, the way things are right now. Already, somehow she is stupid enough to take risks for only fifty dollars a pop. Carrying out that big lunch pail like she does is stupid too. None of the other women take anything out but little purses or folded up paper bags. I've talked to her about that great big metal sandwich box, but she insists on using it.

She could tape ten boxes to her leg down some baggy pants or dress or some-thing, but no, she has to use the box. The damned box! And the company's stupid to not have a guard at the door, management is naïve as shit, who-ever set this place up set it up to be robbed. Back when I started ripping off vitamins, it was too easy much too easy—graduating to Oxycodone was a piece of cake, too, but yes, yes, a much bigger piece. Molly was hungry for the hundred a week. I'd take out more stuff if I could, but how, really, how? Maybe if I hook up somehow with the right people, maybe then I could move more. Maybe someday—

A large bottle of syrup slipped from his fast moving hands and cut off his thought, but he caught it, before—before it smashed on the concrete. Gene was fast, very fast, once he got going.

Still Molly's got to go, she is a liability—and if she likes this new guy Eli—might get too close to him, and tell him about the whole get up, if he catches her eye, you know, like that, if he makes her think crazy like all the girls her age do. Might be she—might look to impress this guy—if he gives her the eye—like I do sometimes—sure she's just a kid—but I'm a man I know how far to go and then stop—kids do and say stupid things, go too far—I know. Yes I'm worried. I'm damned worried. When I was a kid I did a stupid thing—I pulled a fire alarm in the school—they had to empty the whole school out and fire trucks came—I did it three times, pulled the alarm when no one was looking—and I would have gotten away with it but I opened my big mouth on the bus ride home—the girl I was trying to impress turned me in, and I was suspended for the rest of the year, sure I learned the hard way—oh I cried and cried and cried—but no one cared—the girl loved the praise they got for ratting me out—now if Molly blows this it'll be worse than being suspended, it'll be firing, or maybe even be jail—yeah, jail for sure because this is big money, and the drugs, of course the drugs involved. I'm not interested in doing jail time because of some stupid kid who gets carried away and says the wrong thing one time—I mean one time, is all it would take—this is a big operation I've got going on here—I'm not going to let her fuck it up—this is how it always starts—a little comment turns into a bigger comment, which turns

*into an even bigger one—and then I'm popped, stuffed, done! Well, I'm
not going to be popped, stuffed or done—*

Gene half-ran up and down the line, his hands nearly a blur,
filling order after order—and without even thinking, it was that
kind of job—his mind could wander, wander, wander, all over and
do it twice as fast, because every order is just about exactly the
same as the last; it flowed on.

*—yes, yes, I will cut Molly loose. But how, and when, and also; is
it really the practical thing to do? Maybe not, maybe things need to stay
like they are; I don't have to decide today. I won't be squeezed into making
a rash decision. No I won't, will not, no; will stay cool.*

Gene saw movement in the corner of his eye, turned, and
faced Franklin, the assistant foreman, who'd come onto the line
with a sheaf of tomorrow's orders and dropped them into Gene's
box. Gene smiled and waved.

"Hey, Franklin—you're looking natty today! Nice tie!"

"Oh—yeah, Gene. It's brand new. Thanks."

"So, Franklin—any of these orders need to go today?"

"Nope, these are all for tomorrow."

"That's great, I am bushed!"

"Well, you ought to be—you're working this line like
a madman!"

"Hey, hey, I never once claimed to be sane, Franklin. You
ever heard me claim that?"

Franklin chuckled, his dark face full of lines, as Gene went
on fast as he'd been working.

"Lots of money in those orders, man—this place must be
rolling in cash."

"I know—too bad we aren't getting some in our hands."

They laughed together.

"Well—I guess it's in our pay." said Gene. "What the hell.
Somebody has to be at the bottom walking the hard floor all day
doing the dirty work."

"I guess," said Franklin, "But our pay's nothing compared to this. Look at this order. Just this one," he said, picking up an order from the stack. "It costs a hundred and fifty thousand dollars—one hundred and fifty thousand dollars, and that's just for this one order—there must be fifty of them, or more, here like that. They really know how to charge for these damned drugs. You and I should be in the drug business Gene. You know?"

"We are in the drug business. Isn't that where we are now?"

"Yeah, sure! And at the bottom making peanuts. I mean, look—just give me what one of these orders goes for—just one!"

"Yeah, I know. But you know, Franklin, those are just numbers. Unreal. You know?"

"In a way, I guess that's true—but hey. I'm going for a smoke break. Want to join me. You're all caught up, what the hell."

"Yeah, sure—okay."

Gene tucked his trusted pencil behind his ear and followed Franklin off the line, and around past Franklin's mess of a desk to the large gate in the chain link fence that separated the office area from the warehouse. They stood outside the opening and lit up. You weren't allowed to smoke in the warehouse but you could behind the fence.

"Almost tax time, Gene," said Franklin, after lighting up a Kool. "I'm going to owe. I always owe. I really should change my exemptions, but I never do. How about you?"

He took a deep drag, and blew it out joining the smoky answer coming from Gene.

"I usually get something back. I guess I'm set up just right. You know?" said Gene, waving his cigarette.

"I got kids just getting to college age," said Franklin. "I don't know how I'm going to pay for that."

"Been saving for it?"

The smoke cloud grew snaking around them.

"Yeah, but not enough. I got to keep food on the table, you know. I don't make enough to save a lot. But, I'll get by their college and all that, though. I always manage somehow."

"Yeah, I know what you mean," said Gene, surrounded by smoke from their noses, mouths and waving cigarette tips. Ash began peppering the floor at their feet.

"I need to get some kind of side job, like in a store or something. I've done that before."

"Oh yeah? Where at?"

"Men's clothier. There's a few at the mall that always need somebody. I know clothes pretty well. They'd pick me up in a minute."

"That's cool," said Gene, blowing out smoke, looking Franklin up and down.

"It does look like you know clothes pretty well—look pretty spiffy in that shirt and tie, those slacks and those shoes, you know."

"Yeah," said Franklin. "Yeah, I suppose I do. I just got to shake off my lazy streak and get down there and apply."

"Sure. Why not? Hey, I always have something going on the side. "

"Yeah, I know. You tend bar, I think, don't you?"

"Yeah, and here and there other stuff too. You know. There's never enough."

"You can say that again."

The thickening smoke blew up and around and grew out and down and through Gene's mind.

Hah, got this thing going on on the side here at this here warehouse even right under your dumbfuck nose—look, look, look at me, I'm thinking it out loud—I steal Oxys! See! See it in my eyes! Can't get in my head—I steal Oxys—wear your head on your sleeve—men's store, hah—who's going to buy any kind of clothes from a dumb little twerp like you, Franklin? Yeah you—dumb little twerp is what I'm calling you but you can't hear me you can't hear what's in my head—I'm shouting it—We steal Oxys—We Steal Oxys—see you, no one can hear what's in my head—I can scream it as loud as I want—dumb—little—twerp. I am stealing this shithole blind—me and Molly yeah my sweet little Molly yeah—

Franklin blew a perfect smoke ring that caught Gene's eye and contained Franklin saying, "Yeah maybe I'll go down Archie's at the mall, see about getting some Saturday work. Damned College and taxes won't pay for themselves. We need to get the kind of money the big shots get. Like, you see what Panko drives? That top of the line Cadillac?"

"Yeah, I see it. And he's not even that much higher than us."

"That's right—and you know, actually, you don't do that bad either in that department. Where'd you get the money for that big assed BMW you drive? How'd you save that much—"

—we don't save up our money you little shit, we steal Oxys—can't you hear me? I am yelling in my brain, We steal Oxys—you poor ignorant twerp—

Franklin's cigarette waved more ash to the floor as he went on, saying, "I could never afford that—even with a part time job at the mall. Damn, it must be nice to have a good car like that. You see that shit I got to drive, haven't you Gene? My crappy two hundred thousand mile old Volvo?"

Gene took one last deep drag, blew it out to the side slow, and said "You could afford it, Franklin, if you had a couple side jobs. I told you, I don't just tend bar. I work a wheel on the boardwalk at night in the summer, run the rides on the pier, here and there, you know, you just got to pick up what you can here and there and you can afford almost anything."

And pills too, stupid fuck—what I been thinking into your little bitty face—pills, too, fuck, yes, under your little snot nose—

Franklin pulled the cigarette from his mouth and waved it and spoke louder.

"Yeah, but the boardwalk jobs can't pay that much, can they?

"You mean the wheels?"

"Yeah. The wheels."

Gene smiled, blew out smoke and gazed into the distance.

Yeah, you silly fuck, you got it right and wrong at the same time the wheel job pays shit but that's where I push the Oxys—the wheel job grabs in the money at twenty bucks a damned little pill—somebody wants two, or three, or four to get off good—that pulls in the money—forty, sixty, eighty a handshake, a thank you, and a goodbye. Really simple—

"What does Massengill drive? Got any idea what Massengill drives?" said Franklin, blowing out smoke.

"Panko's boss? Oh, he drives shit. A fucking big old Ford."

"An old Ford? What's a big shot like that doing driving an old cheap Ford?"

Gene took a drag, looked down at his feet, then up into Franklin's face.

"I guess he's just too cheap," said Gene. "He got to be pulling down twice what Panko makes."

"Twice? Huh, no. More like three or four times more."

"Think so?"

How would you know you stupid fuck—?

"Sure, I bet. He's up there. Way up there."

A forklift came rattling and whining into the main aisle in the distance, turned again, and headed for them. Gene leaned against the fencepost, watching.

—here comes this new guy Molly almost spilled the beans to, I bet—what about this new guy what's this new guy look like—beard dark hair dark glasses, no, closer, there's no dark glasses the hair and beard say dark glasses but no, no, not—

The fork lift came slowed and turned to pass them. Eli smiled and nodded to the men as he passed. Gene raised a hand waving to him. Eli waved back but did not stop going the other way around and back down the rack aisles and out of sight.

"What do you think of this new guy?" Gene said to Franklin. "He came along all of a sudden. Was there ever talk of a second fork lift? Do we even need one?"

Franklin shook his head and his lips tightened an instant, before he spoke.

"I personally don't see why we need one. But Panko told me it was Massengill's idea—hey, listen," said Franklin, crushing out his cigarette in the beat up ash tray stand beside them, "you better get back on the line now, Gene. It's really not break time. If Panko sees us, he'll ask me later what the hell was I doing stopping you from working."

"You mean he's as big of a pain in the ass to you as he is to us peons?"

"No comment." breathed Franklin, winking.

Smiling, Gene crushed out his cigarette and went back to his picking line to get a start on tomorrow's orders. Franklin returned to his small desk beside the racks. Gene's mind raced fast, where was he, yes he was thinking what before Franklin came, oh, yes—

Yes, the new guy—he was talking to Molly about extra money—from the way she tells it, he seemed eager to talk about it—I need to cut her out—but what about this new guy—maybe he'd do Molly's part—maybe if I pay her off—say five hundred dollars and tell her we're not in the pills business any more—

The green trays slid swiftly through his deft hands and order after order filled getting a jump on tomorrow, yes—

—yes, that's the thing, I'm sure she'd be more than happy—then I could get somebody else who has access to the narco cage to get the Oxys for me—the only people allowed in the narco cage are Molly and the fork lift drivers—and of course Panko, fat assed Panko, but maybe I could work it so that Molly's out of the picture and I could get a fork lift driver to bring the stuff out—this Eli maybe—he's already so interested in making extra money—I should definitely keep him in mind—meanwhile back to these

orders—Panko will be happy to see that I'm starting tomorrow's orders today—a happy Panko stays off my back—what is there like twenty minutes left—I can crank out some orders by then—but—

Gene paused, pulled a tiny pill case out of his pocket, opened it, took one of the two pills it contained, popped it in his mouth, then started again working madly on the next order topping tomorrow's stack, the trays all but racing full down the line.

—see me, see me, they'd never think it's me because I'm such a good worker—I clear the line every day, me and Rose—and when I bartend I'm a damned good bartender, so nobody there knows how many little pills get slipped over the bar, and when I work the wheel I'm damned good at it, they'd never think it was me there either, passing out, after every spin, one Oxy two Oxys three Oxys four—fifteen, twenty times a night— that's big money—a thousand dollars or more on a good night—it gets so it's nothing to give Molly a hundred a week—but yes, I am, I'm switching to Eli; he looks like just a kid, just like her; and kids today, they've got no morals—I remember the day I saw it in her eyes that she needed the money and sure, she said—I'm in. It was easy. I saw it in her eyes you know. They're hungry in the eyes, you know—now Eli, he'll be next I bet—but I've got to see if he's got it in his eyes. He's just a kid like her, but first, I need to look him deep in his God-damned eyes—

The bell rang. The day was over. Gene pulled his trusty pencil from behind his ear, put it in a tray at the head of the line, put his glasses in his pocket, and left.

11 – Bringing up the Dragons at Lunchtime

At lunch, out in the parking lot, Eli sat in his big Dodge, smoking. Blue-black smoke; the smoke only the best designer mix makes curled up from the pipe, slowly snaking across the windshield, catching the noontime sun. Eli had come out to the car every day for lunch, sitting parked at the far side of the lot. The warehouse building stretched across the lot before him, from the four loading dock doors to his right to the brick office area with the fancy windows to his left. Inside that warehouse, he knew that there was so much going on. But you'd never know it. From where he sat grinning, it looked still, like a tree trunk is still, though it coursed with hot sap. The building looked small, no bigger than the hand he brought up to his face to cover it.

See how small it is, see it? See it? Yes, this hand proves it. It's no bigger than my hand. No longer than this pipe. No more solid than this smoke.

The pipe stem went again between his lips and he took a strong pull. He held the smoke long, his lungs close to bursting for air, before he let it go. The smoke mushroomed out across the windshield, the fresh air he sucked in cooling his lungs, the warehouse still there.

Yes it's there, thank God; it's not the hazy long-toothed fiery dragon that you fear; and just like it, the cars around are still just cars, without the wild pale faces that come in dreams—

The low sky pressed down, full of clouds billowing in and out the car, smoky and dark. In his pipe, Eli long since had graduated from simple opium or hashish, to the best designer mix he could dream up. Sprinkle of ketamine, slivers of psilocybin, pinch salvia, and the opium and hashish, smoked nice and slow after a light tab of twenty five micrograms.

Lord God, Lord God, I am a common sewer of drugs, a really common sewer connoisseur of drugs; it's a blessing that you know the parking lot is a sea of seething suckers holding tight to your tires, keeping your car from shooting into the air, but, you wonder, how will you walk back in when your lunch is over? The suckers, the suckers—the suckers will surely hold you tight! You know they are there but you dared not look because the sight of them makes them stronger, as strong as curling lashing tails grown up from the dark between the suckers—the tails that luckily, you've never seen with your eyes because you can't see your car tires from behind the wheel, but you can feel it come up your spine, that the tails were up looped tight around the tires. At least the car will remain on the ground. No worry about that, not yet, not time yet to get out and put a foot on the pavement. Pavement yes pavement, even though a tall grown field of yellowing Indian Grass surrounded the car, like Freddie Mason's car years back—down in the field by the brook—all set on fire yes on fire, in the middle of the Indian Grass field. The boys that set the fire would be gone when the fire department came. Is that a siren? No, no siren. No Indian grass, thank God, now that you have your eyes open; things change like this with every blink of your eyes.

As Eli thought about the boys that set the field on fire, the long low warehouse remained in the grip of the long-toothed fiery dragon billowing, stretching, and rolling when he blinked his eyes and down shut for second, thinking of nothing, and formed back into the warehouse building when he popped his eyes open again.

The heat of the pain the cars were all in from being left alone all day, out in the bleak lot, like when you walk down the block and hear the dogs howling and howling and raging at having been left alone all day by their masters who went to work and yes, each dog knew; as dogs do; that they would never see their masters again. The howling spiraling blowing around under and over the pain-filled cars, you have to get out and fight through it.

His watch slapped in his face shouting it's almost twelve thirty, yes almost twelve thirty, yes, my God, almost time to get back. The hot pipe cooling, he looked in the blackened bowl.

Common sewer indeed, yes—connoisseur, yeah!

And he knew he'd dare it, he knew he had to dare it, God yes they had hired him to dare it to dare him to ride the big mother fucking monster fork machine, so now the time had come.

Eyes open must stay open; the waving grasses and muscular suckers and curling lashing long tails that could trap you on your way back to the safe warehouse, must remain gone, your eyes must not close; you must pushed what was left of your stale sandwich into its bag and let the still-burning pipe out free onto the ashtray. The pipe's a living thing. Living thing, have respect; set it free, onto the ashtray. The burning matter inside would live out its natural life there like all things that God made must do—plus, you know what you are doing. You've done all this before. Okay, now—ready set, shut eyes one last time, the great pink flap of flesh of the door the devil cut off from some screaming sinner, curled away open to let you out, and after a last glance at the suckers and all, you can open my eyes just at the instant the pressing low sky would have crushed you down flat forever. Eyes pushed wide, you go toward the warehouse; eyes burning wanting to blink, like wanting to pee, or wanting to shit, that kind of urge began filling you, but—you must not run across to the place like your mind is screaming for you to do; they would see.

He had to pass the great window of the break room, where he knew they all sat looking at the new guy, coming in from the car.

Lord God it is he odd, he must be a stuck up bastard not eating lunch in here with us, he must be a stuck up bastard not wanting to get to know us better, and what? What? He is running bug-eyed in from the car like a fool where's his fool's cap the red and white furry one with the jingling jangling bells that everybody knew when shaken at court, would mightily please the king and queen—

He kept his fiery burning drying eyes open and made the door. At last able to blink the overhang came over dripping with fat and as he blinked harder because his eyes burnt so, the thick lips of the warehouse door sucked him in and shot him down the aisle through the office, the women all staring and staring.

Yeah look it the new guy what about the new guy, what—

The stares and the thoughts came at him like hail of arrows like he was a naked Saint Sebastian bound tightly to an oak, but still somehow moving, somehow struggling straining and at last escaping back through the yellow door past which lay the super bright super huge hissing, snapping, warehouse. And yes, there it was, still there; his orange fork truck. After momentarily checking his belly for arrows, and finding they had all missed, he climbed aboard. The handle pushed forward, he gripped the steering knob, and was off. He had by now learned to ignore the howling he thought was coming from sinner's faces set in the floor, like sinner's faces in Dante's hell, set in the frozen lake for eternity. But glancing down, there were no faces; and again he knew the howling was just from what he'd read as a boy about how crazy old Ed Gein, the world's most famous body snatcher, had thought he'd seen grinning faces in the piles of leaves that lay around his farmhouse in the fall when he came home buggy-lugging corpses to his barn. Pure craziness it was. Pure craziness guided the fork truck smoothly around the bend and back toward the bulk stock area, where he could sit in the one ray of sun that came down from the skylight, letting the light ray seep into him and slowly bring him back down to the warehouse floor again. He could sit there, idle, not caring what might appear the next time he dared close his eyes; sit mindlessly warming himself, idly thinking this or that thought, until Molly or Frankie came and said they needed something picked or moved, or until Panko came around with some other meaningless task to do. The forklift set in the open space by the corner, between towering walls of mineral oil cases, and, he felt ready, really ready, to deal with the rest of the day, unaffected by the swarms of barking dogs running snarling snapping all around.

Soon, Molly drifted up in the quiet inside. Molly spent the most time alone in the narcotics cage, and he had watched her from afar as she went religiously to the locker room two times, each and every day, between each break. It was clear to him that Molly was best positioned to be the prime culprit stealing the Oxys; but there was probably somebody else involved too. In an operation this big, with this much product disappearing from the place, there had to be at least two or more thieves involved. This was always true on every assignment like this he'd been on. He had already been in the narcotics cage, first thing in the morning after it was opened, and, taking the scientific approach he always took on these jobs, he had counted the number of cases of Oxys on their pallet in the back, and he had discovered that each Wednesday and Friday the count decreased by one case. He had watched the Oxys in the picking rack slanting down toward the picking line where Rose and Gene worked, and he had noticed that they did not get used up there very fast; not fast enough to justify two cases gone a week from the pallet in the narcotics cage, like clockwork; one on Wednesday and one on Friday. Once in a while he had seen a case pulled by the bulk case lot pickers but never more than one every two weeks or so—this broke the pattern but not enough that it didn't matter—he opened his eyes and listened to himself across the table from himself, with the dim lit café all around, smoke rising, branching up, reaching gone into the dark,

waving a smoke back and forth over the large golden ashtray lit-
tered with butts, saying what he thought to himself there alone
on the lift in the crowded café, with no one else around but himself, pointing into his chest and talking.

*Molly! Molly! Molly's is the one, you know it, my man, but she's
such a nice girl you don't want to bust her, no, not yet, the operation is
bigger, she hands the stuff off after she gets it out of this place, who does she
give it to, that's the one you want, not Molly, Molly's a nice girl, the kind
you'd like to marry, the kind like Mom told us we'd both stumble onto
some day, don't blow the whistle on her yet, wait for the big fish to fry, this
is too simple, too simple, too simple, she's such a nice girl, you don't want
to send her to jail—at least not yet—besides you need the work, stretch it
out as long as you can, get to know her, even if you are right, make some
money on this—paid by the day, you know—they pay rats by the day—*

Eli chuckled lightly. He was so funny to himself, when he got
to thinking quietly in the quiet alone place. Money money money,
yes, everything boiled down to money for everyone. Eli knew he
was right, as he always was when he was on cases like this—before
they grabbed Molly at the door, he wanted to know how she got rid
of the stuff, had to break the big chain, whether it was somebody
on the inside or somebody on the outside. Massengill had said, Eli,
get the big picture. The whole picture. How are they getting out,
where are they going and where are they ending up. Every link in
the chain needs to get busted. Don't just bring me one name and
be done with it. Eli scratched deep into his beard, wondering what
Molly would think if she knew that he was thinking she's the first
link in the chain. Would she just stop doing it? No, he thought
now. There's a lot of money in a case of Oxys, each with ten bottles,
each bottle ninety pills. That's nine hundred pills twice a week,
eighteen hundred pills a week, and they go for twenty or so a pop
on the corner these days that's thirty six thousand dollars gross,
cash, per week. And, sure there must be expenses, different people
taking cuts, but that's still a lot of money. Having done all this

math in his head, Eli, exhausted by the thinking, almost fell into the midst of the howling snapping pack of huge redeyed wild dogs swarming around, when he realized the worth of what she was doing—thirty six thousand dollars—the dogs snapping and snarling in a muted silence—but Molly did not look like she was pocketing all that cash alone, no. He had seen her car, an old grey car, maybe a Honda, ten years old and he saw the clothes she walked out in each day at the end of each day and they clearly weren't expensive either, no; the pills were going someplace, to someone else; after she carried them out in that lunch pail two sizes too big for her, that black lunch pail that couldn't possibly attract more attention, it was almost like a metal briefcase, as big as it was. The dogs were silent now; they just prowled about him, probably just as tired as he was, after being punched in the stomach by going through and tallying up such a huge amount of money. The sun had moved the light was gone, but he was warmed. The sun could now march up to its boss's desk and say, Sir, mission accomplished, just as Eli knew he would be doing, in time. Time, yes; yes in time. Yes. His face went down in his folded arms and kept counting through how he would get there, as he lightly kicked the steel panel by his feet on the forklift, and he leaned closer to himself over the small round café table. Some dark girl had taken some huge ashtray away from the table, and emptied it. When she brought it back, he started to tell her; she looked quite interested, stood stock-still, and listened.

—*you know, here it is, the cars, the cars can tell you where the money is. Listen, look, you saw the big brand-new black BMW out there, that one you already know is owned by Gene the picker. So, list him as a candidate. And sure, sure, there's also Panko. Panko had a top of the line brand new Cadillac. Those two, maybe, they're where the money sits. It sits in a pile out there. Every car is a pile of money come bigger, some smaller. All the other piles of money in the lot were much smaller. Even Massengill's pile was small, almost tiny. By the piles of money that became cars when the workers got into them—through what magic, so, through what magic I can see all this so clearly. Why can't everybody see things so clear?*

All at once, the dark girl tucked her tray up under her arm, and said, "Because, Eli, everybody is not you."

The dead quiet space around him spread the words out away as clear and thin as crystal, and all the dogs had been led home by their masters, and the dark girl was around someplace nearby, but no longer anyplace close enough to see. He felt her with his eyes closed, but with open eyes she wasn't around; yes, it would have to be Molly and Panko or Molly and Gene, there weren't any other obvious options. Has to be this way, has to be, Molly's eyes shouted out clearly, when Eli looked into them, "Eli, I hope you can see I clearly am not the type to have street contacts to hand drugs off to. There's somebody else. Somebody else. Somebody—"

—*else*, he intoned thoughtfully to himself, after a long hot pull off the smoke he did not have because there was no smoking in the warehouse; *Yes! There's somebody else. So here's what you do, pal, here; you force the issue—force it yes use force, and, because Molly's the daughter our Mom never had, and Molly's the sister we never had and Molly's the lover we never had, the lover I never will have if I blow it—if she gets busted in this thing there will never ever be another lover like the one she might have been to us!*

The stale warehouse air pressed in all around, opening his eyes. Black birds had just filled the air, but they were all gone now. He was too late to see them, but they had pooped everywhere, because their greasy shit smell hung in the soupy air, and they were gone, probably because one by one they had disappeared when hit by poop falling from some higher bird; every bird had a higher bird to poop on it and then that one had a higher bird to poop on it, and so forth, so on, one by one they evaporated, but there had to be one left at the end; higher than the others, yes. The higher ones maybe. Maybe they were the ones. Eyelids closed, he sat on the edge of the inside of the lids and waved his cigarette at himself and talked to himself where he sat across from himself in that old Amsterdam coffee shop so many years ago

Eli. You need to stop leaving the joint. Forget the fucking forklift and think. Are you serious about this? If so, sit, listen, learn, this; even if we found for sure who it was, Panko or Massengill big birds like that or little Bird Gene or maybe even Frankie or Franklin; the day it comes clean on the wall the diagram in red and blue that shows the whole caper, they will nab Molly, too, and if she is the one actually carrying the stuff out she will do time and the others, well, depending on how solid the case is, the others might just go scot free, and we never will have a daughter or sister or lover ever never—

Eli jogged the forklift forward slightly, seeking the sun again, but no use, the sun was gone. It would not shine again anywhere near this spot until tomorrow—

What you need to do, my man, is to get Molly out of the picture. So, here—listen up, listen good. Yes get between Molly and all the others, knock Molly out of the picture and jump up and pose with the big fish behind this. Yes, come out—just come out and let Molly know you know about this stuff—and suck up to Gene. That big wave he threw at you—too friendly much too friendly, too friendly people are not to be trusted. So yes get in the middle jump in the middle, shield our daughter sister and lover. Yes, here's how. Watch me and listen. Do this just like this—this phone here see it see it? Open your damned eyes so you can see it, for Christ's sake—

Eli had his cell phone to his ear. The phone was ringing. Who am I calling? Who, but—

The phone picked up.

"Massengill here."

So talk say what comes I'm right behind you.

"Mister Massengill—it's Eli—I'm back in the warehouse."

"What's up? Got something for me—is today the day we close this?"

Go on, say the next thing. The very next.

"No, not yet, I need you to do something."

"And what is that?"

Say it, you know the plan, how to do it—here say it with me—

"I need you to tell Panko to keep the narcotics cage locked at all times."

Yes!

"Why—that will stop the pilferage, maybe, but we want to know who—"

Go!

"Yes, I know that's what we want. I think I know who is doing it. But we need to catch the whole ring that's involved. Right after this phone call, call Panko and tell him I should be the only one that has the key to the narco cage."

"How am I going to get him to buy that?"

Oh gosh that's too easy give me a hard one for Christ's sake, big man—

"Tell him you are trying some new reporting chains, and that you are putting me in charge of the cage's security. If someone wants to get something from the cage, tell him that they will have to come and see me, and I will watch over them while they are in there."

"I can't do that—you're just the new fork lift driver there."

"But this is not a union shop. Seniority doesn't matter. You can do it. Promote me. Think of something. You are the big boss. It doesn't have to make sense. You can do anything; it's your distribution center, and there's no union. We got to shake things up back here. You got the power to do it. Just tell Panko."

The quiet came at Eli from the wall behind and the stacks of cases to the sides.

"Why do you want to do this?" said Massingill.

"Because—once we do this, whoever is taking the stuff will need to approach me and I can get in with them and find out more about what's going on—become part of the ring, move up the chain of command so to speak—like the Trojan horse you know, like that."

"All right—makes some sense—but shouldn't Carl have a key then too?"

"No. Just me. Not Panko, either. Listen Mister Massengill, you're paying me and my company a lot of money to find the culprits for you, and I say this is what we have to do now."

"Not Panko? Not Carl?"

"Absolutely not. We need to seal the cage up as tight as a drum."

"How close are we to a bust?"

"Close. But you've got to get me this."

"Okay. It's as good as done."

He hung up the phone, closed his eyes and looked up as he told himself across the little café table what a good thing he had just done.

Yes—great move, Eli. Great bold move to catch everybody involved and get them busted at the door, a nice clean bust, right in front of the warehouse, you might even have made yourself bait—bait now—bait— the rat that has the key, the rat that has the only key—ha this will shake up the big fish it will it'll make them swim—ha I remember when we were a little baby, Mother's sweet little baby boy—even then we always had the best ideas—we always knew how to get the best of everything and everyone—my baby, my baby boy, she cooed to us—rat on the bait hook, hanging in the water, you don't want the bottom feeders, want the big fish, the big assed fat bass—they'll come to you, come sniffing around—step up use the big noisy lure at dusk like we have. The big fish will come, come for the money, they'll take the risk—they won't let anything cut off the money—the big bass down there watching watching tempted tempted yes here it comes the strike, yes, set the hook, wake up, do it—

The break bell rang, lifting his head; open-eyed, he spent the break in the racks, thoughts gone now; listening as the drug afterglow faded, knowing he had just done something big, that he wouldn't understand really until he finally came completely to himself, after the end of the day bell rang. But, it was as always exactly the right thing to do. Perfect, as usual. There was, after all, only one of him, only one, yes; only one Eli the Rat.

12 – The Narco Cage

Molly sat on her cart, vacantly ripping open the tops of antibiotic cases, when Panko came up, his pants and shirt tighter than usual, his tie shorter and wider. Molly put her hand to her face to keep from laughing at how silly he looked, because, after all he was the boss.

"Starting today," he said, puffing himself up to appear larger, "the narcotics cage is locked down. You'll need to ask for the key and have someone with you when you're in there."

"What?" she said, putting down her box cutter. "What do you mean locked down?"

."Massengill's orders. I was told to turn over the key to Eli."

"Eli?" she said, rising, head shaking. "He's just a fork lift driver, and, he's new. Why?"

Panko shrugged narrow-eyed.

"I don't know. Massengill's decided Eli's in charge of the security of the narcotics cage—if you need to get something out of there, you need to go get Eli, and he will stay with you while you're in there and get what you need, then he'll lock it when you leave."

—*what? Why? God, no, why*—

"Why is this? I'm stunned," said Molly, arms thrown out from her sides.

Panko waved her down.

"Molly, don't ask me any more. All I know is what I've been ordered. This is the way it is now. That's it!"

"No, Tom, wait—I could see having to get you to unlock it. You are the boss. Eli's no boss. I could even see Carl before Eli. Eli is brand new!"

—take back what you said take it take it—

"Molly, that's enough," said Panko, lifting a finger. "Honestly, just between us, I don't think it makes sense either. But this is how it is. Massengill has his reasons and he doesn't have to tell us what they are."

"But—you know, it would make more sense for me to be in charge of it—I get stuff out of there a lot, all the time."

Panko's hand went higher now, palm out.

"So do the fork drivers, Molly. They stock it and take out empty pallets. They probably spend more time in there than you."

No no no no please no—the pills the money all gone now no—

"Tom, it's wrong. I need to go in there. You have to talk to Massengill, there's nothing wrong with how we've been doing it—"

"Molly, Molly—why are you getting so worked up about this? I've not seen this side of you before. Take a breath. Your face is all red."

Bug-eyed, stopped cold, she had no answer.

It's got to do with pills, it does, it's hitting me in the pocketbook, it is—but damn I can't say it can't say it need someone to tell Gene yes Gene—

At last she stretched out her hands, palms up.

"I'm not worked up, Tom. I'm just surprised."

It will be okay Gene will know what to do Gene will help me help—

"But," she said, "I guess that's just how it is. Sorry Tom."

Gene—

"Well whatever the reason," said Panko, "go back to what you were doing. I just wanted to let you know about the change."

Gene will help, smile Gene will fix this, smile—

Smiling, she nodded, her tongue pressed solidly into her teeth. She stood there watching Panko turn and disappear up the aisle and around the racks, gone. She gripped the handle of the cart and pushed straight up toward the picking line to tell Gene what Panko said, but was stopped at the end of the aisle, to let Eli clatter by on the fork lift, a huge lopsided load of cases precariously balanced on the forks. Eli grinned and nodded as he passed.

—yes, *no doubt thinking a lot of himself now, no doubt big shot big shit is more like it—*

After he passed her, she hurried to the head of the picking line, left the cart, and went up to Gene. Rose was working on the line a dozen feet from Gene. Rose seemed completely absorbed in the orders, so Molly spoke softly to Gene.

I need to need to tell him need—

"Gene!" said Molly. He turned to her.

"Molly, great! I was going to come looking for you. Some of my stock is low—"

"Gene! Quiet! Rose can't hear this."

"What? Why not. What?"

"I can't get any more stuff for you from the narco cage."

He stabbed his pencil in behind his ear, the blood draining from his face in panic.

"What? Who says? Why? No, Molly, don't say this—"

"It is true. Panko just told me. The narco cage is now going to be locked at all times, and you'll never guess who I have to go to if I need to get in."

"Who?" said Gene, leaning on the line.

"Eli."

"Eli? Who—oh, the new fork truck driver? That Eli? Why the hell—"

"Who the hell knows why, it's down from the big shots is all Panko would say. Eli now has the only key and I need to get him to let me in and while I'm getting stuff from there he's going to be with me to watch me and I—"

"Watch you? Who? Why? Just you? Or anybody who goes in there?"

"Anybody. Even Panko."

Gene bit his lip, and then spoke slowly.

"No, no, this can't be—it just can't—"

"Hey guys!" said Rose, suddenly coming up behind Gene. "What's up? Is something wrong? You two look agitated. What has happened?"

"No, no," said Gene, turning to Rose, smiling. "Everything is fine—it's just this order here—these seventy six fourteens— Molly says we're out of stock—and it's a rush order! And, we don't have the slightest idea what to do."

He waved a blue piece of paper in the air and slapped it back down in its green tray. He shoved the green tray back into the corner and got the next order to be picked.

Molly watched, her mouth a tight line.

"God! You guys are pretty passionate about these orders, aren't you?" smiled Rose.

Gene planted a hand on his hip and leaned on the rack.

"Oh, oh yeah! That's us. Mister and Mrs. Passionate."

The side of Molly's mouth turned up in a slight smile, and, laughing, Rose turned and went back to her section of the picking line.

"So anyway," continued Molly as Gene turned back to her. "I don't think I can get you anything more until we figure something out. But we have to keep doing it. I've got to have the money."

Gene pulled the pencil down and marked the order he was picking. He spoke as he pulled stock from the rack and let it drop in the tray.

"Let me handle this," he told Molly quietly, his eyes squinting almost closed. "I'll think of something. I got to. I need the money, too."

"But what can you do?"

He pushed the full order tray away down the line.

"Don't think about it, Molly. I'll take care of it. I will let you know what to do."

Gene's eyes, father's eyes, calm come in me yes, Gene says there's no worry none—

Molly felt her tense shoulders relax as he went on to say, "We'll figure it out. Give me a day or two. Don't think about it. Let me do the worrying."

Gene. Yes. Thank you, yes—

Molly turned away and left the line. Gene returned to his picking, but faster now, because now something was up, he always worked faster when something was on his mind, he scanned the numbers on the orders and the numbers on the rack and his hands raced, like he was a machine, quickly and noisily pulling the boxes of pills and tubes of cream and whatever onto the row of green trays, one after the other and on and on.

So, I need to get close to this Eli guy. I need to get close and maybe bring him into the scheme. How? There's always some angle, some way, yes—I've seen that he eats his lunch in his car every day, I could go out to my car with my lunch and eat out there for a few days, and then walk over to his car and knock on the window and say hi Eli mind if we eat lunch together, and that way I'll get to know him, size him up, work on his head, he's just a kid like Molly, after all—I got her, I can get him. Money does the talking and plays the best game. Yes that's what to do, but—Lord God, I need a smoke break over by Franklin. A smoke break right now.

Gene put his pencil back behind his ear, laid down his glasses, and pulled out his cigarettes. Leaving the line, he came up past Franklin who stood at his desk counting up orders. As he passed Franklin, he waved a cigarette in the air and motioned for Franklin to follow.

"Franklin! Smoke break! Come on, I need a recharge!"

"Sounds good!"

Franklin put down the orders and the men went to the gate by the ashtray, and lit up. Smoke appeared, curling around and up in the short-lived sulphuric smell of the match strikes.

"Hey Franklin," said Gene right away. "I just heard something interesting."

"What?"

The smoke between them thickened but the words still flowed free.

"Seems like this new guy—Eli? You know, the new fork lift driver? He's in charge of the narco cage now. Keeps it locked, and has the key."

"What?" said Franklin. "Who told you that? That's crazy!"

"Yeah, Molly told me that Panko told her that if she needs something from the cage, she has to get Eli to open it up for her."

Agitation reddened Franklin's eyes.

"I can't believe this! Panko hadn't told me this—though I did notice that the cage was locked up this morning. I just thought Panko forgot to open it today. Panko should have told me this if this is the new rule. It can't be, Gene."

"Oh, yes it can. And it is."

Gene took a long slow silent drag off his smoke as a fork truck appeared far up the aisle and slowly came toward them, humming and clanking louder as it approached like a volume knob was being slowly turned up higher and higher on some odd-ball college radio show of noise.

"Well, there he comes. We're in luck, Gene. Let's flag him down and find out what is really going on."

Franklin smiled and waved Eli down. Gene leaned idly against the fencepost.

—*what luck*—*yes it starts here*—*here we go, play it*—*like a hooked fish yes*—

"Hey Eli," said Franklin. "What's this about you being in charge of the narco cage now?"

"Oh? That? Oh, yeah," said Eli. "Panko told me about it this morning. I was surprised when he told me the whole story about it needing to be locked up all the time."

"Why is it locked up all day now?" said Gene. "What has changed?"

"I don't know. Boss's orders, you know. They are much smarter than us peons, you know!"

The three laughed and the smoke cloud thickened and tightened around them.

"By the way, I don't think we've properly met," said Gene, extending a hand, "I'm Gene. I work the picking line."

Eli shook Gene's hand.

"Good to meet you Gene—yah, you know, I don't really know anything about why I have been given this great honor of being in charge of the cage, but don't worry Franklin—you can tell Panko I am deeply honored."

Eli winked, and Gene and Franklin smiled at each other.

"I've been told that they've got the good stuff in there," said Eli, "I suppose I must be lucky to be the one in charge of the good stuff."

Gene's eyebrows rose.

An opening here's an opening—go—

"Good stuff? What good stuff do you mean?" asked Gene.

"The hard stuff. You know—the stuff that's good for whatever ails you."

Yes—bait—too easy much too easy—

"Yeah, I guess I do know," said Gene, narrow eyes chuckling, before taking a long drag on his cigarette. "I hear some of those pills go for twenty dollars on the street."

"I know," said Eli, hopping down from the fork truck, "Hey, can I bum a cigarette off you guys?"

"Sure," said Gene, shaking the pack toward Eli. He took a cigarette. Gene lit it.

"Didn't know you smoked," said Gene.

Set the hook!

"Oh sure. I started at six months old. Bad parenting you know."

They laughed as Eli took a few drags.

"But seriously, Eli, why are they keeping the cage locked all day now?" asked Franklin.

"Security. Security or some sharp bullshit like that. It's just a new rule. Bosses like to make rules, or else they don't feel like they are doing their jobs."

Eli's cigarette went back to his mouth. Gene's eyebrows rose slightly.

"Bullshit?" asked Franklin. "Why is security bullshit?"

"Oh, c'mon," said Eli, smoke flowing from his mouth and nose. "Companies are all anal about that kind of shit nowadays. It's no big deal. Just a rule."

Eli looked down.

Set the hook!

"Anal," said Gene, chuckling. "That's funny. Companies are all anal. Got a ring to it."

Eli took a long drag from his cigarette and threw it in the ashtray. The remaining smoke curled up.

"Well," he said, "Need to run! Need to watch that damned narco cage, you know. Don't want to be falling down on the job. Remember I'm the new guy here. You know."

"Yeah," said Gene, grinning. "Better make sure. The whole company is at stake."

"I know," said Eli, hopping back on the fork. "I am carrying a very heavy very important load now! See you guys!"

Chuckling, Eli turned the handle of the fork truck, that immediately whisked him away.

"That guy's really funny," said Gene to Franklin, as the truck whine faded.

"I know. Funnier than shit. The big, fat, long, stinky kind of shit—you know?"

"Heh! Yeah, I know!"

Both men stubbed out their cigarettes and left the smoking area. Franklin went back to his tin desk and resumed shuffling through orders. Gene, however, did not go to the picking line. He walked down the aisle the fork had come up and scanned the aisles for Molly. He sometimes looked for Molly to get him some stock he was all out of. He came upon her, in a side aisle, sitting on her cart, again, cutting boxes. She heard Gene coming and stood as he spoke,

"Molly, I started to get our problem figured out. I just introduced myself to that Eli guy—he's pretty funny. We talked, me and him and Franklin."

"Really? So, what did you talk about?"

"Oh, never mind the details. Leave that to me. I think I can use him to fix our problem."

"Is he going to leave me alone in the cage?"

"No, not yet, I'm working on that. Right now I'm just getting to know him, making friends with him, you know, like that. That's how you start dealing with something like this."

"Okay," she said. "Let me know when it's clear."

"Sure will! Just don't worry and don't do anything rash."

"Okay."

Molly sat back down and Gene returned to the picking like. As soon as he came on the line, Rose came to him, an order hung in her hand.

"I saw you over there talking to that new guy." she said.

"What? Where—"

"Over there where you sneak a smoke with Franklin a dozen times a day!"

"Dozen times? Come on, Rose. That's not true—"

"What? You think I'm blind? Anyway. What's the new guy like?"

"Eli?" said Gene. "Oh yeah he seems like a good guy. Franklin waved him down, actually. We were talking about the new procedures for the narco cage."

"What new procedures?"

Gene told her. She listened open-mouthed, and then spoke.

"Wow! The big shots must think a lot of this guy to give him so much responsibility. Next step they'll make him foreman or something. Wow!"

Gene sat back on the line, and folded his arms.

"Well, what do you expect? Word is, he's related to one of the big shots in corporate, and that they made the extra fork lift job just for him. I actually would not be surprised if we're all working for him someday."

She put her order down on the line and leaned against the racks, speaking softly.

"Do you really think that Gene? He's only been here less than a month. Would they really make someone who's been here less than a month foreman?"

"I don't know. It's just talk. He's just a guy. You know what I mean? It's probably all just the rumor mill, you know. Just a lot of crap."

"Yeah," said Rose. "Crap is right."

They stood a minute then went back to work.

Lowering his head once more into his work, Gene pulled the orders, bulling his way mindlessly through the work right up to the break bell. There had been enough stress this morning. The orders flowed by.

To get close to him will be no problem at all, I'm sure we can click, can click—but how to bring him in, suck him into the scheme how to use what to use—Molly? Look. What if Molly and him were an item— that could happen—they're young, Molly could pull it off—I don't know what her reaction would be though—better ease into it—see what happens, ease into it—it would be great if she were his girl—ease into it easy —if she was, she could get him to do anything—yes but yes, whatever happens yes, no, I can't take the drugs out—I can't take that risk—can't be the one—that end stays the same—see Molly the whole deal is not down the drain just because—better ease into it—have a heart to heart with Molly—need to tell her right out, Kiss up to Eli—I'm sure he is single, he looks single, but maybe not—maybe it'll be plan b, plan b will be what need to think will be what—sure, should go out to him while he's in his car at lunch and tell him right out when we're pals, that—at a hundred a pop—he'll let Molly in the cage and look the other way—a hundred a pop is nothing to throw on him—but—but—need to sleep on it—plan a plan b plan c and so forth, no, and wow! Wow what a load of mother fucking work piling in here today good God—what a mother fucking pack of shit to figure out today—

The break bell rang.

13 – Molly and Eli

"Eli!" Molly called out, as the forklift neared.

The forklift pulled up in a clatter of empty pallets; Eli leaned over.

"Molly. What's up?"

"I need to get in the narco cage."

"They got orders for that stuff on the line?"

"Yup."

"Okay, get on the forks—I'll drive you there."

"What?"

Eli smiled and waved a hand.

"Step right on the forks there and hang on. I'll drive you to the cage."

The smile became devilish; making her step onto the forks and grab onto the frame as the machine began to move. They slid along over the concrete floor, the truck whining. She hung on, slightly scared.

Jesus Christ, Carl would never have done this—sour-faced bad-smelling old man that he is—but this Eli seems to be fun—

The clattering whine filled her, as Eli sped up around a bend.

—fun, Jesus, yes; but what if Panko sees? This can't be allowed— this gotta be dangerous, dangerous yes, but; oh well what's done is done— it's fun and fear fun and fear yes it's—

Rows of racks blurred past them; and yes, it was wrong, but it got them there; and, at last they pulled up outside the narco cage. Molly jumped off the forks again onto the solid floor.

—*wow what yes, yes, fun*—

"Hey you look like you got a kick out of that. Did you get a kick out of that Molly, huh?" asked Eli

"Yes, yes—but I need that cart there, wait—"

She turned from him and stepped out and grabbed a green cart just down the aisle, and came back to him, engulfed in the whine of the cart's squeaky wheel.

—*Jesus Christ carts never sound like this but what the hell, everything's different, everything has changed*—

She stopped at the cage, cutting off the whine, as Eli went to the door of the cage, pulled out a chain of keys and after jangling the keys in his hands, searching, he pushed the right key in the lock, turning it, and the big black chain link gate slid quietly open. Molly followed Eli in, and they stood surrounded on all sides by racks full of pallets of small boxes; boxes of the heavy stuff, the stuff Eli had talked about to Gene the other day.

The hard stuff, you know—the stuff that's good for whatever ails you.

"So, Molly. Whatever do you need?" asked Eli. "This is the place!"

"Need a dozen bottles of Noctec," she said, pointing to a pallet across the cage. "Right there. I see what I need."

"Go on to it. I got time."

Molly stepped toward the pallet, as Eli watched intently.

"You don't have to stay with me," she said, pausing and flashing a smile. "I'll be here a while. You are probably pretty busy too."

"Oh I need to stay and watch you," he said. "Massengill's orders."

"Massengill?" she said. "The big bosses' orders?"

"Yup," said Eli, sitting on the pallet next to Molly, as she worked. "He's the one that gave me the key. And he said I am supposed to stay with whoever comes in here, until they leave."

She eyed him as the cases started opening under her knife.

Damned pain in the ass, why—but Gene. Yes. Gene said not to worry—

"So anyway, Eli," she said brightly, her hands busy. "Why did the big shots decide to make you in charge of this place?"

He flicked his hand, like chasing a fly.

"I really don't know. I was surprised. Were you just as surprised, Molly?"

"I—"

The eyes his eyes no the eyes burn, talk so they go—

"Yes. I supposed I am surprised, that no one trusts anybody anymore."

The eyes said, "Trust? Why do you think this is because somebody doesn't trust you?"

She flinched inside at the way his voice had snapped that back at her.

What? What do I say Gene. Where is Gene? Gene yes he said not to worry hang on—

Molly began to answer Eli somehow, but he straightened up to twice his height, spread out his arms, and spoke loudly, as if to a crowd.

"Molly, this is just how it is now! Apparently, this cage is now my domain! Every man needs a domain of his own where nobody else can come into without his permission, and this is mine! Mine, I say! All mine! Ha ha ha ha—"

Molly laughed; he was just like old movies she had seen of some fat dictator in a funny hat on a balcony shouting out into the adoring throngs below. Encouraged, he went on.

"Well, I suppose to be fair about it; I shouldn't just say every man. Every woman has her domain, too—you for example, Molly. Your domain is those racks out there and all those pallet loads, out across this great big warehouse of ours, and the picking racks—that is your domain! And it is huge, much larger and more important than this. Ever think of it that way, Molly?"

"No," she giggled at the tail end of the laugh. "But really, seriously, why do you have to stay here with whoever comes in here?"

He sat on a small stack of empty pallets to the side.

"I will tell you exactly what I was told, and this is all I know. There are a lot of heavy drugs in here—Oxycodone, Oxycontin, Fentanyl—those kinds of drugs—all the drugs the addicts are hungry for and chasing each other down killing each other over to get, out in the streets. Massengill wants to make sure they don't walk out on their own, or to stop them walking away if they already have been. So, he gave me this grand domain! As though I am to be trusted or something! Jesus!"

She laughed, as he went on, hands waving.

"I mean, Molly, think about it! A real kick in the head, it is! I can see it now—the cage is open, and all the little bottles of drugs come hopping out of their boxes, their little feet sprouting out and they all go a-walking out of the cage on their own—can't you see it? Can't you?"

"Yah," she said brightly, pulling back her knife. "I can see it now. Tiny little legs, thousands of them. Hah. Funny."

"Sure, it's funny. But not to the big shots. The big shots for some reason think that with me, of all people, here guarding over them, they won't dare do that. They might poke their little bottle heads out from their boxes, but they won't dare make a run for the door with their tiny little legs. That is why I have to stay in here while the cage is open. Look at those big jugs of Noctec over there that you've got in your hands—can't you see those jugs sprouting arms and legs and hopping down from their cases and through the door and down the aisle toward the door, and on toward the loading docks, jumping in the back of some delivery truck toward freedom?"

"Yeah, sure," she said, brushing hair from her eyes as she stood by the cart. "There, I got all I need right now, we can leave. But I got a question for you, Eli."

"What?"

"Are you married? You're a funny guy. I'm guessing that you are married."

His eyebrows rose.

"What does being funny have to do with being married?"

"Oh—I don't know," she murmured idly. "It seems like you would attract all the girls."

She caught herself.

—my God! Did I say that, I heard myself say that, what did that sound like, what will he think that I said that what—

"Are you married, Molly?" asked Eli, his eyes softening.

—dear God—

"No." she said sharply.

"Well, why not? What's true for the gander should be true for you too. You're a funny goose! It seems like you would attract all the guys!"

Lord God, no, let it go. Let it fall to the floor and get out of here—

"I don't know Eli. What I do know is I got to get this Noctec over to the pickers. All done here now. So let's go."

Without looking at him Molly pushed her cart toward the door of the cage. Eli followed, once more jangling the dozens of keys on his keychain, looking for the right one.

Dear God, why does he have ten thousand keys like that, who has that many keys, what kind of keys so many—

"You know, Molly," he said, following her out. This cage is really a great domain to have! I mean, just put in a big old TV, a nice La-Z-Boy too, and a minibar stocked with drinks and snacks and I could spend the whole day here. It's a nice place. Quiet. Great domain. Don't you think Molly? Why in such a rush? Wait up!"

She left the cage and looked back, saying "They're waiting for the stuff. This took too long. I got to move now. Hey Eli, thanks for the ride up to this end. It was fun."

As she pushed away, Eli slid the big cage door home with a crash and locked the big solid steel lock built into the door.

"I could tell you liked it, Molly. I like doing things people like. Well, now that we're out in your domain, you are the boss! Take it easy Molly!"

"Okay Eli."

She did not look back as she pushed away. Eli leapt on the fork truck and disappeared, the whine lowering and lowering, and lowering, behind her, going away, until he was gone into quiet. The cart did not screech now. Molly did not notice. The cart did not screech now; that was something really good; and she ought to have been glad; but she had a lot more than some forgotten annoying screeching cartwheel on her mind. She rushed the cart to the line and went up on the line to Gene, who needed the Noctec, and who'd been standing idle, waiting.

"Molly, wow, where you been?" he said with a smile and a wink. "You running a little bit slow today, or what—you got the Noctec?"

"Yeah, I got it. I was talking to Eli."

As she brought the bottles around to the line, Gene pushed his pencil behind his ear, took off his glasses, and put his hand on the bottle she held, stopping her.

"Oh yeah? You were, huh? What'd you talk about? You took a while," he said.

His eyebrow rose pulling out her answer.

"Oh nothing really—he talks a lot of crap," she said, cracking a smile.

Gene put his head closer to Molly and talked softly.

"Molly, you know he's our ticket to get the Oxys out again. You've got to play up to him a little. You think you can get along with him?"

"We had a nice conversation. He's pretty funny—not real serious. But what do you mean, play up to him?

"Play up to him, you know. Get him to like you. If he likes you enough, well, I was thinking—we could somehow bring him in on the plan and you could get the stuff out again."

"What Gene? Are you nuts? No one can know what we been doing."

Gene's face moved closer to Molly's, and his voice lowered.

"Hey listen. I talked to him. He's an odd character—there's more to him than meets the eye. I think if you can get under his skin a little—you know what I mean?"

"Gene, yes. I know how you think. I know damned well what you mean."

"What do you think? It's like, you need to act. Play a role. Look at it that way. Play pretend that you like him. Okay?"

She stared him in the eye, unblinking.

No it's wrong but—I know we got to do something, I'm missing the hundred a week—this is all wrong, but I—

"Okay, I'll try." she said, averting her eyes.

"Good. Work on him. Feel him out. I been really looking for how we can handle this, and bringing him in is the only way. You know?"

Her eyes went back at him but his raised eyebrows drove her to look aside again.

It's wrong, all wrong. But—

"Yes, Gene, I know. I will do it. I know exactly what you mean."

His hot greedy crooked smile said, "Atta girl, Molly."

Gene pulled his pencil down from his ear, put on his glasses, and turned from her to fill the Noctec orders. Molly went back off the line to her cart. She picked up the sheet with the stock numbers she still had to pull. The numbers flowed down talking, somehow talking, and saying,

Gotta get close to Eli—suck up to Eli—how the hell do I do that?
Jesus Christ so wrong but Gene's right Gene's always right a hundred a
week, yes—

Molly pocketed the sheet and turned her cart back toward the racks where the Amoxycillin was kept. The pallet was empty. The item was next on her list, and good, the pallet was empty—so she needed Eli again, she'd be able to talk to him again. She walked toward the bulk stock area to find him, and yes, there he was, moving large loads of great brown cases around. She caught his eyes, and he stopped, dropped his load, and drove to her.

"I need Amoxycillin—rack seven," she called out, as he approached, grinning.

"What? You need Amoxycillin—you got an infection Molly?"

"No, no, stop. I need you to drop it for me. You are just full of fun today, aren't you? Your big domain, my big domain—hey you know like you said in the cage, out here in my domain I am the boss. So get moving!"

"Okay. Hop on the forks like before. I'll do it now."

She rode the forks as she had before and together they slid smoothly over the shiny slick concrete floor toward rack seven. At rack seven, she pointed at the empty pallet. He stopped the truck and she got off, coming around beside him.

"Twenty five ninety eights," she said, "Right here—that's what I need. Stop."

"Yes boss!"

They hopped off the forklift and he bent over pulling the empty pallet from the racks and got it out of the way. It slapped to the concrete with a sharp loud crack, and he got back on the machine and pulled around to get a full pallet from up above. As he intently watched the forks rise, she spoke.

"So why aren't you married, Eli?"

"You already asked me that."

"No I didn't. I asked if you were married. Not why you weren't. Different question."

"True," he said, as he moved the machine forward sliding the raised forks into the full load above. "I view marriage as a trap, and it's not good to be trapped. Wouldn't you agree?"

"It could be a nice trap though," she said, tilting her head. "I hope to get married, myself."

"Sure you do," he said, lifting his head as he followed the load down with his eyes. "But why would you want to get married when you can be free instead, free as a bird, free to go with who you want, when you want?"

"That could be lonely after a while, I think."

"Lonely? Why lonely?"

"I don't really know—"

—so intense he is looking at me asking me why—

"Are you lonely Molly?"

What?

"Sure. I suppose, sometimes. Isn't everybody sometimes?"

"Sure, I guess," he shrugged. "But when are you?"

—eyes pulling out something coming up to say the eyes no—

"I suppose, at home, at night. When there's no place to go, and no one to go there with. Working in this place doesn't help. There's no interacting with people. I have nothing in common with most of the people in this place."

"We're interacting," he said with a smile. "Maybe we have things in common."

What—

"Sure, yeah, maybe," she said. "I mean, we probably have more in common than I have with the other fork guy, Carl. He always was sneers and stares and acts like he's doing me a big favor when he gets me a load. Plus he stinks. Have you noticed he stinks?"

"No comment. I am the new guy."

"Hah. Okay. But hey—where is Carl now? I haven't seen him once since you started."

"Carl works the dock—I handle the racks. That's how we've decided to split the work up. Look out Molly; I don't want to hit you."

She stepped back as he moved the load and slid it into the empty space on the floor.

"There you go—plenty of Amoxycillin for your infection—I hope you feel better soon."

His face wrinkled up and his mouth moved as though chewing gum.

Very odd very odd—

"Very funny. Eli. You are a real funny guy. Breath of fresh air in the stale old place."

"I know—and by the way, yes I have noticed that Carl stinks like a dead man."

"Dead man? Hah, funny—like a dead man—"

"How do I smell Molly? Do I smell like Roses?"

"Yeah—just like Roses."

"All right! I am glad to be pleasing you so!"

Their eyes met; friends yes. Friends. Molly warmed.

—I can do this Gene I can really do this he is okay better than okay—

"Well—it is the duty of men to live and to please us women!"

"Hah, funny. I can think of a great comeback, but I'll let that slide. You need anything else?"

"No—not right now—"

"Don't hesitate to come back when you need something. You know where I hang now!"

"Yes, I do."

He turned around and drove away with the empty pallet. She reached up and got the boxes off the load, slitting the tops open and working on the Amoxycillin cases until the lunch bell rang, causing her to drop her knife and rise and turn around and start walking, heading for the lunch room, thinking in time with her step.

—this Eli seems okay—it may work out—this might end up a pleasure to do—

As she sat on the bench in the locker room eating, she stared at the lockers all shut tight across the room. The other women ate in the break room. Molly preferred to eat alone. Every day she had ended up idly counting the lockers from left to right and right to left—but this day as she chewed her tuna sandwich, her mind could not stop thinking through her grin.

—yes it will. It will be a pleasure—Eli, Eli—a pleasure yes it will be, a hundred a week, yes—and Eli too maybe. No harm in a thought. Something in his eye, I—I really can't look away—

Eli.

Several days would go by like this. Molly would go get Eli to open the cage or lower a load, and when they were together they'd talk back and forth about nothing things, about families and friends and small things like that. She like everybody else knew that Eli always spent the lunch hour out in his car—until the day she finished eating early, came out of the women's locker room, and there sat Eli, eating his lunch on a bench outside the break room. She came up crumpling her empty lunch bag in her hands and tossed it into the trash can next to the bench.

"Eli!" she said. "Why aren't you out in your car? Wow! People are going to think something is wrong with you for eating inside, almost like a normal person!"

She cracked a grin; he responded and waved the fragment of sandwich he had left back and forth as he replied.

"Normal person, Molly? Hey! I never claimed to be normal. I just got tired of the car. It's getting toward summer. It's too hot in the car, and I don't like to sit with the AC on, running the engine the whole time. No good for the car, you know—"

"No good? Why is it no good? Isn't that what cars are for? To run?"

"Yeah but not like that—here," he said, scooting over. "Sit down; we got another ten minutes until we need to go back in our cells."

"Cells? Oh, cells. I get it. You're such a card!"

"Nobody calls a funny guy a card anymore."

"Well, I do. My Dad used to say that all the time—God, look at that damned guy on TV! He'd such a God-damned card!"

"Gee, Molly. Girl like you ought not talk like a sailor!"

"That's my Dad, he talked that way. He talked like a sailor. What, do you think it's your job to preach about the evils of bad words and shit? Like some preacher?"

He finished chewing his last bite, swallowed, and said, "Preacher? Why, sure. I'd make a great preacher. But there is one problem."

"What problem?"

"I never go to church at all, and I only pray when I'm scared. God don't like that."

"How do you know what God likes or doesn't like?"

"Just do. Look out. Garbage coming through!"

She leaned back against the wall as he rumpled his empty bag, tossed it in the can down inside next to hers, burped silently, and stared her in the face.

"Tell me, Molly. What scares you these days?"

"What?"

"What scares you? You can tell a lot about a person from what scares them."

She screwed up her mouth thinking, until it came.

"Getting through each day scares me. And knowing that there will be hundreds more days all exactly the same that I got to get through."

"Hey, Molly—every day is what you make of it!"

"I guess so. So anyway, what can you tell about me now that you know what I'm scared of?"

"Shit, who knows. I just said that. Maybe it tells me nothing—"

"What? Then why'd you say that?"

"I say a lot of things Molly. You should know by now. I'm liable to say anything."

Eli's eyes half closed and slowly, as his eyes held hers, his mouth formed to a smile.

—why is he this way he's so different so different why does he look at me this way—

He looked away, and rose quickly.

"The bell's about to ring I bet," he said.

"Yeah. Probably."

"Let's go to it."

"Yes."

They went back out toward their jobs and the bell rang above below and around them, and the day went, and the next, and the next, and they ate lunch together on the bench every day, talking about everything; all things; anything.

"Why the warehouse Eli?" she said one Friday. "How does a bright guy like you work in a warehouse?"

"I don't have a high school diploma," he said. "I'm lucky to have this, without that."

"Some people have said that some big shot over in corporate got you this job—made it for you, in fact. That true?"

His eyebrows rose.

"Really? Who's saying that?"

"It's around. Is it true?"

"No, no way. My father is an electrician in the big plant up north where they make some of the drugs we stock. He did pull a couple of strings and get me this job, but he's no big shot. Why would people be thinking that? I never talked about how I got this job, except right here, right now, with you. God, people are crazy funny."

"Yeah, I know. Me, I just answered a newspaper ad to snag my job."

"That's unusual. Seems like the only way these days to get a job is to know somebody, or kiss somebody's ass, or whatever."

"Yeah, that's funny. Kiss somebody's ass! Very true."

They laughed, and as the dying laughter slowly mixed with their chewing, Eli spoke.

"You know, I could ask you the same question."

"What question?"

"Why are you in this lousy warehouse?"

She swallowed hard and looked away before answering.

"I don't know. It pays okay, for now I'm content here. I keep thinking I'd like to go to school nights and get a college degree and get out, but the money just isn't there. Besides, all the exercise running up and down the aisles is keeping me in shape. All the bending, pushing and lifting, you know, do you see what I mean? I don't want a job like the girls up in the office, sitting at a desk, getting all porky sitting and snacking all day. I'm sensitive about my figure, and so I'm glad this job lets me keep it up."

"I can see that. You know, a long time ago, when we first met, you said that there were easy ways to get extra money here." said Eli.

—oh, he remembers he's been wondering yes, he might—but slow, go slow.

"I don't remember that. When did I say that?"

"The other day. What did you mean?"

—his eyes eager want to know but no, slow it down, slow it—

"I really don't remember," she said. "Maybe overtime or get a night job or something—I really don't know what I meant."

—watch his eyes—

"No, I—I don't know. Maybe you really didn't say anything. Maybe I've been breathing fork truck fumes too much or something."

"Nah, that's not it. I probably said something. Making extra money's on everybody's mind these days, I bet."

"Yeah I bet. But—"

The break bell rang. Molly rose quickly, saying, "Hey, I got to run. All my racks are low. I need to run get them filled or everything will get held up. Bye!"

"Bye, Molly."

She turned from him and went back toward her truck set deep in the maze of drug racks.

—he's been thinking about what I said. He's hungry for money. Yes it's the right direction Gene is always right, this might work, he is thinking in the right direction—

For the next few days the topic of money came up between Gene and Molly now and then, but went easy, easy—but she knew it was on his mind though. She had run it by Gene; she'd told Gene that Eli's interested in some extra money; and to this Gene's eyebrows rose and he grinned and after they talked about it a bit, Gene said what would be next step in their plan.

"Okay. Just keep at him the way you've been—but don't spook him. Let me drop the big question on him, when the time is right. Hey, the way it's going we'll be back in business in no time!"

"I know. It'll be great!"

"Sure will." said Gene, pulling his pencil out from behind his ear and turning to his work, grin stuck on his face.

—Gene is happy, I'm doing good, I'm doing right—but how and when will the big question drop—Gene will know. Trust Gene—

Molly kept working on Eli; they had become friendly as if they'd known each other forever. They talked about anything and everything as the days went. Then, at last, one day as Gene and Franklin took their smoke break by the chain link fence, Eli came by on the forklift and stopped, like he would from time to time, to share a smoke with them.

"Hi Gene, Franklin." said Eli.

Franklin nodded, as he took a deep drag. A cloud of smoke surrounded the men as they stood there by the fencepost. Eli flicked an ash into the ashtray as Gene spoke.

"Hey, you know what, Eli?"

"No. What?"

"The whole place is buzzing about you and Molly being an item."

"Item?" smiled Eli. "Item, like how?"

"Word in the racks is that she likes you a lot."

"Really? And who is that coming from."

"Rose's been telling me. Molly's been talking about you two in the locker room to the rest of the ladies."

"And what was she saying?"

"You know, telling them what a great guy you are, how smart, how interesting, what a good guy you are to work with, all that stuff. Hey listen, why don't you ask Molly out after work for a drink on the way home? Solly's is a nice joint. Right down the road. She's telling them all how much she likes you. I could see you two together. If you know what I mean."

Gene turned winking at Franklin and they both smiled broadly.

"Oh please," said Eli, smoke blowing from both his nose and mouth. "I don't know, I—"

"Hey, don't say no right off like that. Molly's a great girl!"

"I know she is. Okay. We'll see. Hey, look. Gotta go!"

Eli ditched his cigarette and drove off fast on his fork truck.

"What do you think," said Franklin. "Think he'll do it?"

"Could be," said Gene, through narrow eyes. "It could very well be."

"Well. Back to work, Gene. I think Panko's on the prowl—"

"Got it. See ya!'"

The next day Molly brought Gene some Oxy's for an order. He stopped her a minute.

"Hey Molly—you ought to know—I gave Eli a little encouragement yesterday. I told him he ought to stop after work with you for a drink."

"Oh yeah? Is that the big question you were talking about?"

"It's the start of it. Keep softening him up like you been. It's in his court now. He told me he likes you."

"Really."

"Oh yeah. So keep it up. The next move will be from him."

"How do you know that?"

"I'm a man, Molly—I know what men always end up thinking about when they hang around a woman like you for long enough. It's a fact."

Molly's face reddened slightly, but it brought up a grin.

"Yeah, I suppose I know that too."

"Right. We think alike. Keep on."

"Will do."

Things went on as usual for a few weeks, until one day, it finally happened. Eli was pulling a load down for Molly, and as it slid down he turned to her.

"Molly, I been thinking. Why don't we stop off for a drink after work tonight?"

Goosebumps rose on her arms, but her answer was quick.

"Um, okay? Drinks? Where?"

"Let's go to Solly's. Gene recommends it. We could have a few, sit back, and talk as long as we want. No bell will ring telling us to stop. Come on, say yes."

"Okay, you talked me into it," she said, in mock exasperation.

"Hey, great! Let's meet at the front door after work. I can drive us."

"Yeah, yeah—I bet it will be. See you later!"

Molly smiled as Eli drove off. It'd been a while since she'd had a drink out at a bar with a guy. It would be fun. Plus, Eli had a way about him that she was really starting to like, even without throwing in what she and Gene were playing him for.

At the end of their shift, they meet by the door outside and walked down the sidewalk, along the parking lot, toward his car. He eyed her huge lunch pail.

"That's an awful big lunch bucket you got there—why so big?"

"Oh, I eat big. Can't you tell?" she said as she patted her stomach.

"Nonsense Molly, I see you eat every day, remember. You eat like a bird."

"A bird? It might look that way, but not really. At night I gorge."

"Oh sure, I bet—here we are. Get in."

In the car, after jabbing in and turning the key, he turned to her and spoke in perfect tune with the whine of the car engine.

"Mind if I smoke?"

"Oh? Smoke? No, not at all."

He reached over to the glove compartment, and came up with a briar pipe with the bowl wrapped in tinfoil. Her eyebrows rose.

"What kind of smoke is that?"

"A very, very special blend," he said, removing the tinfoil and crushing it into a small ball.

"Blend? What do you mean, blend?"

"Sure. Nice smooth smoke. Like weed, but much nicer. Got a few different things working together, very, very nice. Want to try? I won't be mad if you say no."

Molly sat stunned—*he must really trust her*—she had smoked some marijuana with friends through the years, and she liked it, but she never had expected this from Eli.

"I—I suppose," she said. "Sure. Why not."

He pulled out a lighter, shot the flame in the bowl and took a deep drag, and when his lungs were full and his lips came away, a snaky plume of white smoke rose from the bowl and spread out across the roof above. She took the pipe from him. The bowl warmed her hand. She dragged on the pipe; yes it was like weed, but different, more like weed than weed itself, it seemed. Smoothly it filled her, and she held it in with closed eyes.

My oh my, smooth, good, great—

"Hey, that is something!" she said, releasing the smoke.

"Take another," he said. "One drag's not enough. Take a few. You got to feel it."

She took another drag and held it in, and let it out, and repeated, each time the smoke smoother and more fragrant. Then she handed the pipe back to Eli. Not knowing quite what to expect, she leaned back on the headrest of her seat. Eli put the car in drive and pulled out of the lot. As he drove he took a long drag off the pipe and offered it to her again. She took it, the trees, telephone poles and office buildings and wide rolling bright green corporate lawns all flowing by silently, crystalline, bright, and glowing brighter and sharper under the sun that was hid someplace where she couldn't see it. The smoke filled the car now. She closed her eyes and felt the smoke pressing in all around her.

—drink? What to drink. When was the last time I been brought out for a drink? Much much too long since I been brought out for a drink. What's this Solly's? Never heard of Solly's. Maybe there's not really such a place. Maybe there's really not a world any more either. Or sun or moon or Eli or even not a car at all. Good God open your eyes and see is this really a car ride? Is the car still around me? I wonder, I do, in here—

Molly exhaled, and then took another long, smooth drag off the pipe.

"Hey, Molly! Hey!" he said, laughing. "Don't hog the pipe. Give it here—"

She handed it back to him.

What'd he say what he said oh yes about hogging the pipe, I—

A telephone pole with great green tentacles of ivy wound around and around stood by her as they stopped for a traffic light.

—*it's full of spiders get out get out, deep old ivy weeds crawling with spiders see them there, and there and there and there—*

"Hey Eli," she heard someone say in her voice as she stared at the pole.

"What?"

"Would you sit in a giant nest of spiders all night for a million dollars?"

"What—spiders? I don't know—"

"I would. You bet I would. "

She'd sit atop the telephone pole in the ivy with the world flashing by as though it were really the car, and she would spend the night all night, and earn the money.

—*but how would they be able to deliver the million dollars to me the next morning—*

"Someone's going to pay me a million dollars," said Molly.

—*when I'm up on the top of the pole—*

"Really? A million, huh?"

She nodded as the tree walked away to the left out of her line of sight and the car turned a curve out onto Easton Avenue. The heavy smoke filling he car to bursting, past bursting, was making the pipe hardly even necessary any more.

"Yes," she said slowly. "A million. What they call a cool million. You know how they say that they say it on the TV in the movies and in books all the time—hey! Listen!"

"What?" he said chuckling as he guided the car along.

"What book have you read? I read books when I can, books are supposed to be very very good for the mind—here give me it give me that—"

She grabbed the pipe from him, she took smoke from him, and she took everything inside and outside the car from him up through the pipe.

So need to keep it real all real with more smoke nothing will be anymore—yes, nothing's there really real at all what am I thinking—

The smoke filled her. The dashboard glowed back saying look at me, look; and she did.

Through and behind the dashboard there's wires and further the engine and further the space in front of the car, where, if you stood there, the car would mow you down—

"Jesus Christ, Eli," came in the smoke cloud flowed from her mouth, saying, "God damn your dashboard, your car and all is funnier than shit!"

"So, why are you not laughing?" he said, taking back the hot pipe.

"Oh, no, laughing is never allowed. Never. Never ever ever. Laughing is for sad not funny and crying is for funny not sad, see, see? The world is fucking upside down. But your car, I swear, your car is just too funny—"

"Well, funny girl, snap out of it. We're here."

The blacktop under the car swiveled around and became gravel and the barroom building came up before them. Eli pulled on the emergency brake, with a sound that ripped down through Molly like a great big old fashioned telephone book would sound, being ripped in half by a big oily strong man in some TV show.

"What did you just do?" she asked. "You made that noise there what did you do?"

"I pulled the emergency brake. What'd you think I did?"

—tore a hole yes tore a hole that swings open and closed and let me get out see I knew it was a car all along you tried to trick me that is was something much more important than a car, and I almost believed it until you made that noise, I am no fool, now I know, yes—I know for sure, Eli, because I am standing outside the car now and it's real because my hand's flat on the roof—you, yes you, coming around the front of this car, see? See? My hand's flat on the roof!

"Hey, you okay? Why'd you jump out so fast?"

"I didn't know," she said flatly. "Why? Isn't it time to get out someday, after you've been riding in a car—like this one!"

She slapped the top hard.

—see car big car shaped balloon bulging with smoke packed full—

Eli gently took her hand.

"Here, come on. We're at Solly's, here let's go in."

"And leave this here?"

She slapped the car top smiling; this made Eli's cartoon face split at the mouth bringing out the words.

"Yes, of course! This is a parking lot."

"Oh. Yes okay. I guess it's safe to leave the car here."

She stepped away following him toward the door. The spongy blacktop was hard to walk on, but she managed by keeping her eye dead in the center of the back of his neck. The door held open and his neck went away and she went into the cool dark.

—what's there a doorman here somebody opened it to let me in and took the sun out of the way so I could go through without more sun—

"Isn't it odd for a bar to have a doorman?" she whispered to Eli, as he let the door close over her, once she was inside."

"Doorman? What doorman?"

"Somebody opened the door for me; I didn't have to open it—"

"That was me, Molly—hey, shape up, are you okay?"

"Shit. You're a damned doorman. Why do you come to the warehouse every day then? This your second job? You really are some silly—doorman?"

"Molly, no. Come in. The pipe is talking through you. Here come in, let's get a couple of stools."

"Sure."

Stools. Sit on the stool. Everybody sits on their stools! Yes they do!

As they sat at the bar Molly breathed, "You are so wise, Eli. How did you learn to know everything in the world like you do?"

He just smiled at her with a nod, as the bartender came up, and he said to the bartender, "We'll have two beers. Whatever's special today on tap will be okay."

"Sure thing—that it to start?"

"Yeah, that's good."

The bartender nodded and Molly jumped inside herself seeing him do so.

—he is all lizard skin down below the collar. Eli, Eli. The bartender is all lizard skin—

"Molly, said Eli. Why are you holding the edge of the bar so tight? Relax. We're here now. You're here with me. Just relax."

Yes I suppose so—I suppose that's true enough—

"Okay," she said, assuming that even if the bartender was a lizard hungry for their flesh, Eli would fight him off to protect her. So it was safe. She let go the bar. The tiers of dark bottles behind where the lizard-man had been, all glowed; light bulbs, she guessed—light bulbs were invented to give people light. She turned to Eli.

"You know, I can't imagine how anybody got by before there were light bulbs."

His eyebrows rose.

"Light bulbs? No, I can't imagine how either. Why? You into light bulbs?"

Sure why not whatever you say.

"Yeah, kinda. I suppose. I don't know. Yes, I guess."

The lizard-like bartender stood at the far end of the bar, getting their beers by pulling back human hands stuck up in the air like tap handles.

—lord God to be under the bar with that job to have your hand up to be yanked on all day yanked on yanked on what a shitty job what shitty jobs we have Eli a hundred a week you know, is a lot. A hundred a week, not beer, no—just a hundred—

"Hey, Molly, you with us? Why the face?"

The labels of the bottles on the wall looked like they were smiling, each whispering out about their contents.

"I'm Stoli," said one.

"I'm Jim Beam," said another.

"I'm—I—"

"Molly? Hey? What planet are you on, do you know?"

She looked down from the bottles as the lizard bartender put the beers in front of them. The bulky man leaned back and said, "So Eli. Who's your new friend here? Usually you're solo."

Lizard eyes twinkling on faraway stars said to answer, but be polite.

"This is Molly," said Eli. "We work together. Molly, this is Tommy."

"Yeah, good to meet you, Molly." said the bartender. "But you can call me Thomas."

"Okay," she said—"And Eli, yes, this is planet earth in case you didn't know."

She grinned and pulled a riot of laughter out from them encasing her so she knew she would be safe. The laughter died in a moment. Three in silence were there. Three—

"Great to meet you Molly!" said the bartender, who slithered off around to the other side, and was gone.

"So Molly," said Eli, as they both began sipping the beer. "What are you planning on doing tonight?"

"I don't know. Probably watch TV."

"What will you have for dinner?"

"I've got some good leftover Chinese at home that I'll heat up. Orange chicken."

"Oh, orange chicken. That sounds good."

Eli drained his beer and motioned to the bartender for another. Molly pushed her hand out on the bar top, and then recoiled. The bar top felt scaly. Snake scaly. It didn't look it, but it was. Very, very snake scaly.

"Eli—Eli, feel the bar top."

"What?"

"Feel here, on top of the bar. It's all covered in scales."

He laid his hand on the bar, touching hers.

"Oh, gee, yes!" he said, in a joking tone. "It is all covered in scales! That's awful Molly, just awful! Pull your hand away! The bar might bite you!"

She obeyed, and where unseen scales had been appeared ancient rings from years of glasses left standing there too long. She put a finger into the center of one of the rings, and a tiny spider popped out and crawled onto her finger, which now rested atop the telephone pole wrapped all in ivy that she was owed a million dollars where Tentacles of ivy atop the telephone pole started to encircle them, the ground far below her.

—it is so so wrong. I took the dare, spent the night in the nest, but how on earth will they get the million dollar prize to me up here—

Eli's voice came instead, scattering the million dollars all around in a green shower.

"So what about your family, Molly?" he said.

The green money the green money all the green money is mine—

"You live at home with your family, right? What are they like? What do they do?"

"Oh," she said, pulling her hand back from a second spider crawling from a second ring. "I live with my mom and dad. She's on disability and he's retired."

Spiders everywhere.

"What are they like?"

She moved her hand around the bar top and everyplace she pulled her finger away from another spider popped into view.

"They're weird," she said, trying to remain calm, though she hated spiders. "It's a long, ugly story."

"Ugly? Why ugly—"

Spiders more spiders—

"I don't know, just ugly. You know? But tell me about your family."

"I live alone. I ran away from home when I was eighteen, and never went back. I can't hardly remember my parents. Maybe I had it ugly too."

She drank her beer, spiders appearing and disappearing and walking all around as they drank, and talked. The scaly bartender had been wiping his way down the bar toward them and reached them and his white rag swept over and took all the spiders away.

"Eli—I feel pretty weird." she said.

"You know why that is though, don't you Molly? Keep telling yourself why that is. Then whatever is weird will go away. I told you the smoke was good."

The row of bottle-faces set along the counter behind the bar began to softly hum a gentle tune, one that she'd heard before, but couldn't place. They sat for a while drinking their beers, the humming winding around them, all gentle and warm and Molly felt good, calm, content—

"Well, we better scoot now, Molly," said Eli after a while. "I'm expecting a phone call at home and I need to go to be there for it."

"Oh?" she said, opening her eyes. "Who's going to call you?"

"A friend. Lives on the coast. It's where I get the stuff from."

"Stuff?"

"Yeah," he winked. "The stuff you're on now," he whispered.

"Oh," she said. "That's important." She sat up tall, and drained her beer, as Eli put money on the bar. Molly slid from the barstool, thankfully and surprisingly there was now a solid floor under her. Not a spongy soft and creepy one, like all dark old barrooms tend to have. The hard floor creaked, but thank God it held her nicely as she stood. The humming music from the bottles stopped. The spidery scaly bar top moved away too as she stepped back.

"See you later, Tommy," Eli called out to the scaly skinned bartender. "Say hello to Solly for me!"

"Okay Eli! And Molly—good to meet you."

He waved his gleaming wet towel. Eli waved back.

"Okay, let's go." he told her; she obeyed; and out the door, the sun setting half hidden behind the tall tree line across the road. They got in his car and headed back to the warehouse. As she pulled over her seatbelt, it rattled out, as if it were a large chain. Thus chained into her seat, helplessly held, she let Eli drive her out of Solly's lot.

—*chain is strong chain is safe chain is good chain is*—

"I'll take you back to your car. Do you want a little stuff to take home?"

"No, I don't think so."

"Are you okay to drive?"

"Yeah, I think so." she sighed.

The million dollar pole and unlit boxy corporate buildings went by as she came down. When they finally arrived at her car in the company parking lot, Eli reached into his glove compartment and pulled out a small leather pouch. From this pouch he took a small cube wrapped in tinfoil, and handed it to her.

"Here—enjoy yourself, maybe while you are watching TV some night."

"Oh?" she said, taking it. "What is it?"

"Red hashish—Lebanese. Very hard to get in the states. Very expensive. You're worth it."

"Okay. Thanks, I guess."

She popped the foil cube into her bag and got out of Eli's car. He waited until she was safely inside her car and had started it before he pulled away, waving. She felt light and bright and fully fit to drive. She would have to tell Gene all about tonight. Gene's face floated across her windshield. He had a narrow-eyed knowing look, like he was there with her, and already knew what had happened between her and Eli. When she got home she put the hashish in the bottom of her sock drawer, got something to eat, and watched TV, just as she had planned to do all day.

Different somehow though. Better. Nicer—yes, yes.

Eli took her to Solly's three more times that week. They shared more of his special blend and eventually just some very potent very rare opiated Lebanese. After their third time together, Molly figured that with all their shared drug use, the time was ripe for Gene to approach Eli about the Oxys in the narco cage. She was convinced that Eli was a definite fit in the deal. He would go for it, for sure. Plus she had decided that she liked him. She would tell Gene first thing in the morning. As she fell asleep a tiny fairy flew around her head, twinkling her with fairy dust and disappearing into the darkness above her bed with a tiny last spark of light.

14 – The Deal Goes Down

Molly came onto the picking line to see Gene. As always, he tucked his pencil behind his ear when he saw her coming, removed his glasses, and carefully folded them into his pocket. Rose was far enough down the line for Molly to speak freely.

"You can talk about the Oxys to Eli," half-whispered Molly. "He's okay. He's one of us."

"I know," said Gene, smiling. "You and him are getting to be quite an item—going to Solly's every night, like you are. Good work, Molly. The money will flow again soon."

"I've been trying to get close to him like you said. I think he's at the point to take money to let me get the Oxys."

Gene's eyebrows rose.

"Why, what'd you say to him about it? Did you tell him we—" She waved her hand.

"No, no, I told him nothing. That part is up to you."

Rose suddenly came up gripping a green tray.

"What are you two all whispering about? What's the latest gossip, hm?"

"Nothing Rose." said Gene. "Just chatter, chatter, and chatter, you know, I'll jump on any excuse to keep away from real work!"

"Huh! Very funny Gene—hey Molly—I hear you've been going to Solly's every night with Eli. Ain't you been?"

Molly smiled.

"Yes I have. He's a nice guy, a fun guy."

"I bet that's what you two are all whispering about, right? Hey, what's the latest? Clue me in, come on."

"Yeah, that's it for sure!" said Gene.

"Well what about it? Molly?"

Molly and Gene laughed, and Molly said grinning, "Nothing, Rose. There's really nothing. We just go out to have a few. Not really too exciting."

"One thing can very quickly lead to another," said the older woman. "Hey guys, keep me in the loop. Love a budding love story!"

"Oh, please," snapped Molly. "Hey, I need to get back out to my cart. It's all loaded up."

As Molly left the line Gene threw her a wink that Rose could not see, and she cracked a grin as she rounded the corner. Gene put back on his glasses, and got his pencil down from behind his ear. He began to work; Rose drifted away. The orders slipped through his hands all by themselves; by now Gene had done this so many years, he was a machine. He sped up faster—faster—fastest and yes, here it comes, in his head, the plan, and the next step.

Let's see, at break I will walk with Eli and chat him up—I'll tell him that I want to talk with him in private—real private. What will I say to him—I don't know—I guess I'll tell him what Molly told me about the stuff he smokes—what will his reaction be—I don't know—I just got to go up and break the ice and get things moving along—I don't know—been suffering too long now for lack of selling Oxys—only got a few bottles left at home that I save for my regular buyers, but I haven't had any for walk-ups for a couple weeks now—I don't know—it's got to break through soon—I'm sure that after this talk everything will be okay—I don't know, but it has to—and it will—

The break bell rang. Gene came off the line and waited for Eli to walk up from the back of the warehouse, and Gene stopped him, with a raised hand.

"Eli, hey—wait a minute. We need to talk."

Eli wiped his nose with his blue sleeve.

"About what?"

"I can't tell you here—too many people around. It's top secret!"

"Okay—top secret? Give me a hint."

Everyone was drifting past the two on their way to the lunchroom. Gene slowly followed the others and told Eli, "I'll meet you here, after break. Then we'll go to the back where nobody ever is but you. We can talk there."

"Can't we talk at break?"

"No way. No one must hear us. Just trust me. Meet me here after break."

"Okay. You got me interested. See you then."

"Great!"

They went to the lockers and got their snacks. Gene ate in the pastel painted break room. There was only fifteen minutes to wait for the bell to ring them back to work. After fifteen minutes went by the bell rang. Eli and Gene walked together quietly toward the open spaces of Eli's usual haunts. Once there, Eli got on his fork truck. Gene came up leaning on the chipped up, yellow steel truckside.

"So what do you want to talk about?" said Eli, his eyes planted firmly in Gene's. Both men's eyes glowed, black as coal, in the false shadowy light from the neon tubes overhead.

"Okay." said Gene, laying a hand on the edge of the fork lift. "First, this conversation isn't happening—agreed? You got to agree to that. Or this conversation is already over."

One of Eli's eyebrows rose, his mouth a line.

"Fine. Agreed—so what's this all about?"

"I've been talking to Molly."

Eli lowered his gaze into Gene's.

"What about?"

"Molly tells me you have a private preference for weed and hash and that kind of product."

Eli slapped the side of the truck, threw his head back, and rolled his eyes.

"Oh, God, Molly just couldn't keep it to herself could she. What—are you tight with her?"

"Sort of. We've been working together a long time."

Eli leaned at Gene.

"This conversation isn't happening you say? You sure?"

"Swear on my Mother."

"Okay, I've got stuff. Use it and spread it around a little. Why do you care?"

"I want to buy some. Hashish is impossible to get."

"I'm not a dealer."

"But you can get me some, right? Some nice Lebanese? You gave some to Molly."

"I suppose. But it'll be expensive. More than you probably think."

The eyes locked tighter.

"I got the money. And you can take a cut for yourself in the deal. But one thing; when you get it, I want to try it before I buy. I've been ripped off before. I won't get ripped off no more. If you know what I mean."

Eli abruptly leaned back, smiling.

"God, no. I wouldn't rip you off. I'll be straight with you, and since this talk never happened—I got some out in the car right now. Come out with me at lunchtime. You can try some. The afternoon will be really funny in this silly place, when you've had some of that shit. You got money with you?"

"I do."

"Then meet me out there at lunch time. We'll go out for a drive."

Gene held out his hand, and they shook, and he said. "I've got to get back to my line now—I'll see you at lunch. And thanks."

Eli watched Gene walk back up toward the picking line and then immediately opened up the truck full speed toward the racks, to search for Molly.

—this is starting to work—no, it isn't starting, it is working— huh. Yeah, huh—

He ran up and down the racks until he spotted Molly slowly pushing a cartload of big heavy brown boxes. He drove up behind her.

"Molly," he said, coming off his fork truck. "Why did you tell Gene about smoking with me at lunch?"

As he talked, he feigned mild anger, and fought not to crack a smile.

"Oh yeah, I won't lie. I told him—Gene's a good guy, Eli. We can trust him. I told him how good the stuff was. I know he likes the good stuff; he's always looking for it. You know, the Lebanese—"

"You know I really ought to be very, very pissed."

"I—I don't know what to say," she said, box cutter hanging at her side.

"But guess what? I'm not," said Eli, letting loose with the smile. "If you say we can trust him, I'll trust him. Me and him are going out at lunch today, so he can try some of the stuff. I think you ought to join us. It'll end up a blast of a day!"

"Oh, yeah! Great. It will be really funny!"

"Out to my car then, at lunch."

"For sure!"

Eli smiled, nodded, backed down the aisle, and was gone. Molly pushed her cart up the picking line, springing up on the line and up to Gene.

"Gene. You talked to Eli?"

"Yes I did."

"You took a hell of a chance." she said slowly, her face solemn.

"I know, but sometimes you need to take a chance to get something going. Besides, like you said, I've noticed that he drives his fork lift around after lunch stoned out of his mind."

They exchanged narrow-eyed chuckles.

"I'm going to go with you to lunch today," said Molly. "He asked me."

Gene spread his hand out on his chest.

"Jesus Christ no, no don't do that. Let me alone with him."

"Why? It'd be fun—"

"I'm going to ask him about the key to the narco cage and set things all up."

"Why can't I be there for that?"

He put his hand onto a cardboard tray on the line, and pressed it hard as he spoke.

"I'd rather you weren't there. You just need to trust me. You could spook him. You've never set something like this up. What if you said the wrong thing? Listen, trust me. Please. He and I got to be alone."

"Okay, if you say it's best—"

"Good. Yes, it's best."

As they both exhaled, Rose rushed up behind Gene with a pack of cellophane wrapped tubes of cream in her hand.

"Molly, you put the wrong stock in the sixteen eleven rack. Things seem a little mixed up. Want to come look? Come on down."

"Oh—okay. Where? Come on and show me."

Rose and Molly rushed away from Gene, toward the far end of the line. Gene turned back to his work, picked up the next order, and shook it out.

I can't wait till lunch—share some good stuff, and solve this Oxy problem—I knew Eli was a head from the minute I saw him down the aisle—I just knew—you could tell by his lopsided smile—his look. After lunch he's just too damned happy, driving around, damned crazy. We'll

have solved our problem—just got to schmooze with him now—schmooze
him good—I hope they keep him in charge of that key—that damned key
to heaven—money talks you know—my money talks—and money will
talk again to me—money from heaven again, from above—

Gene's hands shook with excitement as his mind raced faster
than his hands eyes and pencil picking orders so fast, faster even,
so fast that Rose called up from her end, yelling, "Gene, Slow
down. I can't keep up!"

"Oh, sorry. I'm just in a good mood Rose! You know how I
get when I'm in a good mood!"

"Yes. You turn into a maniac!"

They exchanged sharp grins and Gene pushed and pushed
for the time to speed by, until, at last, the lunch bell rang. In five
minutes Eli and Gene met by the front door and started toward
the parking lot, Gene leading.

"Come on Eli—I can't wait to see what you got—"

"Hold up, wait—where's Molly?" asked Eli, looking around.

"Oh, she told me to tell you. She can't come."

"Why not?"

Gene flicked out a hand.

"I don't know. Something about not feeling well. Some
woman problem, probably. She said she wanted to stay in and
relax and we should go ahead without her."

"You guys really are tight, aren't you?" said Eli.

"Yeah," he said, smiling. "Pretty much. Molly's a really
good kid."

"I can see that."

As they moved through the sunlight, a mild breeze blew
across them. The grass spread out around them as they moved
faster. Down the slope, a man on a loud riding mower was cutting
the weeds along the fence by the highway. Eli pointed at him.

"Now, there's a good job—outside, in the sun, sitting down."

"Please, no. In bad weather, jobs like that are no picnic."

"Oh yeah," chuckled Eli.

They reached Eli's car and got in. The pounding sun all morning had heated it way up.

"So Gene, what do you want to try first? I have opium, opiated hash, plain Lebanese."

Gene rubbed at his nose, his eyebrows raised.

"A damned supermarket you got. Hey—you've got opium?"

"Yah of course. That's my favorite."

"No weed?"

Eli frowned.

"I don't bother with weed. Far too weak for me."

"I agree."

Gene opened his lunch pail and got out his sandwich. Eli did the same. They ate a few minutes in silence until Gene spoke.

"I'd like to try the opiated hash,"

"Really? Great. Okay."

Eli reached into the glove compartment, took out his briar pipe, and a small foil-wrapped cube. After a few minutes of preparation, he lit the pipe, and thick white smoke curled from the bowl. He took a drag, held his breath, and handing the pipe to Gene. Gene took a hit, the smoke curling thicker and sweeter around them, forming heavy layers in the car drifting slowly up through the sunlight.

"That's strong," exhaled Gene.

"That's the idea, isn't it?" said Eli, grabbing the warm bowl. He took another drag. Gene took a bite of his sandwich before taking the pipe again.

"Whew!" said Gene, his eyes rolling.

The inside of the car expanded. Eli looked miles away from Gene, but he tried to give him the pipe anyway, and Eli's hand was right there to take it even though the rest of his body seemed far, far away. The sun coming in the windshield felt blinding. Gene pulled down the visor on his side, and took the pipe back from Eli. They exchanged the pipe several times before Eli placed it carefully in the ashtray. Eli sat a far off shadow, way, away from Gene. The shadow picked up a sandwich and ate it. The shadow's teeth made tiny clicking sounds. The shadow was faceless, and blurred, and Gene rubbed his eyes and squinted as the shadow said, softly, "How about we talk business now?"

Gene opened his mouth floating out words from deep inside his belly. He read the words in the air to the shadow beside him as though reading from an ornate floating scroll.

"I want to buy some of this," he said, and the shadow sent the words back to him, and he caught them, and to his surprise he held in his hand a tiny, shining, foil-wrapped cube. Looking up, he almost missed hearing the words he read on the scroll, "Here you go," at the very instant the scroll rewrapped and became Eli's smiling face. Gene fumbled with the cube—it was as hot as a hot potato, but it cooled quickly, and he raised it before his face and squinted at it, all cross-eyed, he couldn't really see the cube until he heard himself say, "What? Yes. How much?"

"Free," smiled Eli. "You're a friend of Molly's. That's good enough for me."

Gene seemed startled as Eli's body absorbed all the shadow and became Eli again.

"Free? Huh. Thanks. What does it go for normally?"

"About eight hundred for a quarter pound brick," said Eli, flicking off a bug.

"Wow!" said Gene, eyes popping. As he considered the gesture, Gene's fingers were tying themselves into knots at the end of his arms, forcing him to press his hands to his thighs to make them stop; *knots, no good—must not tie into knots when it's all this close; listen.*

"That's a little flick off the brick," chuckled Eli. "About fifty bucks worth."

"This is pretty funny," said Gene, pocketing the hash with some difficulty, as his knotted up fingers had grown clumsy and numb. The bowl in the ashtray continued to curl smoke, and Eli picked it up again, took a smoke, and spoke, his eyes tiny slits— mere lines drawn on his lids, saying, "What's so funny Gene? You say very funny, why very funny eh?"

"You are funny! This whole deal is funny!," said Gene, raising a hand, "They put you in charge of the narco cage and you come out and smoke all this stuff and come back in all messed up, and all—yet you still have the key, right? You got the key?"

"Yep."

"So tell me. Why'd they give you the key to begin with?"

Gene took the pipe and smoked as Eli told him.

"Panko said it was because I had to go in and out of there a lot, anyway, so—I guess he didn't want me bothering him a dozen times a day for the key, you know? Panko is lazy. Like an old fat worn-out dog he sits and reads the paper all day—pretty good deal, eh?"

"Yeah, yeah, funny good deal. Yeah. Very funny—you know I—"

A genie of smoke instantly dropped from the words Gene had sent to Eli and settled down on the console between them in the car, as it inhaled Gene's words and told Gene that he really ought to get it together and get to the God-damned point.

Get to it—tell him what you came out here to tell him—about the Oxys—now that the ice is broken, you can tell him—

"What'd you say Gene? You were saying something. What?" said Eli, taking the dying pipe from Gene, and relighting it with a giant flame right in his face. Unfazed he took a drag, killing the flame, and held the pipe back out to Gene. Gene took another smoke and as he inhaled, the genie on the dashboard swirled about and was dragged down into his lungs with the hashish smoke. The genie was now in Gene—a genie in Gene—so appropriately named it seemed inevitable—

"Hah!" exclaimed Gene, handing the pipe back to Eli.

"What's funny, please share," giggled Eli.

So much smoke boiled about in the hot car, their visibility was zero. The genie in Gene spoke out through Gene's overheated mouth, bugging his eyes, and flapping his lips like a puppet to make Eli think it was Gene not the genie that was talking, and said straight out, hard, sharp, "I haven't said this to you Eli, this sentence is between you and me and after I say it, it never ever happened—but listen, I'll pay you five hundred dollars a pop to let Molly into the cage, and then look the other way while she does what she has to do."

"What will she be doing?" said Eli, his eyes narrowed.

"You don't have to know, said Gene, fully Gene again, the genie done and gone, having done his work to get the conversation started. "The five hundred dollars is all that matters—five hundred is a lot of money Eli," said Gene, hard-eyed. "A lot of money to be paid, just to look to the side and see nothing."

Eli's mouth just opened a crack in his stony face and the words drifted toward Gene, whose ears went up, *like what will he say will he say yes will he say no will he flash a badge now and say you're busted or*—

"Where are you getting five hundred dollars from?"

"Never mind. Five hundred dollars is a lot of money. Where I get it, you don't need to know."

The pipe pulled out from Eli's lips and the words showed in the smoke.

"Yes, yes, yes. I suppose that is true."

Eli made motions with his hands over the pipe, snaking curled smoke up and forked out into the layers of smoke in the car; like some sort of magic—

"Okay, I'll do it," said Eli. "I think you and Molly are both crazy to be doing anything in there, but I'll do it."

A great smile came out Gene's face. It left him hollow, all hollow inside where the Genie had been and any doubt that Eli would join them had been; so he wolfed down the quarter sandwich he had left, and lifted his thermos to his lips toasting Eli, the smoke in the car whirling heavily around his arm, forming into a point, the words poking Eli in the face.

"Here's to a long and fruitful business relationship," the words said, causing Eli to smile, and then the words fell useless into the dark by Eli's feet. Eli's hugely dilated eyes glowed and answered back to Gene, which made him smile too.

"Yes. To a long, long, and very very fruitful relationship."

Eli tapped his warming coke can against Gene's thermos and they both drank to their toast.

"Five hundred cash, each time," said Gene. "Probably twice a week."

Eli's jaw dropped, his eyes bugging.

"Huh? What? Twice a week? That's a thousand dollars a week! What do you guys got going on that you got a thousand a week to piss in my face?"

"Look at you, good at math. Like I told you before. You don't need to know where the money is coming from." shrugged Gene, his eyes buzzing silently behind his lids.

"This whole thing seems like some funny joke," Eli said bluntly. "But yes, I will take it. And I won't ask you again what's going on. I can use a thousand a week. Use it good I will!"

"Who couldn't these days?" said Gene, twisting around, reaching for his wallet in his back pocket. His eyes buzzed as he twisted, his fingers gripped the wallet finding that it was burning red-hot. Gene dropped the wallet into his lap so his fingers would not burn and the wallet came up and opened and gave his hand ten one hundred dollar bills which were also hot and so Gene quickly handed the glowing bills to Eli. Eli took the bills and flipped through them counting them as Gene said, "There. That's your first installment, ten bills. Let Molly into the cage alone tomorrow afternoon and Friday afternoon. You do not know what she's doing, get it? Make sure—you don't know or see what she's doing. Got it?"

The hot potato of a wallet then slid coolly back down in his deep pocket.

"Yes, I got it, and thank you sir! It's all here."

"Okay. Are we done out here then?" asked Gene, waving a sudden swarm of smoke tendrils from about his face.

"I suppose we are." said Eli.

At that Gene smiled and then he crumpled up his wax paper sandwich wrapper and put it in his lunch pail. The smoke in the car faded to nothing as Eli stuffed the pipe bowl with tin foil, killing the flame, and then put it away in the glove compartment with the money he had just earned.

"Twenty five after," he said, slamming shut the glove compartment and pointing to the clock in the dash. "Time for us to get back in there."

"Yeah. Work time always comes too quick."

"Sure does. Come on, let's go."

Gene got out of the car only to discover that his legs were still the Genie's and it was only by the good graces of the Genie that he'd be able to get back to the warehouse. Luckily the Genie was happy too about how everything had gone, and Gene's lunch pail lapped against his thigh as the Genie walked him along, his own legs numb.

"I feel like I'm floating," whispered Gene.

"Hah," gurgled Eli, who had since sprouted horns. They were black and matched his jet black curly hair almost exactly, almost completely hidden.

"Eli."

"What?"

"You have horns," said Gene.

The genie walked slowly on, Gene's dead legs dragging behind him.

"I have horns? Does that make me the devil?"

"No. Not the devil. Just some weird thing with horns."

The walk went by under them and the grass was green. The man on the riding mower had long since disappeared. When they got to the door, Gene's leg again had become his own and the horns on Eli's head had retracted back under his hair. Together they went in. Gene rubbed the side of his face. It was numb. He led the way toward the warehouse door. Eli was gone all gone, all gone, nothing for Gene to worry after anymore, now that the deal was done.

—*okay, okay; now off to tell Molly. Molly deserves all the credit—she did all the work—tomorrow afternoon and Friday afternoon she will get ten bottles each time, and we're back in business—this Eli is all right—*

Gene shook his face loose as he entered the warehouse; so dim and ugly in there, so—so ugly and dim. Eli went straight out toward the racks, and Gene turned to stop in the locker room to put his lunch pail in his locker. Bobby the packer was in the locker room, too. He slammed his locker shut, as Gene approached.

"Hi Gene," said Bobby, "I see you ate outside today eh? Great day for it, huh?"

"For what? Oh—yeah—lunch—outside. Great day yes, a great day."

"God!" said Bobby—"what's that funny smell?"

"Smell? I smell nothing. Why?"

"Don't know. Its weird."

Gene could not think what else to say to Bobby without the Genie inside to advise him. So he went out through the chain link fence toward the picking line. He came onto the picking line and looked over a spread of new orders Franklin had brought during lunch. Rose came onto the line behind him.

"Hey—Rose. You seen Molly? I need some stock. I got some new orders and don't have the stock—"

"Here I am, Gene." said a voice behind, turning him. There stood Molly, with her box cutter hanging in her hand. He held out the clipboard with the order sheet on it.

"I need some of this stuff. A whole lot—here let me show you—"

As Rose drifted away, Gene spoke softly to Molly.

"Molly, listen. I got great news for you. For us, I should say."

They stepped behind the rack out of view or earshot of anyone else.

"What happened? What's so great?"

"Tomorrow afternoon, and Friday afternoon, ask Eli to let you in the cage. Get the usual we always get on those days. Eli will look the other way while you do it. He's agreed to know nothing and see nothing and say nothing. He's on our pay now. He is one of us!"

"How'd you manage that?"

Gene gripped the rack as it swayed unsteadily above him.

"Just like you get a few dollars to bring the stuff out, he gets a few dollars to see nothing and know nothing. Everybody is going to be happy ever after, after all! Dollars make everybody very, very happy! You know that—"

A fish jumped from the concrete floor and splashed back in, as though there were a river running between the racks. Gene wrung his hands together, and swallowed hard. As they stood beaming at each other, fish of all sizes began breaking the surface all around them, and Gene struggled not to sink into the grey waters rushing by.

"So what you paying him, Gene?"

The current got stronger—he held on with his words.

"He gets the same as you. Fifty a pop."

"Where you going to get an extra hundred every week?"

The smell of mud pond water hung all around, though the current was subsiding.

"I'll just raise what I charge for the stuff when I sell it down at the shore."

"And what do you charge for them down at the shore? You know, you've never told me."

His hand rose panicked, even though the danger of drowning had passed.

"We shouldn't talk about all that right now. Just know that we're back in business. A hundred a week for you. A hundred a week for him. Even, equal and fair, good money for everyone involved."

The fish swimming about just under the surface of the concrete made Gene very uneasy.

"I got to get back on the picking line. Now, remember—tomorrow and Friday afternoons—you can take what we need. He'll stay quiet."

"Okay Gene, if you say so, you're the boss."

Gene returned to the picking line. For the rest of the afternoon he had trouble with the fish swimming just under him beneath the surface of his picking line. He couldn't see them but he knew they were there, just under the thin concrete, thinner than ice; people have died falling through the ice. Fearful he worked with gritted teeth, but would make it, safe, to the final bell.

Molly did not see Eli at all that afternoon. It was as though he had disappeared someplace. She had hoped to go with him to Solly's tonight. She then heard from Carl that Eli had gone home right after lunch. Said he had had an appointment. She left Carl and bit lightly on her tongue.

Funny that should happen right after Gene made the deal—funny that should happen then—I wanted to go to Solly's, but—a hundred a week again. Yes. Good. Great, in fact—

Molly worked to the end of the day, feeling lighter now that they had pulled this off. She slit the box tops open, smooth as silk.

Sharp knife, deal done, yes, things were good—but somehow it's too easy. Nothing's ever this easy—no, no nothing—

This churned her stomach so, that she had a hard time finishing out the day.

15 – Eli and Molly

Eli now had enough to bust Gene and Molly. But he had grown to like her. He sat on his forklift in the bulk stock area the day after he had lunch with Gene, waiting for her to come to get him to open the narco cage, like Gene had said—and he would look the other way. But he would know what she was doing. And he would feel terrible for her to be in the trap he had set. Yesterday after he had lunch with Gene, he had gone to see his dealer, nicknamed Parkie, to pick up an order of high-quality hash. Eli never even knew Parkie's real name; just knew he was an ex-California surfer type, who'd got kicked out of the Army years ago for spiking an officer's coffee with LSD. That was in Germany, many years ago, now Parkie lived in an apartment near from where Eli kept his place. He went to Parkie's third floor room, knocked three times, and the door opened a tiny crack.

A tall blue-eyed blonde man in a green bathrobe stared out from the cracked open door.

"Parkie! You're home!" said Eli.

"Eli," said Parkie, who shut the door to undo the safety chain and then flung the door open, his blonde head nodding, shaking hands as Eli slipped in. A cheap card table stood in the dead center of the room, two folding chairs set up across from each other. There was a hot plate set on the counter to the side of the room, and a small refrigerator stood over by the sink. Otherwise there was no other furniture, not even a couch. A door led to the single bedroom. On the card table was a large green bowl, piled high with foil-covered slabs.

"Sit down here," said Parkie, motioning to one of the two folding chairs. They sat down across from each other as Parkie smiled.

"How's the rat business going?" he asked Eli.

"Oh, it's going," said Eli. "I'm on an easy case right now. They're stealing prescription drugs from a big pharma warehouse down in Somerset. I'm almost ready to close in, you know, squash the bastards!"

Eli raised his arms and opened his hands like some beetle was flying around waiting to be grabbed. Parkie laughed, the dirty shade on the single window behind him pulled down halfway, causing everything in the room including Parkie and Eli to be a dull shade of grey. Eli kept on talking.

"There's just one problem. A girl is involved. A nice girl that I don't want to bust—"

"Jesus Christ, man," said Parkie, slapping his forehead. "With Eli there's always a girl involved, isn't there?"

"So true!"

Their laughter washed across the bowl of hash in the center. Parkie produced a small pipe from the pockets of his green bathrobe, and a lighter, and they began to smoke, as they continued to chat about the case.

"So, tell me about this girl," said Parkie.

"She's taking Oxycodone from the warehouse and transferring it to another worker, who is then selling it on the street."

"Does this other worker ever take any out the door?"

"No. He's got her doing the dirty work. He says he pays her."

"Peanuts I bet."

"Yeah, probably peanuts, right. Anyway, he's the one I'd like to bust, but I can't figure out how to keep her out of it."

"Well, as long as she's carrying the stuff out, you can't."

"That's true. I know that."

Parkie passed him back the pipe, but Eli waved it away. He had smoked enough for a day. He spoke through a mild pink and yellow buzz that came from the four faded walls.

"So what have you got for me today, Parkie?"

Parkie waved his hand over the bowl.

"What you see before you. Nice big fresh hot red Lebanese hash."

Eli took one of the slabs from the bowl, nicked a corner open and sniffed at it.

"Smells damned good."

"Only the best here, you know that. So—how much do you need?"

"I'll take five hundred worth."

"That's a good bit. Now, you know you still get a nice discount here."

"That's true. Maybe I'll take a little more. Six hundred, how's that?"

"That is very, very good. Wise decision for such a young man."

The men smiled. Parkie took four large slabs from the bowl and put them before Eli. Eli produced the money from his worn out wallet and gave it over. Parkie stuffed the money into a pocket of his dingy frayed bathrobe.

"You know, you could make those two hate each other."

"Who—?"

"This girl you don't want to rat out. And the dealer she's in with. You could make the girl hate the guy and stop bringing the stuff out for him. Then he'd have to bring it out himself—and then buzz, buzz, buzzzzz—busted! Hah! Easy, peasy, yes, easy as pie."

Eli placed a hand on the four slabs of hashish.

"How do I go about doing that? I can't see—"

"Hey, the details are your problem. I just come up with the big ideas—I'm a big idea man. Never handle details."

"Right," chuckled Eli.

"You fucking the girl yet?"

Eli's face froze.

"No—of course not."

"Is the dealer fucking her?"

"No."

"How do you know?"

"I think I know her pretty well at this point."

"Yeah? How?"

"We've been out after work drinking and smoking. About four or five times."

"She tell you she's bringing the stuff out?"

"No."

"So then how do you know?"

Eli shifted in the chair and put his hands behind his head. The colored buzz twinkled in the air before him. He felt much too tired to go over the whole thing.

"I just know," he said. "The other guy told me some stuff. It's complicated, you know."

Parkie nodded, blinked, rubbed at his eye as though something was in it, then rose and went to the sink, and washed his hands. He returned.

"Anyway, that's my suggestion. It's really so simple. Make them hate each other. That's the way to bust him. You're already tight with this girl so it ought to be easy. Is she good-looking?"

"Very."

"Figures, they always are," smiled Parkie.

Eli glanced away, then back.

"Enough talk about me now. How's your business humming?"

"My business? Take a look. Business is great. Humming like mad. Good word, that—humming. You are very good with words, my man. But why do you ask?"

"Just curious. A lot of good stuff in that bowl there. Probably a lot more around the place too. Bowl of hash makes a really nice centerpiece."

"Hah. Sure. Great centerpiece. Yes. But you know what's really even funnier than that?"

"No. What?"

Parkie laid down a hand, palm up.

"Look at you. Just look at yourself. Here you are a, professional rat, who gets people busted—and then after work comes to see me, and we do business together. That's funnier than shit."

"Sure, very funny. I am always good for a laugh, aren't I?"

"Oh yeah, yeah. Hey listen—do rats make good money? Are they paying you what you're worth?"

"I got no complaints."

Parkie's hand flipped over, palm down.

"Every time you come back east for a job, I can't help but thinking that you ought to go into business with me instead of playing the rat game."

"With you? Doing what?"

"Dealing. To the street dealers. Not to the users. The users are trouble. Stupid, and trouble."

"No, sorry, I probably make better money as a rat I bet. What money are you talking about?"

"Oh, plenty. Lots. It would flow to you like water. I could put you in charge of my whole east coast operation. Know that? That's a big deal." said Parkie, lifting the pipe and lighter, lighting up again.

"Maybe someday. Maybe, if they ever let me go."

"What security firm you with again?"

"Pennington's."

Parkie nodded, as he offered Eli the bowl again.

"More for the road?"

"No thanks," said Eli. "I've had enough."

Rising, Parkie slid the stack of hashish toward him.

"You got a bag I can put this in?" Eli asked.

"What do you think this is, a five and dime?"

"Very funny."

"In the cupboard over there, there should be some bags."

Eli took down a paper bag and put in the slabs.

"Got to run, Parkie."

"Okay—and remember."

"What?"

"Make her hate him."

"Yeah right, that too," Eli said, leaving.

That was yesterday afternoon. He opened his eyes, and there he sat in the bulk stock area, waiting for Molly. Gene had said that it would be this afternoon, and Fridays. Eli figured that for appearances sake he should remain in the cage while Molly took the drugs. That is what everybody expects. It was what he'd been ordered to do by Massengill; Stay in the cage with her, and watch what she does. It's also what Panko expects to see. It would not be good if Panko walked by and saw Molly in the cage by herself. Eli could sit looking the other way, and still be in the cage. After all, Gene was paying for that too. To be looking the other way, but knowing damned well what was happening. That is how it would be.

He jerked out of his doze as Molly came out of the racks with a smile, stopped, and waved for Eli to come down toward the narco cage. He drove up beside her.

"Narco cage?" smiled Eli.

"Yup. Gene told me about the arrangement. You ready?"

"Sure. Get on."

She stepped onto the clattering forks and gripped the truck frame as Eli started down the aisle. At the narco cage, Eli stopped the truck, got off and pulled his chain of keys from his pocket, and fumbled through finally thrusting the right key into the lock.

The cage door slid back and Molly and Eli entered the cage. Molly paused looking at him.

"Are you going to stay in the cage with me?"

He nodded.

"Yes, I got to. Wouldn't be good if Panko came by and you were in here by yourself. I'll just hang out. Take your time, do whatever you have to do."

"But you're supposed to look the other way. Gene said."

"Don't worry. I know nothing. Just go on do your thing so we can leave."

She pushed her cart to the Oxycodone pallet, sat, and began ripping open the box tops. Ten bottles to a box; a hundred tablets to a bottle. She emptied one box onto the cart, then rose and pushed over to the veterinary section. Again, she sat, and began ripping boxes open. She referred to a piece of paper she pulled from her pocket, with stock numbers penciled down it. She had been given this list by Rose, who picked the veterinary drugs off the racks. Molly's hands were very fast, and her cart piled with stock of all colors shapes and sizes very quickly. The Oxycodone set safe deep inside the pile. She rose, threw her knife atop the load, and pushed toward the door to leave the narco cage.

"Okay Eli. Let's go, I got everything I need."

"Yes, great! And I know nothing! Isn't that funny!" he said, cracking a smile. Rolling her eyes, she smiled back. She pushed the cart out and headed toward Rose's veterinary racks, which were over near the locker rooms. He watched her go, her hips gently swaying.

Ten bottles, thought Eli, as turned locking the narco cage door. She took ten bottles. There are a lot of pills in there. A hundred pills a bottle. That's a thousand pills. Now, say that Gene sells them for twenty dollars a pill. That comes to twenty thousand dollars in street value.

I will be God damned—

This was stunning; twenty thousand dollars, twice a week, on and on through weeks months and years—a warmth rose inside him. This was going to be his biggest bust ever—by far. Gene had clearly said Friday afternoon too; so that's forty thousand of street value a week, if she takes the same number of bottles—Christ!

No wonder he's driving a God-damned BMW—he could buy a brand new one every other week.

Eli watched Molly unloading the vet stuff for Rose.

Shit! And—who's he selling all these pills to—maybe he's not and he's selling whole bottles to street dealers for five hundred a bottle, that's twenty bottles a week, that's ten thousand a week—and what was Molly getting paid to take the pills out from the warehouse and transfer them to Gene? Was she getting paid what Eli was? Five hundred a pop? That would leave Gene with eight thousand a week—Jesus Christ, got to think, can't think, but—must.

He chewed his tongue as her cart slowly emptied.

Now—yes—get them pissed at each other—like Parkie said— how, how—money that's it. People fight about and for money all their lives, yes—money—

Eli drove back away to the bulk stock area and looked idly up at the corrugated steel roofing. He began to count the trusses running across holding the roof up way up there.

One, two—yes I got to somehow get under Molly's skin—three, four, five—yes maybe I should take Molly to Solly's tonight—six, seven, eight—yes ask her at break yes—nine—yes she always said yes before and she will say yes now—ten, eleven—in Solly's I'll get a few beers in her and tell her all these numbers—twelve thirteen fourteen—yes there's fourteen. There always has and always will be fourteen trusses across up there—the last truss, the last step of the plan, this means it's right, this is what to do, yes—

Yes, he gripped the handle and nodded, looking down from the ceiling. He would drive a wedge between Molly and Gene. Greedy Gene would then be forced to work alone, and that's when

Eli would blow the whistle and they'd grab him going out and he would take the fall for the whole operation—all by himself.

Sweet. Always fourteen trusses always have been always will be yes, very sweet—

Just then Molly came up through the racks, pointing.

"I need eleven twenty fives." said Molly, coming up, laying a hand on the truck.

"Okay," he said, straightening up and gripping the truck handle. "Hey listen, how about you and me at Solly's after work today? It's been a few days. It will be a celebration of, you know—our new relationship."

"Okay," she said brightly, "I'll meet you there. Can't ride there with you."

"Oh yeah? Why not?"

"Got to stop off someplace after work. It'll just take a minute. Then I'll come to Solly's."

"Oh? What you stopping off for? I could drive you."

"No you can't. Trust me. I'll meet you at Solly's"

"All right, if you say so. See you at Solly's, then—come on, hop on the forks!"

She hopped on, and he drove her to the stuff she needed. As he lowered the pallet he noticed that her cart was clear of any boxes or bottles. The Oxycodone had to be in her lunch pail now, most likely in her locker. The tall green and orange racks cast strange shadows around them. A neon light high above them had flickered on and off and on and off and was getting ready, rehearsing over and over, to burn out for the last time.

"Funny light up there." he said.

"That thing's been doing that for a month. Panko's too cheap to replace the bulb. I told him, he said, 'Well, work in pitch black just like there was light. Black, light, makes no difference—the work will stay the same either way.' And then he just walked away. Now was that a weird thing to tell me or what?"

Her voice wavered as she brought box after box onto the cart, all the while talking. She talked and the boxes moved and the light flickered, and Eli watched her, until, again, the break bell rang. Once at the locker rooms, he went in the men's and she went in the woman's, and when they came out, they sat on the bench. They chatted and the bell rang and the rest of the day wore on until, at last, at four twenty five, the bell rang saying the day was again over. He hung back and waited near the veterinary racks, from which you could see the main doors out of the warehouse. He saw Molly leaving, her large lunch pail in her hand. She walked out with long, strong, confident strides, the lunch pail hanging at her side—she went out the door into the office and he knew, he could see, what he could not let happen.

Out there is exactly where she would be grabbed—this is where security and the police would come out of the offices and stop her at the door and demand that she open the lunch pail. But no, no—this cannot and will not happen—I got to save her, need to save her, got to save her yes because I—no. no. Can't be, no can't.

Eli stepped out quickly, left the building, went to his car, popped open the glove compartment, and pulled out his opium pipe. Just opium today, just pure; just sweet. Not a job for hash or any stronger stuff today to get things all twisted and funny and nuts—the talk at Solly's called for pure opium and straight sharp lines of facts and figures. He lit the pipe, and took a long, deep drag. The smoke wreathed his head as he started the car and slowly pulled out of the lot, steering with one hand and holding the pipe in the other. Slowly he drove toward Solly's, smoking, the passing trees all bowing, the sun above smiling. He drove slightly faster than usual—he decided that he would bring her into the car to smoke some opium with him before they went in Solly's—yes, they'd smoke together, laugh, get all casual—and then inside, he would do it to her, crush her with the math that was in his head. The twisting tendrils of smoke rising from his pipe's bowl told him yes, yes. He would do it to her good.

—Get them pissed at each other, Parkie had said.

The smoke went down his throat easily. It warmed Eli. He rolled down the driver side window letting in the mild day. After several turns, Solly's came up. Small squat green building, an old man funny kind of bar—but Eli liked it. He liked that it was funny. The smoke continued to go down easily. Solly's was a palace. Solly's was like Xanadu, golden spheres and towers topping it. Sure yes, the perfect place. The crunching gravel under the car's wheels pulling into the lot ripped at his ears. The perfect place, yes—he braked the car and the ripping in his ears stopped.

—Get them pissed at each other, Parkie had said.

Yes, indeed—Solly's is the perfect place to get somebody totally totally pissed off.

The pipe lay warm in his hand. He took a last drag. He did not want to smoke too much before Molly got there; he needed his wits about him. After thumbing out the pipe, he put it in the ash tray. He switched on the radio; some mindless talk began that he could not possibly pay attention to. Switching channels, he found none better. He turned off the car, killing the radio, engulfing himself in silence, the layers of smoke slowly dissipating. It had been a long day, he was tired. His hand went up against the windshield. It looked just like any other glass, but it felt different. Very, very soft, like some clear paste. His finger went right through the soft glass, just as Molly pulled loudly up beside him. His finger came back out the soft glass, and surprisingly, yes—it left no hole. It was good there was no hole, because—but before the reason came to him, his door window slid down and he yelled out at her after she got out from her car.

"Molly!" he called out. "Hey Molly, I'm right here. Come on in the car with me!"

She muttered something too low, it seemed like just a sound, not a word—and with it before him she came around through it and wet across to the passenger's door and got in Eli's passenger seat.

"Hey, Eli. I took a bit longer than I thought. Have you been waiting long? Uh-oh, I smell something in here. And there—right there's the pipe. You naughty boy!"

"Yes, that I am, that I am. Hey Molly—how 'bout you try this before we go in. Pure opium, plain and simple."

"No, no, opium makes me see things all hazy. All it does is make me tired. I'll pass."

"Oh no, come on—just a little bit? Just to get a buzz. Not enough to nod off. C'mon!"

"All right, okay, maybe just a little. That's all though. Just a couple of hits."

Molly would not look Eli in the eye; she did not seem herself.

"Here, take the pipe. That's right. Hey, you've got something on your mind, don't you? What's the problem?"

At last her eyes focused on his.

"Can I be honest?"

"Of course. Why not be honest? Come on—"

"Okay, all right—I don't like that you know what I've been doing, me and Gene. It's wrong what we've been doing. I worry that you'll think less of me."

Her eyes.

"Oh, Molly, Jesus—of course I don't think less of you. Look; I'm part of it now, too—if I thought it was so wrong I wouldn't be part of it. This is a big company. They'll cut your throat for a buck. The bastards deserve to be ripped off. We're doing right."

"Are you sure?"

Her lips.

"Yes I am. Go on, time's a-wastin'! Come on, take a smoke."

He lit the pipe for her, and she took a big hit, held the hot pipe in her hands and the hotter smoke in her chest, then exhaled; and inside the smoke surrounding her head, she took another faster and deeper drag.

"Hey, go easy there kiddo!" he said. "Not so fast. It's strong stuff."

He laughed as she smiled, eyes bugged out, and blew the smoke straight into his face.

God, that's strong stuff. But—her teeth—so perfect and—but no no no yes my job is not this like Parkie said—said—don't look at her do it do your job—"

Roughly snatching back the pipe, he took a final hit, crushed out the embers, and coughed hard three times.

—do it yes, get them pissed at each other—

One more cough, made her say, "Are you all right Eli? I—"

"Oh sure, oh sure. What's a tickle in the throat when you got something going that makes you five hundred a shot for unlocking some cage and looking the other way?"

He sniffed back hard, his eye on hers.

—get them pissed at each other—right eh—

She had been brushing stray hair out of her face, but his words froze her hand in midair, her eyes bugged as before, and her eyebrows rose painfully high.

"Five hundred dollars a shot? What do you mean? Who makes five hundred a shot?"

"We do! Isn't it what we get paid every time we take the stuff from the cage? I get paid that to let you in the cage—and you get paid that to take the stuff out. It's great!"

She looked at him gravely.

"I don't get any five hundred dollars a pop."

She held the unlit pipe to her lips, but did not smoke.

"But I thought—Gene said he was paying you big money."

She flicked out a hand and half-shouted.

"You're not serious about that, are you Eli? He's paying you five hundred dollars—a thousand a week? What the hell is this?"

"I don't—what? Why? Don't you get five hundred twice a week too?"

"Shit no!" she yelled. "I get fifty dollars. A hundred a week!"

"Fifty dollars? Lord God, that's nothing for the risk you're taking of getting busted—"

—Get them pissed at each other—go—go—

"—you could get hard prison time for stealing so much for so long. I can't believe it!"

"How can he afford to pay you a thousand a week for doing nothing?" she said loudly.

Eli sat up, pressed his right index finger into his right palm, and strained to remember the numbers he had worked out earlier.

"Well Molly—look at it this way. You're taking twenty bottles of pills out a week. He's probably selling the stuff to dealers for five hundred a bottle. So, he's probably making ten thousand dollars a week!"

—Get them pissed at each other—go—go—

"What—ten thousand? Ten fucking thousand?"

"At least that, yes. And the street value of twenty bottles, if there's a hundred pills in a bottle, is probably around forty thousand."

"Forty thousand?"

"Yes. That's if they sell for twenty a pill on the street. That what they go for these days."

She slapped her hands hard on her thighs.

"Christ! I never added all that up before—I don't know where my head's been all this time—"

—Get them pissed at each other—

"—that's criminal!" she yelled out, glancing from Eli to the window, and back. "Absolutely criminal!"

He smiled inside.

"You're damned right it is," he said smoothly.

—Get them pissed at each other—go—go—

She sat back in the passenger seat.

"Sounds like I need to have a talk with Gene."

"Yes, you ought to if you think he's just using you—which he is."

—*Get them pissed at each other—go—go—*

"And plus, Molly, think about it. Who gets sent up if one day they search you? You are taking all the risk. That's not right. The company starts to dig when they wake up and realize so much is being taken, well—you're the one they'll take away in handcuffs. He's got you all set up, Molly. All set to take the big fall!"

—*Get them yes pissed at each other yes, keep on—*

Molly's jaw set hard, and her eyes half closed, as a hard angry look melted tight on the curves of her face. Eli then decided to close in for the kill. His hand sought hers, and squeezed it tight, and he spoke in the soft tones of a priest, a confessor. His hand squeezed hers tighter by degrees, as the talk went on.

"Molly, listen. Would you like me to be there when you talk with Gene? I swear to God, I never dreamed he would do this to you, you guys seemed so tight. I feel it just as if it was me."

She shook her head hard, slapped her thigh harder, pushed her face at Eli, and said "No, no, no. I can handle this jackass. Right now, I am just numb. Stunned, and numb. Let's go in, I need a beer. Maybe a dozen. Maybe a thousand. Maybe I'll just stay inside and drink so many I drop dead right there, right then. You know what I mean, Eli? You know what I mean?"

"Yes," he breathed, and he meant to say more, but her door sprang open and she shot from the car and rushed toward Solly's door. Eli followed, tiptoeing slowly over the spongy ground, holding his breath all through the thick air, and rushed into the silvery bar, which once entered, seemed to always slap a ripe smile tight over every patron's fat face.

16 – Molly and Gene at Dunkin's

Gene sat in his big BMW in the parking lot of the Dunkin' Donuts, about a mile from the warehouse, waiting for Molly. He had
not seen her since Wednesday's drop-off, the first one involving
Eli. He wrapped his hands around his coffee and the warmth came
up his arms, slowly increasing as the people went in and out of
the coffee shop.

*You don't know why I'm here—you can't know why I'm here—I'm
into the big money—big, big money—more money than any of you can
imagine, and easy money too—so so easy money—money is all it takes—
money can do anything—I sell a pill here, a pill there—behind the bar,
by the wheel—they ask you if you got some, they tell you what they need,
and the money comes and and again and again—just like that it keeps
moving, yes just like that—*

Gene felt good about the deal he'd made with Eli, and was
glad he would be getting another ten bottles of pills today from
Molly. It was all back to normal; except for now having to pay Eli,
but the money he paid Eli was a drop in the bucket next to what
he himself would begin raking in again. Gene smiled and sipped
at his coffee as he watched a large woman in a brown coat drag
two recalcitrant children from the coffee shop—both held huge
donuts in their hands— and they went back toward the rear of
the lot where their car was as Gene said to both them and himself,
You, you can't know, you can't imagine—

Suddenly Molly's small Pontiac pulled up beside his BMW. She got out without waving, carrying her lunch pail, and came around. Gene put down his coffee, unlocked the doors and she got in the passenger side.

"Molly—"

"Gene, listen." she said. "We need to talk. First, here are the bottles—"

She opened the lunch pail and there were the ten yellow boxes each containing a bottle of Oxycodone, ninety pills each, the usual score—

—but something's wrong—her face is not her face—but there's the stuff—it looks like she got the stuff—that's okay I can handle whatever her problem is as long as I get the stuff—

"Thanks, Molly. You did good again—but what's the matter, you seem on edge—"

"We need to talk about what you pay me. The fifty dollars—"

"What? Why? Sure, I'm going to give you your fifty dollars. That's the deal."

She pointed at his chest, her eyes ablaze.

"Eli told me that you are paying him five hundred dollars each time to open the cage for me—twice a week! What the hell are you doing paying him five hundred when you're only paying me fifty?"

Gene's face set in anger as he slammed shut the glove compartment.

"Jesus Christ, Molly, what the hell are you two doing talking about this deal—he's not supposed to know anything about what you do!"

She raised a hand.

"Never mind what we were doing talking about this—it was obvious to him what I was doing, I didn't have to explain anything to him. And besides, Eli and I are tight—and he told me what you're paying him. Why would you pay him so much more than me? I thought we were friends, Gene!"

Gene leaned back, and pounded his hand on the steering wheel.

—Jesus Christ I knew this would blow up somehow—I knew it—I really really knew it—I could kick myself in the ass—right square in the ass—

Turning to her, he tried to speak calmly.

"Molly, I know I told you to get tight with him, but not that tight—not talking about money tight. Why the hell did you do that?"

Again, she raised a hand to shut him up.

"Never mind all that," she snapped. "I should be getting more money than a lousy fifty."

—but fifty dollars is what I've always paid you—you ought not be talking to me like this—no not like this—this can't be happening—

She pointed at his face, almost stabbing into it, her voice sharp, clear.

"And you, you bastard!" she said, "You're making thousands of dollars every week off these damned pills—thousands! You can afford to pay me what you're paying Eli—I'm taking all the risks, carrying the pills out—listen, Gene. Starting right now today, I want more than Eli—I want fifteen hundred a week. To include back pay."

Tiny hairs stood up on the back of his neck.

—what?—that's ridiculous—that's a joke—no way—no way she said that—

"What? Wait a minute—Molly just shut up a minute!"

"Shut up? No, I won't shut up! You just listen, and do it! Pay me that much, as much as Eli, plus an extra half to make up for all the times you didn't pay me right, or you can carry out your own damned pills!"

"But I—I can't go in the cage, how will I get the stuff, I—"

She waved his words aside.

"That'll be for you and your butt-buddy Eli to figure out! Not my problem, Gene! All I know is that a hundred a week is chicken feed! And my God, the jail time I've been risking for you! How stupid have I been—but I'm not stupid anymore! You're the stupid one now Gene!"

—wait a minute—this can't be—Molly's just upset, it always passes and this will too—calm, calm, take a breath, talk to her calm—

Raising his hands, he spoke calmly, as Molly fumed.

"Wait a minute, Molly—calm down a minute. It's all a question of what is the most difficult thing to do. Think about it. Eli has been made responsible for the total security of the cage. If they find out he let you steal pills, it'll be worse for him than for you."

She shook her head violently.

"Bullshit!" she said. "If I get caught taking them out the front door, that'll be worse for me—no, no Gene—I'm not budging—fifteen hundred a week or no more pills!"

—no, no way, never—

"Molly, take a deep breath, be quiet a minute, and think about what you are saying."

Her head tilted and she pointed again.

"Think about what? What? How bad you ripped me off? Why are you so God-damned greedy, Gene? We figured out that you're making something like ten grand a week selling those bottles. Ten fucking grand!"

—what? Now this is quite a talk they had didn't they these little filthy insects—they are quite a bunch of shitty little insects when they get together—

He raised a finger and spoke smoothly.

"That's nonsense. I make nowhere near that."

"Nonsense? What are you making then, Gene—mind telling me?"

"I maybe get a couple thousand a week, if I'm lucky. If I pay you fifteen hundred, and Eli a grand, that'll wipe me out! Just can't do it, kid! Just can't no way, no how."

She threw up her hands, jerking back her head.

"You're such a pile of bullshit Gene!" she shouted.

—all right time to take the gloves off Molly—you need to see reality—

Turning to her more fully, he jabbed his finger at her face.

"Listen Molly—I take the most risk of all—I sell the God-damned things—you know what you can get for dealing stolen pills? I could get twenty years! Or maybe life! Do you think I got nothing to worry about like you got, Molly? Are you stupid enough to really think that?"

—yah—yah—that got your attention—what do you God-damned think of that little bitch—

She threw up her hands and yelled faster, louder.

"That's your problem Gene, not mine! It was you that dreamed up this whole damned thing, okay, yes! Maybe you ought to be sitting in jail! Might wise you up, Gene—that's what you need, is some fucking wising up!"

Hurt, he pointed at her gently now, and spoke slowly and softly.

"You don't mean that Molly, come on, think—we've always gotten along so well—I'm very, very sorry that you're so upset—tell you what—I'll pay you what I'm paying Eli—a thousand a week. How's that? Is it a deal?"

—there that ought to do it—will that shut her up—

Her hands came up waving.

"No! No, that's chicken scratch too! Fifteen hundred a week or nothing! I carry the shit! The risk is all mine!"

Her face flashed as lightning.

—Idiot! Greedy God damned idiot little bitch!

Gene gripped the steering wheel and stared out the windshield at the people coming in and out of the donut shop. He slowed his breathing, turned to her, and tried to speak evenly.

"Molly, I will think about it. Give me a little time for that. Okay?"

"There's nothing at all to think about, Gene! I'm not going to budge. That's it, or nothing."

—Never! Little baby bitch, no never!

She gripped the door handle.

"I got to go now. I can't stand it here with shit like you—yeah you think about it—think about it really, really hard—you got me so pissed off that I can barely think!"

—you bitch, you little damned bitch, to talk to me like this—

"I can tell, Molly—sure, you're so pissed off! Poor little baby, go ahead, be pissed off! See where it lands you! Yeah, see where you end up!"

She made a rude face, opened the door, picked up her empty lunch pail, got out, and slammed it shut. Gene watched her go to her car. He touched his breast pocket. A fifty dollar bill was folded down in there. Molly's fifty—the fifty she doesn't want anymore.

—why did damned Eli and Molly talk about the money—this is a bad situation—Eli is going to get hell for this—this is all his fault—you're not supposed to share what you're making, regardless if it's a salary, or something like this damn deal—sure I could afford to pay Molly what she wants, but why should I just because Eli is so damned stupid and can't keep his damn trap shut—big stupid ugly hairy bastard Eli. I jumped too fast I guess. Maybe it's that I'm slipping. What the hell made me think I could trust the bastard—

As Molly drove away, Gene started the big BMW, throwing it into drive. On the way home, he stonily refused to think any thoughts about the situation. He still got his ten bottles of pills out of it. And she didn't even think to ask for the fifty. So it's his fifty now. Her loss.

—one day at a time, you've got to take these things one day at a time—that's what gets me through all this shit—its nerve wracking—didn't know exactly how he and Molly got teamed up like this in the first place—it started with one bottle, two bottles, some vitamins, some other stuff—was selling to pharmacies, no hard drugs back then, giving her fifty was fair back then, but; now with how much they are taking and how big it's all got, fifty isn't so fair—what to offer her, though. What

do I need to offer her—I know it should be a bit more, but what—but oh, wait until I get my hands on Eli—I could wring his neck—I probably should—maybe I will you know. Maybe I fucking will—

The next Monday, after he had picked a few orders on the line to get things started, Gene went looking for Eli back in the racks. He caught up to him way at the back wall, stacking loads of empty pallets high up, so high, dangerously high. The conversation they would have was not one for the break room, or the locker room or anywhere within earshot of Rose, Franklin or Panko—

"Eli!" said Gene, stepping up to the fork truck and pushing his pencil behind his ear.

Eli turned.

"Gene? What brings you back here? You need something? You never come back here."

"Why the hell did you tell Molly about our deal?"

"I—what?"

"That was a big fucking mistake Eli! A really big mother fucking mistake!"

Eli got off the fork truck.

"What do you mean Gene? We're all in this together—you, me and Molly."

Gene laid a fist on the fork, and pointed at Eli.

"Well then, if that's the case, I'll tell you what kiddo—you're down to a hundred dollars a week from now on—it was a mistake on my part giving big money to you! You'll be getting what Molly's getting, so it's all fair and square!"

Eli folded his arms.

"Then I won't do it Gene. I'll just stop letting her in the cage for you."

"God damn you Eli! All right, good move, but—I don't know what else to fucking say—you're fucking the whole thing up, you know. The whole damned thing's down the drain now, yes right now, because of you! Think it over!"

Gene turned his back on Eli, and stormed away, leaving the smiling Eli to climb narrow-eyed back into the truck of the forklift.

—*this is all working—all working—*

Gene went back to the picking line. He dropped his pencil multiple times and nearly had his glasses fall off his face as he was quivering so much from anger. As he got on the line, he began frantically picking faster than ever. Rose called out to him from her end of the line.

"Whoa, Gene! What're you trying to do, set a record again? You are killing me!"

"I'm just excited today, Rose. Ever have a day where you're just so—so happy and excited you almost want to kill yourself?"

"What are you so excited about?" she smiled.

"I love my job Rose. That's exciting, isn't it? To know you love your job?"

"Oh, yeah, it is—it's very exciting when you get that lucky."

—*oh yeah, exciting, my whole world's falling apart and I'm supposed to tell you about it, you stupid old bitch can of shit just shut the fuck up and go away leave me alone. I have to think about this mess—I have to think this all the way through—there's no way that bitch gets fifteen hundred from me—not from a hundred to fifteen hundred—no way, no how—never no never, no—never, now!*

Meanwhile, Eli drove around the warehouse, until he found Molly seated on her cart getting stock, ripping the tops off with extra gusto, lost in thought.

He drove up, got off the fork.

"Hey what did you say to Gene, Molly? He is really really pissed. Damn, tell me—what exactly did you tell him?"

"Nothing—just that I want fifteen hundred a week to take the pills out."

"God! Wow! What'd he say to that? He seemed pretty agitated—he really tore into me."

"He's thinking about it. Said he needed some time to decide. He offered me a thousand."

"Well—that's pretty good—"

"Yeah, but not good enough. I take the whole risk, Eli—fifty dollars a pop for me is a sin, plus I think I deserve some back pay. Don't you?"

Eli's eyes narrowed more with each slow nod of his head, until words got forced out.

"You still taking the stuff out Wednesday and Friday afternoons?"

"Yes, but it'll be the last time unless he coughs up fifteen hundred. Or, like I told him, he can do it himself. He thinks he's so damned smart—let him find a way!"

She pulled her box cutter savagely across the carton in her hand.

He stepped back, nodding.

"Well then, I guess we'll see. Hey listen, I'm leaving early today. If you need any stock tell me before noon. Carl is out too. He's sick."

"Why you leaving early?"

"Yeah I got another doctor's appointment this afternoon—I'm leaving at noon."

"Doctor? Again? What's wrong with you anyway? What hurts?"

"Nothing I can tell you. Trust me on that—see you around."

Turning, he drove off from Molly. As he drove, he felt every bump in the concrete surface beneath his rubber and steel wheels.

—everything is set up perfectly—looks like my job here is nearly done—too bad that after next week I will probably never see Molly again—she was fun to meet—really fun to know—

Good kid damned good kid.

Soon these thoughts began to drag him down, so he blocked them out and thought about how to deal with tomorrow.

17 – It is Finished

Eli left that afternoon at two. When he got home he went right to the phone to call Massengill. There was a lot to talk about. He settled back into his easy chair in his room and faced the TV which was on, but with the sound muted. An attractive woman was talking excitedly on the TV, but he had no interest in knowing what she was saying. After lighting his hash pipe and taking a couple hard drags, he picked up the phone and dialed Massengill's number. The curling smoke twined in and out of the ringing phone sound and hung in the air behind the receiver.

Then came a click that sounded like a gong; a great, big, round, bronze gong.

"Massengill here," oozed a voice.

"Mister Massengill, this is Eli. Glad I caught you."

His voice echoed into the phone hollowly.

"Eli, yes—how's it going?" said Massengill.

Smoke snaked about Eli, and into his words.

"It's going good—you don't need me anymore. I know the who, what, and when."

"What do you mean?"

Eli squeezed the slimy phone struggling to escape his grip. Putting down the pipe, he held the phone in both hands, forcing the words.

—I've got to say it got to say her name—got to—I have got to—
I'm a God-damned professional—

"Gene Adams, and—and—Molly Crew, are the two employees who have been stealing bottles of Oxycodone from your warehouse."

"Really? Never heard those names before."

—no not really—I'm just pulling your God damned hairy leg—
but excuse me now, fraternal order of professional undercover investigators,
I have to lie—I have to bend the truth a little just a little because of the
way I have things set up—

"Look them up. They work under Panko. And you need to know, it varies which one actually takes the drugs off the premises. The day your guys hit, they should grab both of them. They take the stuff out on Wednesdays and Fridays, every week, like clockwork."

The cloud between them blew away, Eli heard clearly through the slice of clear air.

"Why always the same schedule?" asked Massingill. "And why does it vary which one's carrying the stuff?"

The smoke from the pipe in the astray rose, curled, and branched, and Eli read the answer it was writing for him even though it was a lie.

"They vary it so—so the odds are lower they'll get caught. They think they're really playing it smart."

—there you go—got to believe that—that almost makes sense—it
really doesn't actually, but who gives a shit—thank God I'm not stut-
tering—when I lie I tend to stutter—my stuttering is like God's way of
saying to me 'don't lie, Eli, Eli, don't lie, don't lie'—

"It just seems like that would make them easier to nab," said Massingill. "Twice the chance to slip up."

Nab. Funny word. Who says nab? Nobody says nab—

Eli giggled under his breath, then picked up his pipe and took another drag before speaking, his voice strong with authority.

"They don't think that they're ever going to get caught," he said, smoke curling from his mouth and nose. "I've seen this before; on other cases—they get arrogant and into themselves and people take risks. That's how I got them. They risked confiding in me. Like we planned."

"So, tomorrow's Friday. Should we grab them on the way out tomorrow?"

—no! Molly will be carrying tomorrow she told me no no—

"No!" said Eli, suddenly realizing he spoke a little too strongly, so he went on to say more calmly, "Get them next Wednesday. There's a possibility they might not do it tomorrow. You wouldn't want to stop them and have them have nothing on them. And there's more."

"How do you know they might not do it tomorrow?"

"I'm tight with them. They told me why, but why is not really important."

"Okay. I'll get everyone on board to grab them next Wednesday. Anything else for me now?"

—yes get Gene—make sure, no matter what, get fucking Gene—

"Let's see—oh, sure. Gene's the one who's selling the pills down the shore where he lives. You got to take this all the way, you got to arrange with the cops down there to hit his house down the shore with a warrant, at the same time the other guys grab them at the door. It doesn't matter which one's holding the stuff. Gene is the mastermind. He's the criminal. There'll be plenty of your drugs at his house, in his car—"

"What about this—let's see, I wrote it down where is it—yes, here. Molly. How about this Molly? Shouldn't we hit her house too?"

"No. She doesn't take any there. Gene takes all of it from her after she sneaks it out and gives her some money for her trouble. Then he takes it all down to the shore. Make sure he gets nailed and nailed good!"

"We will, we will—just wait, I need to write all this down—"

"Oh, yes—one last thing. Like it says in our contract, I fade out of the picture after the bust. Tomorrow's my last day. I'll tell Panko I quit. Make sure you tell Panko that after I'm gone, he's to leave the cage unlocked just like he used to—don't give the key to Carl, or anybody else. Just make very sure to tell him to leave the cage open."

There was silence on the line—it was too long.

—*Massengill what are you thinking, speak already, speak*—

"Why don't you just not go back to the warehouse tomorrow? Just stop showing up? You really could just call and leave a voicemail with Panko that you quit the job. That would be easier for you."

"No, I got unfinished business to clean up there. A couple little loose ends I need to take care of, to make sure it all goes down like I said. Then, I'll be out of the picture, and you can bust them next Wednesday."

"Okay, Eli. Great work by the way. I'm going to write a letter to your firm for this."

"Great."

—*Molly*—

Complete lucidity engulfed Eli suddenly, as though he had smoked nothing—tomorrow would be the last day he would see Molly—very sobering, yes, quite so. Tomorrow, he though to take Molly to Solly's one last time after work; but—

The last time with Molly. The last time, no, please but, yes—

"Eli you still there?" said Massengill.

—*yes, face it. There's always a last time, make the most of it, of every second to the last*—

He had blown the whistle hard on Molly—he had had to—it settled on him as though the ceiling was set to come down and crush him like in some silly video game—he grabbed for his pipe, yes it was lit, he dragged out the smoke, and came back to himself.

—I am a professional, yes this had happened before would happen again, so get real and face it. Life is this way many many times before it's all over—

"Eli?" Massengill said, more loudly. "Our connection cut or something?"

Eli opened his eyes; he had not even known they were shut.

"Yes—yes, Mister Massengill. I'm here—sorry; I hit some button on the phone. Damn these fancy phones, you know—but anyway. Is everything clear? I'm going to write you up a report and send it to your email tomorrow or the next day. Watch for that—and don't forget, make sure you tell Panko about the cage when he calls you. Make sure you order him to leave it open at all times. This is the most important part of the whole plan."

"Calls me? How do you know he will call me?"

"Mister Massengill, he almost calls you every time he needs to wipe his ass. He'll call you to kiss your butt like he does. Doesn't he call you at least once a day about some petty shit?"

"Yeah, yes, I guess he does. That's pretty funny to hear you say that. But anyway, I got to run now. I'll arrange for the warrants to search Gene's house, get corporate security alerted, contact the police—all focused on Wednesday. I'll need your final report, like you said, by Saturday at the latest. I'll need to have documentation to get warrants—"

"You got it, Mister Massengill. Anything else?"

"No, it looks like you've done your part. Good job, Eli. If this works out like you are saying it will, I'll be sure to recommend your company again. And don't forget—I'm going to send them that letter about you."

"Thanks."

"So long. And good luck."

"Right—"

The phone slid down out of Eli's grip and banged hard on the table. Before it clattered around and made more noise, he grabbed it and banged it down, hanging up. The pipe was out. He put it to the side. He was quite high enough—he had done it again. The TV picture flickered, with the sound still muted down. He looked around, but the remote was lost, but that didn't matter—TV is better silent anyway. A bright kitchen full of animated, heavily made up, oddly dressed people was on the TV. They were all madly cooking, and talking, and laughing, and running back and forth—it was a cooking show—he thought of what he was going to have for dinner tonight. As usual, he would eat alone. The oddball people in the TV went on and on with their funny nonsense—and one last time for today, he went over what he'd set up between Molly and Gene, and he even had prayed a few times to God earlier, that this is what would go down, the way it's set to, to save Molly and bust Gene dead, right at the door.

—*she'll refuse to work unless he pays her the money I got her to demand—and it's certain as anything that he'll never pay that. He needs the drugs, he'll take the chance, and carry the pills out himself, tomorrow, yes—and since that will go well, he'll be asshole enough to believe he can do it again and again but Wednesday, he will learn, he will hit the wall, and it will be all over—yes—*

With all the foolish people running around the kitchen wilder and wilder on the muted TV as a backdrop, the hashish worked harder and harder, taking him through the plan again and again, and he let it go, for God knew how long, until his stomach churned. He was not hungry, but he did have to use the bathroom. In there, it hit him, and he leaned over the bowl, and all at once threw up nothing, just some great false blur, instantly dissipating down the drain.

18 – Eli's Last Day

"Panko!"

Eli knocked on the doorframe of Tom Panko's office. Panko looked up from the newspaper he had spread on his desk.

"Eli? Hey, Eli. What's up? What do you need?"

Eli stepped in fast without a word, pulled the key to the narco cage out of his pocket, and tossed it out in front of Panko with a grin.

"There it is my man. I'm done."

"Why—what? Done? What do you mean, done?" said Panko. "What—"

"I don't need this key anymore."

"Why not?"

"It's my last day," said Eli. "I'm giving my notice."

"What?" said Panko, mouth hung open, eyes stretched wide.

"I said I'm giving my notice. Pretty simple concept, I think."

Panko's hands formed into fists on the desktop.

"How much notice are you giving me? Are you serious Eli?"

"Dead serious. And I guess there's no notice. This is my last day. Got to catch a plane to the other coast tonight. I start a new job tomorrow."

Panko stood shakily, and rubbed his hand over the side of his head.

"I'm—I'm just stunned—I thought you liked it here, Eli—I think you could have had a good future here—there was some talk of making you management—"

Eli raised a hand.

"I'm not interested in warehouse management." he said.

"What kind of job is this new job?"

"That's my business—I don't like to share my business—but it's a big jump in pay—big—anyway—there's the key to the narco cage—that's about it, I don't owe you anything but the rest of this day. Then I will be gone."

"I—I've got to find out from Massengill what he wants to do about this—God damn, Eli—I am stunned. Massengill recommended you. He pulled strings to get you the job. Doesn't that mean something?"

"Oh, sure. But this new job is much too good to pass up."

"I didn't know you were looking for another job!"

"I wasn't—they came looking for me."

"Who will you be working with? You say it's out on the coast?"

"Yes it is. And I don't want to say any more about it. Here—"

Eli pushed out a hand, and Tom Panko took it. They shook hands.

"I had fun here," said Eli. "You've got yourself a good crew here."

"I—I suppose—listen, Eli, are you sure you can't give us a few more days—having an extra forklift driver really helped."

"Nope. Got to go. I'll finish out the day—I'll contact you with an address in a few weeks once I get settled, you can send my last check to me there."

"What about the narco cage?" said Panko, fingering the powerful key.

"I'll tell Molly to come see you if she needs something from the cage. So. That's it! Nice to know you, Tom."

Before Panko could say another word, Eli turned, went out and jumped on his truck, faded off down the aisle, turned the corner, and was gone. After quickly shutting his office door, Panko picked up the phone to call Massengill, to tell him and so they could figure out what the hell to do now. He jabbed the buttons on the phone and it began to ring.

Eli was already halfway across the warehouse. He had not smoked anything today, and wasn't planning to. Everything in the warehouse seemed completely real. Everything had sharp edges, solid colors, nothing hazy, and nothing blurry. No snakes catching the corner of his eye. No fish jumping in the concrete pond beneath. He rode the forklift up and down the empty aisles. The rumble of the truck sounded naturally off the racks and the corrugated ceiling. He saw Carl on his fork truck in the bulk stock area. He pulled up beside Carl.

"Carl!" he said.

"What?" snapped Carl, as always, rough and scowling.

"After today you're the only fork truck driver again."

"What? Why?"

"I just quit."

"Quit?"

Carl's mouth hung open as Panko's had.

"Nobody quits," said Carl. "There are no jobs out there! You can't quit, nobody quits!"

"Well, I am. After today, I'm gone."

"What? Not even two week's notice?"

"No, this is it. Today's my last day."

"God damn, shit. So, what are you going to do next?"

"I'm moving to the west coast. Got a job out there."

"Shit! The west coast, eh? Doing what?"

"Top secret. Couldn't tell Panko, can't tell you, can't tell nobody."

"Why not?"

"Don't feel like it. Simple as that."

"Should I go see Panko about carrying the narco cage key like you do, and will I have to jump and get down loads to go on the line, like you do? Is Panko going to expect twice the work from me? Shit! What do I do?"

"Panko's the boss. Ask him."

"But he's an asshole. I never talk to him."

"Oh yeah, well—don't worry, I'm sure he will come to see you about all that."

"Eli, this is shit!"

"I know. Bye Carl!"

Eli pulled his forklift away from Carl's scowl and decided he would tell Molly next—he cruised the aisles looking for her and then saw her sitting on her cart by a pile of huge cases. He pulled up. She stood and spoke first.

"Panko told me you quit. Is that true? Are you quitting? Just like that? Is today your last day? It can't be true."

"Panko already told you? God, he's fast. Yes, it's true."

"Why are you suddenly quitting?"

He told her about the job on the west coast, and about having to fly out tonight, and how if he didn't there'd be no job for him there tomorrow.

"That's amazing," she said. "Panko said the narco cage will be open from now on like it used to be. Why don't they give the key to Carl?"

"Maybe they think he's too big an asshole!"

They laughed together.

Silence came up around them and the tall racks leaned to hear what they would say next.

"I know it doesn't mean anything to say this now, but I'm going to miss you, Eli."

"I know, I'll miss you too. You know, I was going to ask you if we could go to Solly's after work today, one last time. Get high as shit!"

"Okay," she said, perking up. "What about your flight to the coast?"

"I'm taking the redeye," he said.

"Good—I'm glad we can go to Solly's for one last time."

"Yes we can—and we can keep in touch, you know. Molly—you just need to give me a phone number that I can reach you at—so it's not like this is the end. You know what I mean?"

Eyes—

"Yes," she said slowly. "I think I know what you mean."

He stood up straight on the truck and gripped the handle.

"I got to run now, Molly. Maybe see you at lunch—but then for sure after work?"

"Great! Absolutely."

They waved at each other as Eli drove the truck around a bit and then stopped by the picking line. He went onto the line and up to Gene.

"Eli," said Gene. "Is it true, what I heard that you're leaving us?"

"My God, word gets around fast in this place—who told you?"

"Franklin. Plus Tom came around. He is all confused about what to do now. Pretty funny."

Eli leaned close and whispered, "So that's a thousand dollars a week that you don't have to throw away on me. You know what I mean?"

"Yeah—yeah I know what you mean." Gene smiled.

"And my lips are completely sealed Gene. I wish you and Molly the best of luck."

"We'll keep on, keeping on, as long as the taking is good."

"Atta boy, I knew you would—stick it to the man."

Rose came up with an order sheet in her hand and put her hands on her hips.

"So, Eli, I hear you're leaving us, so soon after your arrival," she said. "Where are you going next?"

"I got a job on the west coast. More money."

"That's great—good for you. Doing what?"

"I'd rather not say."

"Why not—"

Gene came up, saying, "Oh, Rose, he got to keep it secret. This is a man all full of secrets!"

Eli smirked at Gene. When Rose glanced away, Gene winked too.

"Seriously though," said Rose, "I wish you all the luck in the world doing whatever it is you are going to be doing."

"Thanks Rose."

She turned and went back toward her end of the line. Gene waved his pencil and spoke low.

"I hear the narco cage will be open all the time again now. Why is that?"

"Can you see Carl taking care of that?" said Eli to Gene, leaning on the line.

"What—unlocking the cage? I don't know—"

"I do. Carl is an asshole. He'd lose the key every other day!" said Eli, narrowing his eyes.

They laughed, and then Eli stepped away, hands up.

"Gene, got to run—I'll see you! Good luck!"

"Sure thing, Eli," said Gene.

Eli left the picking line and got on his forklift and drove down to the back of the warehouse and stopped on the loading dock, by the open bay doors. The day outside was sunny. The trees and lawn flared green—too bright—too real—the sky blue—

Everything is much too real today. Oh what the hell—it's my last day—what the hell what the hell what the fucking hell! Go!

He jumped down from the loading dock bay onto the black-top and walked out to his car. The keys pulled from his pocket as he reached the car; once inside, he went for the glove compartment. The briar pipe fell into his hand. He unwrapped the foil from the bowl; he couldn't remember what was in it today, he could not think really, it all was good, always.

—*shit! A smoke is a smoke is a smoke is a smoke is a*—

It lit; he pulled; and in a few minutes, the car was full of curling snaking smoke. As he smoked, he looked from one end of the warehouse to the other. And then; there, in the loading dock door stood Carl, his hands on his hips, squinting hard, watching. He had probably seen Eli go out the door.

Fuck you Carl.

A whole lungful of smoke blew over the windshield. Behind it, Carl floated away from the door; Eli imagined he had made Carl disappear, using the smoke.

—*God damn! How easy it is to make someone just go away*—

Carl did not reappear. The smoke continued going down smoothly, and out over the warehouse came a scrub brush field dotted with lush kitchen gardens, staked goats and chicken coops. It was how the land had been before the warehouse was built—Eli couldn't know it, but he was looking straight into the past. All the way before Gene, Molly, Massengill and Panko, a field you'd never dream that someday would change to a place upon which so much drama would occur. Then a garbage truck roared down into the lot, turned just before smashing into the building, and backed up to a cluster of chicken coops, where the rightmost loading dock would someday be. Yes, they had come to collect the garbage from the invisible warehouse of the future, and the garbage men were young men with both bushy hair and bushy beards, and they dressed in tight dark t-shirts and filthy loose jeans, and wore big rotting boots. Seeing this Eli decided to go across where the field used to be and go up to them and offer them a smoke. He got out of the car, shuffled through the scrub brush, accumulating burrs on his pants, and went up to the young garbage man in the pitch black t-shirt, and with the heavy black bushy beard, which marked him as certainly the leader of the crew.

"Hey man," said Eli to the leader, holding out the bowl. "Want a smoke?"

"What is it?"

"I'm not sure. Here, try it."

"You're not sure? Wow! You're not sure is the best kind! Give it here!

The leader took the pipe from Eli's hand and had a large drag. Soon the other garbage men were coming around, and doing the same, to which Eli said "Hey wait a minute, wait, Let me go in and get something really good for you."

What the hell, this is my last day—anything goes on the last day—

He took the pipe from the smiling leader, and taking a smoke, blinked as hard as he could, forcing time forward a step at a time until the warehouse bays reappeared. He climbed up, got on his truck, and drove to the narco cage, avoiding the scrub brush, and the flapping, scared-to-death stray chickens; thinking about what he could give his new friends.

A big juicy jug of Noctec—they would love that—and a case of Oxycodone—twenty bottles—two thousand pills—what the hell what the hell—

The concrete floor slid by smooth, all laughing and joyful underneath. No souls locked in ice in hell today, none. The felt covered racks went by in smooth waves; whatever had been in the pipe today was coming up, and coming hard; once in the narco cage he threw the jug and the cases onto his forks—*lord God let them balance there let them be balanced*—and the truck reversed out of the narco cage. Then Molly was there—in all blue—bald, with a blue dome cap on, pushing a circus cart with a monkey on it which sported a tiny cute red tasseled fez.

"What are you doing," echoed her voice—though it did not look like Molly, it was Molly.

"Oh, they need these for an order down on the loading dock."

"Oh! Well since it's your last day, Eli, listen to this, and listen good!"

At the touch of her slender hand, the circus cart began to play music, steam blowing out the pipes, the monkey danced and danced. After watching this go on for several very long days, Eli at last said, "I'll see you Molly—at lunch—"

"Yeah."

He drove away, the circus music receded behind him, the hidden happy faces in the floor all laughing. On the girders above holding up the roof, there must have been clusters of laughing faces too, people that Eli had known, from other places and other jobs. He could not look up to see them though. He had to look straight on ahead. Accurately and quickly he reached the loading dock bay, never having been seen by another living soul. The garbage men were waiting for him, the black bearded leader out in front. Eli jumped down, took the cases under his arms, and said, "Here—Merry Christmas—a jug of Noctec, world's happiest hypnotic—and a case of Oxycodone—about which I need not speak, but to say, there's twenty bottles, a hundred pills in each. Take, take! Come on! Christmas is here! Or has come! Or, whatever!"

They looked at each other stunned.

"Why are you giving this to us?" said the leader. "You some kind of narc?"

"No—it's for Merry Christmas—my pipe told me so—give me back my pipe by the way, I can't let you keep my favorite pipe!"

They handed him the pipe, and quickly stashed the cases in the back of the garbage truck.

"Thanks man," said the leader out his beard, and through his slaphappy eyes.

"Hey, what the hell are you doing?" said another voice.

Eli turned and faced stinking rotting Carl, who'd driven up on his fork the moment after the boxes and bottle became invisible down in the trash.

"Hey Carl! I am just talking to these guys. They are my new friends—"

Their smiles engulfed Carl, calming him, as he pointed.

"What's in that Pipe, Eli? I never saw you with a pipe before."

"I like to smoke—I'm taking a smoke break—want some?"

"No. I shouldn't smoke, bad for my health."

"King Albert tobacco," said Eli. "Good stuff. Come on, have some. Toast my last day!"

He extended his arm with the pipe to Carl, who came up and took the pipe.

"Okay," he said. "I always did like a good puff on the ol' pipe. But, Jesus Christ it's hot—you sure this is King Albert?"

"Oh yeah. For sure. Go on, enjoy."

The garbage men rolled their eyes, as Carl took a long drag. He blew the smoke out immediately, saying, "Strong stuff, really hot. Doesn't taste like any King Albert I've ever had before—kind of rough going down."

"Oh, right, I forgot, it's got an extra blend—I spiced it up some with some Drum Blue."

"Drum Blue? What the hell is Drum Blue?"

The garbage men swallowed down what ought to have been gales of laughter as Eli said calmly, "Yeah, Drum Blue's the strongest pipe cut tobacco you can get—like it?"

Carl smoked some more.

"Sort of," he said. "It's sure got a bite to it."

The garbage men giggled, bubbling around the edges.

Carl stood up with the pipe in his clown-like hands. Grinning there, he made Eli and the others at last laugh. He smoked a few days, or more, then handed back the pipe.

"Thanks Eli. And good luck, wherever in hell you wind up!"

"Yeah! Thanks!"

Carl turned away shuffling his big flapping loose clown feet to the circus fork truck, which was now festooned with festive streamers, as he drove away.

"He'll have a good afternoon," said the garbage crew leader.

"At least a weird afternoon," said one of the others of his crew.

"Say, what do we owe you for the stuff?"

"Oh nothing," said Eli, raising his arms. "This is my last day—I thought I'd rip them off a little—you guys okay? Want another drag?"

He extended the pipe.

"No," waved the leader, "—but, hey, what the shit! Okay. Give it here—"

Several weeks later, Eli walked back to his car, put out the pipe, put it away in the glove compartment, locked the car, and walked back to the docks. He climbed up the jagged rocky cliffs to the snowy top, with his last breath making the very summit, and got onto his fire-truck forklift. He wiped the snow from his hands as Panko came running up, wearing only a diaper.

"What'd you leave the warehouse for?" said the big bellied bare-chested Panko.

"I needed something from the car." said Eli, trying not to laugh. "A cough drop. Had a tickle in my throat. Needed a cough drop."

The air between them boiled with the sudden smell of shit; as if someone should change the foreman's diaper. Panko knew that people could see that he was full of shit up to his big brown eyes.

Panko said fast, "Massengill told me that he wants the narco cage open from now on, like it used to be. Thought I should tell you. I opened it up—"

—you smell of baby shit—

"I know it's open. I was in there before. But, you'd better go back to your office, Panko." he said, sniffing the air.

He knew Panko's Mother would be there waiting for him, and she would be the one to change him. Eli pictured it, giggling.

"Okay." said Panko, as he waddled his tight packed ass back to his office.

As he drove back, all around him, Eli could see that the warehouse was festooned with colorful streamers. Streamers were all over the ceiling and hanging halfway down the stock racks. As soon as the streamers started to blow in the wind, the break bell rang. Eli jumped off his forklift and went down to the bay doors and saw that the green garbage truck was gone. He would never see those men again but he hoped he would remember them and they would remember him. He sat on the edge of the truck bays, the sun coming in over him, his eyes closed, the rays warming him pleasantly.

Carl came up. Carl always took his break down at the loading docks.

"Eli," said Carl. "That smoke you gave me before—I really liked it. Gave me a real pick me up. This is really a great day!"

"That's great, Carl. I think it's a great day too!"

"I feel a lot more—wide-awake," said Carl. "What did you say that tobacco was—King Albert and what else—?"

"Drum Blue," said Eli. "You can get it at any good tobacco shop."

"I'll have to mix up some of it—I've always liked a good pipe, even if it's not so good for me. Wouldn't have figured you for a tobacco man, though."

"No? What'd you figure me for?"

"Nothing. All straight edge. No booze, nothing. You seem pretty clean cut."

"Right! I am clean cut."

Carl talked faster and faster as much with his hands as his mouth.

"—I'm going to be sorry to see you go—you helped me out a lot—you took care of all those racks—now Molly and Frankie will be coming after me—I don't like that—going up to those racks is a pain in the ass—you ever have a good pain in the ass Eli? Ever had something to do that was a really big pain in the ass that you knew you'd be doing the rest of your life?"

"Sure, all the time," said Eli.

"Like that Molly—and that Frankie—when they need stock, you got to jump for them—but I'd fuck that Molly, I'd give her that, Eli—I'd fuck her in a minute—wouldn't you fuck Molly in a minute, Eli?"

Carl's grin loomed closer. His multicolored stench enveloped them. It really was true that Carl smelled bad, he was filthy and he did smell really bad. Eli at once wished him away but he stayed.

"—how about it Eli, be honest—"

"—I'd fuck her in a minute, Eli. Come on, admit it—"

The end of break bell rang.

"My eyes feel funny," said Carl, rubbing at them. "Ever since that smoke you gave me—my eyes feel really, really funny."

"It's just your mind Carl. Anyway, break's over."

"Right. Yes. True. Okay Eli—"

Carl stumbled away babbling, toward his fork truck. His diaper was fuller than Panko's had been, and the air around him filled with shit smell too. Eli smiled and hopped back into his forklift, the controls like jelly in his hands, all soft and slimy and hard to manipulate. He drove back to the bulk stock area to hide until lunch but found he had sprouted horns. He rubbed at his head hoping to make the horns go away and luckily, mercifully, they dissipated and were replaced by thoughts of how funny it was that Carl was on some hot drug mix now, for the first time in his life, and didn't even know it. The man was so stupid. All everybody ever talked about Carl was how bad he smelled, his rank breath and his overall look of never bathing or washing his clothes. Eli drove along slowly and thought of how everybody said that Carl was living way over his means and how he paid bills every other month instead of every month because he never had the money on time. Up the aisle he saw a newly green-haired Molly pushing her cart with ten big bottles of Oxycodone in it as she headed for the locker room. Apparently she was still working with Gene—that devil—and he prayed that Gene would be the one carrying the bottles out next time—but then, all of a sudden, Molly stopped her cart and slid the yellow bottles down the racks on Rose's end of the picking line. He was relieved to discover that she had not been taking the Oxys to Gene and was not heading for her locker; this was just a normal order. He drove up to Molly with her now purple hair, which he guessed was the color of the drug in him, so he spoke to her normally.

"Guess what Molly? Guess what I did?

"What?"

"I gave Carl my pipe to smoke—he's totally zonked out of his mind, and doesn't even know it!"

She turned to him with a huge grin.

"What! That is perfectly hilarious! How'd you do that?"

"He thinks he smoked strong pipe tobacco—you should see him—he's talking a mile a minute about all kinds of crazy shit."

"That's ridiculously funny—"

"And I got plenty more in the car, for when we go to Solly's tonight."

"That's good, it being your last night and all."

"Yeah. Hey, I thought those bottles you took to Rose were Oxycodone for Gene. I thought you were heading for your locker to store them."

"Gene? Oh no—not today—Gene's got to decide if he's still going to raise my cut—now that the cage is open and all."

—*I hope he doesn't—then he will be carrying Friday and*—

"I don't know if he will but he better—or no more Oxys from me. With everything that's been happening, the risk is too high—"

—*and that's as it should be* —

"Molly, listen. Make sure you stick to your guns. Take nothing out—not even a single fucking pill—until that greedy bastard gives in!"

"Yeah I know," she said—and suddenly she too, sprouted horns—a lovely rack—he waved his hand over her head.

"Hey what was that action with the hands?" laughed Molly.

"Oh nothing. I'm just blessing you. Here."

He placed his hand on the top of her head. The warmth from her head went in his hand. It traveled down his arm, across his body, and into his heart.

He could love her.

—what could top that thought? Leave with that thought yes leave—

A great shiver went through him, he looked her in the eye, and she looked back with a sparkle. No horns, no more.

"I got to go. See you at lunch."

He turned the forklift around, went again back toward the bulk stock area, parked in the corner by the stacks of palleted boxes.

After today, never again will I bring these boxes to the packers.

From where he was parked, he could see the loading dock bays off in the distance. Carl was driving in and out of a truck on his fork lift loading it. Watching Carl, Eli idly wondered why he hadn't thought about Molly in the way he just had, before. Her heat still stuck to his heart and all around him there were great smiles as if the warehouse, the racks, the pallets were all saying it was the right thing to end up with her.

—it was the right thing to think about such a nice girl—

He gripped the handle again, wanting to go see Molly again, and to shoot the breeze with her, just to be close to her, but instead, the lunch bell rang. He was right under one of the red bells mounted on the wall, one of dozens on the walls all around the warehouse, and the ring jarred him toward the locker room. This was the last time he would go to lunch; once in the locker room, he came upon Gene and Bobby. Bobby slammed his locker shut and sat on a bench with his lunch bag, as he saw Eli come in. As Eli went to get his lunch, Bobby half-shouted at him, making all the faces in the locker room frown.

"I hear you're leaving us! Nobody leaves this place! Who the hell do you think you are?"

"Yeah," said Gene, looking from Bobby to Eli, smiling. "Who the hell do you think you are, leaving us?" He winked at Eli.

"A free man!" said Eli, as he shut his locker with a bang and rummaged through his lunch pail. "I am a free man—or I will be at four thirty."

"So what kind of job you getting?" Bobby asked, as he got his lunch bag out.

"None of your business," smiled Eli.

"What do you mean none of my business?"

Gene laughed, his eyes narrowing.

Eli shrugged and stood up, leaving the locker room with a smile as he headed for his bench outside in the hall, where Molly was already sitting eating a sandwich. There was scrub brush all around nearly hiding her. He sat down into the bushes with her.

"God, I'm high, Molly." he said very slowly.

"Must be nice—so what are you going to do with yourself after today?"

Eli ate his sandwich, brushing aside the weeds.

"I got lucky, got myself a good job lined up. Didn't I tell you?"

"Yeah, right, you did—but why does it have to be on the west coast? Why can't you stay around here so you and I can hang out?" she asked.

"I guess I'm always looking for an adventure. But I'll keep in touch."

Lunch went by and before long the end of lunch bell rang. Eli drove his forklift into the narco cage and looked at the pallet of Oxycodone. He thought of how many times Molly had sat there opening those cases, taking a bunch out to her locker and being Gene's goat. He sat there staring at the yellow bottles, thinking about Molly, until the end of the day bell rang. He drove the forklift down to the chargers and plugged it in, fighting the big black cables and plugs that felt like they wanted to wrap him and squeeze him dead, like some boa constrictor. Then he walked up and waited for Molly to come out of the woman's locker room.

—should I tell her? Should I tell her? Should I tell her about Wednesday? No, I can't—I'm a professional and I have worked other jobs like this and I have gotten close to people and I have not blown my cover—I have had people go down. I get paid too much to blow it—

Smiling, Molly came out of the locker room with her lunch pail.

"To Solly's, right?" she said.

He wanted to say No, to my place—we'll go to my place and smoke and drink and fuck—but he said "Yes,—to Solly's." They walked out to his car together. Inside, out came the pipe.

"I've been looking forward to this all day." she said.

He loaded the pipe with a fragment from the small black foil wrapped cube. He looked out at the warehouse stretching across the parking lot.

—I have just walked out of that warehouse for the last time—the last time, and I didn't even savor the moment—here Molly, here Molly, take it take it take it—

Molly took the pipe and lighter from Eli. Wordlessly, they smoked. She smoked. And then he smoked. Over and over like that, all the way to Solly's. Driving there for the last time, yes; the smoke made him acutely aware of this. The trees, houses and telephone poles all went by, waving good-bye—Eli saw faces peering out somehow, someway—

"Do you see those faces watching us, Molly?"

"No, no. I just see dreams."

They got to Solly's. They went in. They talked as they always had. They had a few beers.

The smoke took all the words out of the air. It would be their last time.

At some point they left Solly's.

He drove her back to her car. He pulled up beside it.

She leaned over from the passenger seat and handed him a small piece of cardboard. It had her phone number on it. He hadn't had her phone number until now.

"Make sure you keep in touch."

"Yes, for sure. Bet on it."

Their fingers touched. They joined hands. They kissed gently. His eyes closed and the sun moon and stars came in her kiss all black, with fields of stars all swarming around him.

She said something and left the car.

He never remembered what she said last.

All he could remember was being surrounded by fields and fields of stars.

She drove away in her Pontiac, waving.

Eli sat in the idling car, dead pipe in the ashtray.

The warehouse, empty and silent, set across the parking lot.

She had smoked his pipe with him.

She had sat in his passenger's seat.

She had laughed with him.

His was the only car left in the lot. He held up the small piece of cardboard with ten numbers on it.

She was just a series of numbers on a little piece of cardboard.

He laid his head on the wheel, and he cried.

—the nighttime stars above will hold her kiss, and those same stars will settle down on me at night, and stay with me until sleep takes me—lord God let sleep take me yes—

After midnight, he drove home. After this biggest last hell of a day.

19 – New Lives Ending Starting Out Ending Again

Molly pulled in to her driveway just as dark had fallen, after her last night at Solly's with Eli. For the first time ever she did not gaze out into the overgrown neglected cemetery before going in to face the exact same thing she faced everyday and always believed, until now, that she would always face. Leaving and locking the car she looked at the house first and not the cemetery. It felt very different. Yes, yes, different—it repeated in her head, so much so that on the ride home she'd stopped listening; but it still came up in her, still true. Her life could be different—

Molly, listen. Make sure you stick to your guns. Take nothing out—not even a single fucking pill—until that greedy bastard gives in—yes, Molly, listen—

Yes, a way to remember him; to remember someone; she remembered him one more time as the door opened and she went directly to her Mother, like every other day, but tonight her eyes glowed somehow different. Though Molly did not know this, her Mother saw it when she opened her eyes at Molly's step. The eyes caused her hands to grip the comforter draped all day over her, harder, and she said. "Molly—what is wrong. You look all worn out. Why are you so late? What's wrong with you, what? Don't look at me like that, God—"

"I'm going to go back to school, Mom. I'm going to save money and go to school and get a Dental Hygienist's degree! I'm going to quit that lousy warehouse!"

Mother blinked hard and fast so her eyes would stay open wider. *Important, this was; very important.* She pulled down the comforter, and began talking fast.

"What? What brought this on? You talked about that years ago, but—I don't know why you got away from it, but it is a really really good idea—"

"I know Mom. I am so excited—"

Yes Mom it's good to see you change, too—change at this news what will Father say what where is Father—

"So, how will you save this money, Molly? How can we help? Can we help—?"

"I—"

The phone rang. The phone seldom rang. The phone never rang. Molly went for it; it came up over her ear.

It has to be Eli lord yes it has to—he's going to stay around the kiss, the kiss and everything else met something he has saved my life he has, Eli—

"Hello," she said.

Eli Eli yes—

A voice came in her. But it did not say what she wanted to hear.

"Oh, yes, she replied—yes, yes, don't worry. Sure, yes—okay. So long."

The phone went down. She turned from her Mother and went to the window.

"What's the matter Molly, Molly, why that look?"

"Nothing, Mom."

Out the window stretched the cemetery. The phone call somehow made her remember; she had forgotten to look into the cemetery when she came home. Not looking into the cemetery was wrong.

Yes not doing what you have promised to do is very very wrong—

Mother's voice came around over her shoulder blended with the cemetery which was slowly dissolving into the night.

"Molly, what's the matter? I am happy for you! Who was on the phone? Is something wrong Molly? What is wrong?"

After the dark had taken the cemetery, Molly turned and told Mother.

"Nothing's wrong Mom. Everything is right. Again, it is. Everything is right again."

Though it hid all night out in the dark, the cemetery was still there always again, when every new dawn came.

***

Gene took his wife out to Blondie's that night. He was bushed, yes, but very, very excited.

"I did some things today, Sarah, that are going to make even more money come in than is already."

"Really? I don't know how you do it. But I'm done asking where all the money's coming from. I don't want to be a nag. Especially not on Friday night, especially not here."

"Yeah, I know, but you know, I can sum it up for you; whatever you do, don't get the whole world involved. Too many people involved in something that just leads to trouble, costs extra money too. Do things yourself. Depend on yourself—"

Blondie came up and slid their hot dinners onto the table under their noses, and the two of them, at that instant, settled deeply into the warmth of a contentment neither had felt for years. They ate slowly, savoring each bite. They did not speak; there was too much to feel, the feelings came up in Gene, smooth as silk.

Yes the future is bright, will be brighter, I am slick. I am slick. I am almost too slick, too much—but how do you know when you get too slick? What happens to tell you—?

"I love you, Sarah. Really, I do."

"Lord, Gene, what brought that on? You don't say that unless something has happened that's really special. What might that be, Gene? Why so happy?"

"The future."

"What about it?"

"It's going to be happy and happier—"

In her smile, though, came up a question under what he was saying.

Everything ends, though, everything—

Sarah's smile stayed and stayed, and stayed.

But that is tomorrow's problem.

Fuck tomorrow. And all the coming ones all up the line.

"Gene you look so happy."

"You too."

So, they ate until they were full.

20 – Eli's Report

Eli sat at the table in his room and typed up the final report for Massengill. This was no time for smoking, he had to be plain and clear, names, facts and figures. The thousand dollars Gene had given him lay on the table, as evidence. It took him about two hours to write the report, and to push the button to e-mail it to Massengill. He rose from the table, disconnected his laptop, folded it down, and went to sit on his couch. He sat back in the cool of the cushions. Across the room lay his pipe, and his foil wrapped hashish and opium. He had no desire for any of it. He left the TV off. He said a Hail Mary, and prayed.

I pray that Molly's greed got the better of her—I pray that she demanded all the money and forced Gene to carry the stuff out himself. True they are both greedy, but greed may be the end of one and the salvation of the other. I pray it will be according to my plan.

Amen.

He rose then, dressed in his black shirt, snapped on his ecclesiastical collar, put on his black hat, and went up to his room to pack for the redeye. He looked to his future. Back to the real job. The sabbatical was over—secular life was fun to sample, but— time to return to the covenant, to his God.

21 – At the Front Door

It's time.

    Go to the Narco cage.

    Slit open the case of Oxycodone.

    One, two, three, four, five, six, seven, eight, nine, ten boxes.

    Franklin is not at his desk.

    Take the boxes to the locker room.

    Unlock the big lock.

    Put them all in the lunch pail.

    The bell rings marking the end of the day.

    Get the lunch pail.

    Head to the door.

    "Stop."

    "Gene—Molly—both of you! Step over here."

    "Open those lunch pails."

    Lunch pails opened.

    "—look at that—"

    "You are under arrest—"

    "You there—you may go—but you, yes you! Stay!"

    "Turn around, put your hands behind your back."

    "You have the right to remain silent—you have the right—"

22 – VNA Corporation

At a gleaming conference table high in the headquarters of the VNA Pharmaceutical Corporation, two crew cut men sit across from one another with a spread of paperwork on the table between them. The men's hands rest on the table and their fingertips drum the tabletop in unison.

"It was a good operation. Good work, Massengill. We got justice."

"Yes, thank you," said Mister Massengill.

"—do you know why I called you in here this time—do you know what these additional reports show?"

—what the hell is it this time, how would I know what those damned reports show, the world is too full of damned reports and too full of men like my boss and his boss and all—I am tired of being dragged here to corporate with some corporate agenda, downsizing, off-shoring, what the hell could it be this time—

"No I don't," said Mister Massengill.

"This!" said Mister Jacobs. "The numbers show that there is more pilferage—this time in the Fairhaven distribution center— it's the damn Oxycodone again—see these numbers? See them? Oh and another thing—you never figured out how they defeated the inventory system in Somerset—that was something you were supposed to find out too. Why didn't you?"

Massengill scowled at being reprimanded.

—*it isn't good enough that we busted the damned crook, there won't be any more of those pills walking out of the Somerset warehouse on my watch, what do you want from me—everything—you're just like my father, nothing was ever good enough for him, you're no different, it must be something in the genes, something in the DNA that makes you a very special class of big assholes—just like my father, you are one thing after the next, each one a bigger asshole, worse than the previous—*

"My rat didn't get into any of that, Mister Jacobs—we weren't looking at that then, but we're looking into it now—I got a man on it—we're going to revamp the inventory system—we'll get to the bottom of how they did it."

"But you should be at the bottom of it right now! You have the same problem in the Fairhaven center! What are you going to do about the pilferage there? And how are you going to find out what's spreading this damned disease across your distribution centers?"

Mister Massengill bit his lip.

—*well I guess I'll have to hire another rat, maybe even Eli again, no, no, I can't use the same person twice, as far as why they're stealing, poorly paid employees are generally dishonest, they're generally shit and greedy just like you, Mister Jacobs, you in your office looking at reports raking in a salary that they would all find outrageous, greedy even, and you forget there's people, real people at the bottom who want what you got and the only way they can get it is to steal, like you do, off our backs—off our fucking rotted stinking backs!*

"I'll get to the bottom of it Mister Jacobs."

"Yes, you will get to the bottom of it."

"I'll hire another Rat."

"Good thinking!"

"Can I take the reports with me?"

"Yes you may!"

"Bye Mister Jacobs—I will keep you informed."

"Good bye, Massengill."

He left the room and made his way through the maze of corridors, elevators and stairways toward his car, each step bringing him new thoughts.

Why on earth are these places built this way—they're like a rats nest—Jacobs trusts me to find these new thieves again—who should I tell about it—I'm dying to tell someone about it—but no, better not tell anyone about it—I am a professional—I hate thieves too—I am supposed to hate thieves in this job—I am supposed to listen to Jacobs—after all he is my boss's boss—I am not supposed to raid Kotex machines for candy money—though I do and I'm grateful for the extra change it brings me to buy a candy bar from the snack vending machine—I am not supposed to steal fragments of tombstones from cemeteries and carry them through school all day and then bring them home and hide them in our back yard like I did—but I did—because I too am a thief, I understand thieves—oh I do not steal any more—unless you call accepting my overblown salary stealing, which it is—I will get to the bottom of this—like when I caught the worst bully in the school masturbating up in the beams of the trestle bridge—and I said what is it you're doing, because I had never masturbated—and he said I'm working up a boner—don't tell anybody about this—make sure you don't ever tell anybody about this—and I didn't, to show that I can be trusted—I think I parked my car that way—I won't be telling anybody that somebody is masturbating VNA off—Hah—ha ha ha ha—there's my car. Damn it. Pinkerton he said—Pinkerton. Look it up in the Internet—but Pinkerton. Kotex. Candy bars. Trestle bridges. Boners—who imagines it could have started with Kotex and candy bars—I'm clean now—and the big shot. This big super quiet, don't tell a soul—This brand-new top of the line Cadillac makes me a big shot—a company car, of course—big shot. Nine hundred thirty six thousand dollars—all total from my warehouse. That's pretty sweet. It's getting dark-twilight—best time to steal—you can't see people in the twilight. Let alone what they're doing—I will catch him—what will the rat be like this time? Larger, stronger, tougher, tougher talking? Older or younger—a big mouth I bet. Bait is all. Bait is what he is. Bait to attract the bad guys, get in good with them, then squash them; like Eli did. Just like he did. He was a fine boy—a good rat, that Eli. And there are more where he came from. Relax.

Acknowledgements

I wish to give credit to my wife, Mary Beth, without whom "Eli the Rat" would never have existed. Traveling together through the years of learning, struggling, trying, and failing, the bond between us held fast through everything. She was always there, encouraging, reassuring, and loving me through all the years; and I her. Without her, there would have been no writing, no books, no family, no nothing; in fact there would have been simply no value to be derived from my having lived at all.

Jim Meirose is the author of the previously published novel "Mount Everest", and of three upcoming novels, which will also be released by Montag Press. Nearly three hundred of his short stories have appeared in various literary magazines and journals over the past twenty years, such as The Fiddlehead, Witness, Alaska Quarterly review, Xavier Review, New Orleans review, South Carolina Review, Whiskey Island Magazine, Ohio Edit, Bartleby Snopes, and many others. His short work has been nominated for several awards including The Shirley Jackson Award and the O. Henry Award (for which his story "Fair Morning" was short-listed). Jim lives in Somerville, NJ, with his wife, Mary Beth. Together they have one married daughter, Noelle Heber, and three beautiful grandchildren.